Parisian
LEGACY

Published in the UK in 2021 by Cool Clear Press

First edition published 2021
This second edition published 2022

Paperback ISBN 978-1-7399780-3-7
eBook ISBN 978-1-7399780-1-3

Cover design and typeset by SpiffingCovers

for the latest information visit:
rosaliejamesauthor.com

Parisian
LEGACY

ROSALIE JAMES

For my late father, James Michael

PART 1

ALICE

I have lived two brief lives, the first ended when I was just 16, the day my parents were killed. The second will end far sooner than I could have imagined.

For now, I am focusing on the small joys of each day; the birdsong in the tree outside my window, a golden slice of sunlight across my bed, the sweet, painful perfection of a rose petal as it falls; but I'm getting ahead of myself.

I was born in a tall house in Meard Street in London, it has been in our family for three generations. My great grandfather, Joseph Gardener, imported spices and tea from the Far East. It was his fortune that enabled my parents to live as they chose. My father, David, went to Italy in his twenties to indulge his passion for working with stone. He apprenticed Master Carver Giovanni Ardini, and together, they studied the luminous works of Michelangelo in the Medici Chapel. In the studio, Ardini showed him how to let the stone speak through his hands. The hand holding the hammer, he told him, would be his working hand and the other his listening hand, relaxed and sensitive to the rhythms of the stone.

As a child, I would sit for hours in my father's studio as he worked, watching beauty slowly emerge from an unpromising lump of stone. I remember him saying that he used his chisel in time with the beating of his heart, becoming one with his sculpture, losing all sense of time. He especially loved marble, the way the light slid over its curves, conveying a depth and luminosity that took his breath away.

He met my mother in Paris in 1934. He was there to take part in a meeting of the Abstraction-Création group, along with another student of Ardini, Barbara Hepworth. Together they visited the studio of Picasso, among others, and it was there that my father first saw Amélie. She was sitting for a portrait, her creamy shoulders emerging from a yellow bodice. He said her smile lit up the room. She was wild and beautiful then, and my father could not keep away from her. They went to clubs and parties together, and when her portrait was eventually finished, he asked her to return to London with him.

He was not prepared for the opposition he would encounter from her family. The d'Apidaes were wealthy and well known on the Parisian charity circuit. Amélie's older sister, Clémence, formal and glamorous, was already a leading light at charity balls and functions, but Amélie refused to toe the line. It was all such a bore she told him, 'Darling I am a butterfly, I need to fly!' Then she would laugh and lift her arms above her head, so that the silk sleeves of her kimono fluttered in the breeze.

So, it was with some trepidation that my father presented himself at the grand family apartment, to ask for Amélie's hand in marriage. The meeting was short, Julien d'Apidae would not give them his blessing. Flitting about, he said, mixing with ne'er do well artists and other unsuitable people (at this, he paused and looked my father up and down) was a waste of Amélie's expensive education and unlikely to get her the right sort of husband.

It left them with no choice but to run away together to London. They cut themselves off from Amélie's family and married a few years later in a low key ceremony at the local registry office. When their doctor told Amélie she was expecting me, nothing changed for them until I arrived and upended their routine. Amélie was prone to mood swings and bouts of depression, so they took on a nanny for me. Bella was warm and kind; we played, went for walks, she told me stories and I loved her. It was really Bella who brought me up, while my parents' lives carried on much as before.

My mother was a painter, drifting about the house in colourful smocks, unconcerned with practicalities. They would sleep late, spend afternoons in their studio, then socialise into the early hours. Sometimes, late at night, I would be woken by the sound of my parents stumbling about, bumping into furniture and laughing helplessly. Artist friends would arrive at all hours of the day and night, their cigarette smoke floating up the stairs and the sound of clinking glasses and uncontrollable laughter filling the house. Sometimes Amélie would stumble into my room and bring me down to the garden to watch fireworks with them, or join in a toast to a finished painting. I was in awe of her glamour and exuberance and I wanted to be just like her. To my lasting regret, we were never close. I can see now that I was in love with the gloss of her, but I never really knew her, not outside of her studio anyway.

The one thing we did together was paint. From an early age, I watched my mother setting up her canvas and brushes, and laying out her tubes of paint. Even now the smell of oils takes me back to those rare times when we had a common purpose. Maman encouraged me to feel while I was painting, to withdraw into myself where she said I would find the muse. I didn't know what she meant then, but I felt she could only really 'see' me when I was painting with her. For the rest of my life I would return to painting to find comfort and a sense of belonging.

It is only now I look back, I see that my home life was different to most. At the age of 12, I was sent to boarding school. It was strange at first, having the company of girls my own age. I had been used to adults around me and struggled to fit into my new life. There were rules to follow and dull routines, so when my mother occasionally arrived at school unannounced, in a cloud of perfume and billowing silk dresses, I was overjoyed and relieved to see her. She would insist that nothing was more important than a mother and daughter lunch in the middle of the week, and the headmistress could do little to dissuade her. The other girls regarded me with a mix of fascination and horror, as we sped away in Maman's open top sports car. Later, they would beg me to tell them stories of my French mother and our unusual home life.

Art became the highlight of my week and in my second year I joined the painting club. Miss Lovegrove told us stories of Paris, the French painters and their studios in Montmartre. She would get a faraway look in her eyes as she talked of partially clothed models and love affairs; of friends gathering to drink in cafés and bars, exchanging ideas on art and life. I could not get enough of it and begged her to tell us more, visualising myself in the role of muse to a painter, or wandering the romantic streets of Paris.

Soon after my sixteenth birthday, everything changed. Our science lesson had just begun, Mrs Mead was writing noisily on the blackboard as we waited, pens poised, to copy her notes into our books. The lesson was interrupted by a knock on the classroom door, and without waiting, our headmistress strode into the room. Her sensible shoes tapped on the lino floor and her heavy tweed skirt rustled, as she briskly made her way to the front of the class. We all hastily stood, the collective sound of our chairs drowning out her initial words.

'Good morning girls,' she paused, 'quiet please!' There was a pause as we waited expectantly, all eyes upon Miss Tucker. 'Thank you, you may sit, except for you Alice. Please leave your books on the desk and follow me to my office. Carry on Mrs. Mead.' Miss Tucker turned and swept out of the room, and I followed her, watched by my surprised classmates. I closed the classroom door quietly behind me and walked quickly along the corridor, smoothing my hair and pulling up my socks, as I hurried towards Miss Tucker's office. She was a formidable woman and I was surprised, when upon entering her office, she smiled at me and spoke gently.

'Please come in Alice, sit yourself down over there.' I walked towards the wing back chair by the fire and sat down, wondering why she had called me in. Miss Tucker's dachshund trotted towards me and nuzzled my ankles.

'Hello Pierre' I said, reaching down to stroke his soft ears. Miss Tucker said nothing, but allowed me to continue fussing the dog until I looked up and straightened myself in the chair, my hands resting in my lap.

'My dear, I'm afraid I have some very difficult news to tell you.' She paused. 'There has been an accident, a car crash. Alice, I am so sorry my dear, both your parents have been killed.' Her words hit me like a hammer blow and I gasped, taking noisy gulps of air.

'No, it can't be true!' I said, as tears began to pour down my cheeks.

'It seems they had been at the,' she hesitated, trying to hide her disapproval, 'the Colony Club in Dean Street. They left in the early hours of the morning and decided, for reasons unknown, to climb into their car and go for a drive.'

I realise, looking back on it after so many years, that they must have been drinking, and there was no knowing what else Amélie might have taken. The Colony Club is still well known for the most outrageous gatherings of people from the theatre and other artistic circles. It was one of her favourite places.

Miss Tucker waited while I sobbed, hands pressed over my face. I could picture them in their little car, heading down to the coast to watch the sunrise. Maman had always loved the sea and the sky. Tears seeped between my fingers, rolling down the backs of my hands and I drew deep, gasping breaths of shock and pain. Miss Tucker stepped forward and patted my shoulder, pressing a clean handkerchief into my hand. The little dog, seeming to sense my distress, nuzzled my ankles again. As I wiped my face, I reached down, finding comfort in his warm little head and smooth fur.

'I know this is a terrible shock for you Alice, I am so very sorry my dear.' She paused for a moment. 'I have been in touch with your aunt in Paris, they are devastated by the news of course. They are going to discuss your future, and have promised to contact me again at the end of the week. In the meantime, they think it best for you to be among your friends and stay close to the routine that you know. Do you think you can do that?'

I broke down again and fresh tears of shock and grief rushed down my face.

'There, there my dear.' She looked at me with sympathy, then said quietly, 'I have asked Matron to take you up to your room so that you can lie down for a while. Have a good cry into your pillow my dear and then dry your eyes, try to put a brave face on it. You will continue with your lessons tomorrow. Do your best Alice and we will speak again at the end of the week.'

There was a quiet tap on the door as Matron looked in. 'Ah Matron, please come in. Could you take Alice upstairs to rest for a while, she has had a terrible shock.'

Matron, who had been briefed earlier, reached out to me, 'Come along my duck, you come with me. Let's get you up to your bed for some rest. I'll give you some medicine to help you sleep and get over the shock.'

I dried my eyes with the now sodden handkerchief and reached out once more to touch the soft fur on Pierre's warm head, before standing up. Matron put her arm across my shoulders and we left the room together.

The rest of the week passed in a blur, I walked mechanically from one classroom to the next, performing my tasks as usual, my heart aching for my loss. I cried into my pillow each night and spurned the kind efforts of my classmates. The whole school had been told of my tragedy and asked that extra special kindness be shown to me. I think they were all thankful that this tragedy was not their own. It was almost unimaginable to them that the vibrant woman they had seen in her sports car, had met her death.

Finally, on Saturday morning, Miss Tucker called me into her office again. 'Hello Alice, come in and sit down my dear. How are you feeling now?'

'I am not sure Miss Tucker, alright I think.'

'Well, that is to be expected,' she said gently, 'it is a very gradual process. Although you cannot imagine you will ever feel better, I promise that in time you will,' she paused, looking at me kindly.

'Now Alice, I have some news from your aunt in Paris. Madame d'Apidae telephoned me this morning. She said that they will be unable to travel from Paris for your parents' funeral, which will take place at the end of next week. It has been decided that I will accompany you in their place, along with Miss Lovegrove.'

'Thank you Miss Tucker,' I said, relieved that my austere aunt Clémence wouldn't be coming. I had only met her once on a brief visit to London when she had invited us to tea at the Ritz.

'Soon after the funeral,' Miss Tucker continued, 'your aunt has asked that arrangements be made for you to go and live with her in Paris.' I looked up, eyes wide, as she continued, 'Miss Lovegrove has kindly offered to take you to your home in London to prepare for your departure and I have given her leave to accompany you to Paris, to ensure your safe arrival into the care of your family.'

'I hardly know my aunt and uncle!' I burst out, 'I have met them only once before, I can't go there, I can't.'

'My dear, you are still a child and your aunt is your closest family, I am sure you will be happy there in time. She has your best interests at heart.'

'Can't I stay here Miss Tucker? I will work hard and do my best. Please don't send me away!' I implored her. At least here, I knew what was expected of me.

'I'm sorry my dear, I did suggest to Mme d'Apidae that you stay on here, but she would not hear of it. She wants you to become familiar with life in France. After all, you are half French and will soon be a young woman.' Miss Tucker paused, then added more gently, 'I'm sorry Alice, but unfortunately the decision is final and out of my hands. Matron will take you to the school clothiers tomorrow to purchase a suitable outfit for the funeral.' She looked at me kindly before continuing, 'That will be all for now my dear. Please return to your room, wash your hands and brush your hair ready for supper.'

'Yes Miss Tucker,' my heart was heavy. The course of my life was about to change and there was nothing I could do about it. I turned and left the room, closing the door quietly behind me.

THE FUNERAL 1953

My parents' funeral was to be held in the church of Notre Dame de France near Leicester Square, close to our family home. It was a sculptor friend of Pa's who suggested the venue. They had spent many weeks together carving the beautiful stone statue of the Madonna and child, now standing above the main entrance to the church. As we arrived, I looked up to see her hands spread open, her robes seeming to offer sanctuary. My Pa told me once, quietly and almost reverently, that the work had been a religious experience for him. It changed his inner life, like a light shining into his soul. Through it, he told me, he found unimaginable tranquility and serenity. The recollection of his words as I passed through the entrance to the church, Miss Tucker on one side and Miss Lovegrove on the other, was a great comfort to me. It pleased me that at the end of his life, he had found peace.

Inside the church, I was greeted by many familiar faces, their colourful cravats, bright dresses and brocade waistcoats brightening the sea of black. Miss Tucker, who had visibly blanched at the sight, hurried me forward. 'Come along Alice, let us take our seats at the front.' Bella, dressed all in black, smiled encouragingly as she wiped a tear from her cheek. Two of my parents' closest friends, George and the flamboyant Alexandre, were already in the front pew. They smiled warmly at me and Alexandre stood up and bowed low to kiss my hand, the feathers from his hat tickling my cheek as he moved. I wanted to hug him, remembering the last time I had seen him. I was home for half term, my father was away and my mother had not left her bedroom for two days. Alexandre swept unannounced into the house and took me out for lunch. When we returned, he did everything he could to bring my mother out of the doldrums. I could just make out their conversation, or at least his part of it, from the bottom of the stairs.

'Come on Amélie, make an effort darling, Alice is hardly ever here and she needs you.' The memory of it was painful and I took a deep breath.

I was conscious of the Headmistress beside me again, waiting for me to sit down. I gave Alexandre another small smile and lowered myself into the pew. 'Close your mouth Miss Lovegrove,' I heard Miss Tucker whisper to her colleague, whose cheeks had flushed beneath the small veil on her pillar box hat.

A reception had been arranged at Brown's Hotel in Dover Street, which passed in a haze of condolences. Many of my parents' friends tearfully wished me well and said how very sad they were for my loss, what a shock it had been for them, and wondered how I was going to cope in Paris, all alone. Alexandre was the only one who made me feel better. 'Daahling, just say the word and I will pop over to gay Paree and pay you a visit!' He tapped his nose, 'Rest assured, I have friends in all the wrong places! It will be such fun!' I smiled, doubting that Tante Clémence would take the same view should he visit, but glad I would see him again. George meanwhile clicked his fingers for a waiter and almost immediately, a tray laden with glasses of champagne and sherry was brought. George whisked two glasses of sherry off the tray and placed one each in the hands of the Misses Lovegrove and Tucker, whilst procuring two glasses of champagne for himself and Alexandre. 'Alice darling, I don't think it would hurt you to have a little nip under the circumstances either, perhaps a mimosa?'

'Just orange juice for Alice I think, thank you,' said Miss Tucker, in a tone that brooked no argument.

By the time the orange juice arrived, the charming George had coaxed Miss Tucker into taking another small sherry to fortify her for the afternoon ahead and Miss Lovegrove had accepted a glass of champagne. Despite the unhappy circumstances, both ladies began to enjoy themselves. Miss Tucker's face relaxed a little and gained colour, as her hat gradually slid to a jaunty angle and Miss Lovegrove found herself deep in conversation with a rather attractive older man.

I glanced across at them, the man looked familiar to me. It was only when he approached, holding a lovely teddy bear that I realised it was Alan Milne, a friend of my Grandpa. He was a writer and the bear was the subject of his beautifully illustrated books.

'My dear Alice, what a surprise to see you and in such sorry circumstances. I happened to be here at the hotel when I heard the terrible news about your parents. My dear girl, what a tragedy.' He thrust the bear into my arms and gave us both a big hug. 'This bear is the most wonderful cure for sadness. He will listen to all your woes and he won't tell a soul, I promise you!' Miss Lovegrove stepped forward smiling.

'It so happens, Mr Milne, that I am Alice's teacher and I am to accompany her to Paris later this week.'

'Well Alice, you will be in good hands my dear. A spell in Paris will be just the thing, help to take your mind off things. I expect you will enjoy it too Miss Lovegrove.'

'I have always wanted to go to Paris,' she replied. 'It is a wonderful opportunity. Alice and I will be just fine, won't we,' she smiled encouragingly at me.

'Yes Miss Lovegrove' I replied, not at all sure that I would be, but glad not to be travelling alone.

The mourners gradually drifted home, each taking their leave, sad faces entreating me to keep my chin up, be brave for my parents' sake and so on. I can hardly remember it, still being in a state of shock. I imagined even then that my parents might breeze through the door at any moment laughing, calling for more champagne and saying it had all been a terrible mistake.

Finally, Alexandre and George reappeared. 'Daahling, we must leave you now, duty calls us away. Come, give your Uncle Alex a hug, yes, the bear too.' he wrapped his long arms around me and pulled me to his chest in a warm hug. Tears sprang from my eyes and I pulled away, afraid of spoiling his beautiful blue waistcoat. He pressed a large silk handkerchief into my hand. 'There, there, no more tears darling. Don't forget, I will see you in Paris! We have adventures to plan! You too, Miss Lovegrove! Remember, chance smiles upon the brave!'

He took my hand and kissed it once more, before taking a low bow towards Miss Tucker and Miss Lovegrove. 'Goodbye ladies, what a delight to meet you both, be good!' before looping his arm through George's and sweeping out of the room.

Miss Tucker cleared her throat and straightened her jacket. 'I must visit the powder room and then, I believe, we should take our leave.'

Miss Lovegrove turned to me, 'Let us fetch our coats Alice, I will ask the hotel to arrange a taxi for us.'

When the taxi eventually pulled up in Meard Street, Bella came out to greet us with a curtsey. I had only seen her briefly at the church, and guessed she had hastened home to prepare for our arrival.

'Oh Bella,' I said with relief, rushing forward. The sight of my nanny brought fresh tears to my eyes and she threw her arms around me.

'Oh Miss Alice, I can hardly believe that they've gone. So good to me they were and now you a little orphan girl.' Bella's words made me ache for my loss and I laid my head against her solid shoulder as she hugged me tightly. Then I remembered my manners and pulled away,

'Miss Lovegrove, this is my nanny, Bella.'

'Welcome Miss Lovegrove, such a sorry day for us all.'

'Thank you Bella, it is,' she said kindly. 'Perhaps you could show us to our rooms now, it has been a long day.'

'Yes, yes of course Miss, sorry Miss, please follow me.' We walked over the black and white tiles of the large, familiar hallway. A palm at the foot of the stairs grew from a Chinese urn, towards the double height ceiling and a glass dome of fading afternoon light. The white staircase was brightened by a red kilim carpet winding its way to the top, one of Maman's finds in Istanbul before I was born. As Bella led the way through the house, I broke away from them and rushed up the stairs to my parents' bedroom.

I shut the door and threw myself across their bed, burying my face in their pillows. Surrounded by the familiar scent of patchouli and lemons, I cried the tears I had been holding back all afternoon. Bella came in every so often to stroke my head, eventually helping me to change into my nightdress. She brought me some hot chocolate and as it grew cool on the bedside table, she covered me gently with a blanket and quietly left the room. My sobs gradually became deep rasping breaths, and I fell into a deep, dreamless sleep.

The next day I woke early and made my way into my parents' bathroom. I looked into the mirror, my eyes were red rimmed and my cheeks flushed from exhausted sleep. I drew a deep breath and pulled my shoulders back, I would try my best to be brave. The house was still quiet when, after a long bath, I emerged steaming from the bathroom. I pulled on some clean old clothes of my mother's, finding comfort in their familiarity. She and I were the same size and I resolved that it was her clothes I would take to Paris with me, so that I could secretly wrap myself in her embrace each day. I pulled out a suitcase and filled it with her colourful dresses and scarves, tunic tops, floppy hats and beautiful underwear. I took everything including the smocks and slim trousers she wore in her studio. Then, I plundered her cosmetics and creams, I even found her long cigarette holder and threw that into my case as well.

I had a few days before the trip to France and I spent a lot of time with Bella in the kitchen, finding comfort there, sitting by the Aga or helping her bake bread and biscuits. There was a soothing rhythm to kneading the dough, folding and pushing into it, stretching and folding again. Miss Lovegrove left me to it, recognising that this was what I needed before the proper work of packing my things began.

On the second day, I began to gather things from my bedroom, not knowing when, if ever, I would be back. I took out the small gold cross my father had given me and clipped it around my neck, I packed a photograph of my parents standing together on the cliffs with a view of the sea. My father was pulling her into an embrace as her dress billowed and flapped in the wind, both their faces turned, laughing to the camera. I had outgrown most of the clothes in my bedroom, so I left them, bringing only a couple of cosy nighties and my old teddy.

Miss Lovegrove encouraged me to walk through the rooms with her and tell her about some of my memories, perhaps wanting to make sure I didn't forget something important to me. When we entered the studio, I felt as if my parents had been working there just moments before and I gasped, covering my face with my hands. Miss Lovegrove put her arm across my shoulders and said kindly, 'I know dearest, this is so difficult for you.' She paused, 'Do you think there is anything here you would like to take with you?' I nodded, knowing exactly what I would take. I picked up my father's bag of sculpting tools and my mother's roll of paintbrushes.

'These,' I said, 'just these.'

We took the Night Ferry to Paris at the end of the week, sleeping in our own compartment on the train. Miss Lovegrove explained that it would roll onto the ferry at Dover, and arrive in Paris the next morning. Bella and the remaining staff would close the house and cover the furniture, continuing to live in their quarters until a decision was taken about their future. I hugged Bella tightly as we said our goodbyes, promising to write, then took a deep breath and turned away as I stepped into my future.

JUNIPER

It would be another month before I met Juniper de Montfort for the
first time in Paris. She was a few years older than me and lived with
her parents in London. Their house overlooked Richmond Park,
the Thames meandered in the distance and deer grazed within
sight of their garden. When I visited the house years later, I found
a tranquility and charm I had rarely seen. Pale pink roses rambled
over its white walls and two large, oval flowerbeds, presided over
manicured lawns. A wide balcony on the first floor overlooked
the garden to the left side of the house, and at the back, facing
south, another balcony swept around in a semi-circle, supported
by elegant white pillars.

Juniper came to Paris with her mother, a month after my
parents' funeral. She later told me that that day changed the
course of her life, and even years later, she recalled every detail.
She remembered gazing wistfully out of the glazed drawing room
doors to the garden in London, so badly wanting a change. Usually
open during good weather, the doors were closed that day against
the January chill. The room had high ceilings, and was hung with
hand painted, silk wallpaper; exotic birds seemed to flutter from
golden trees, set against the mysterious depths of dark green bushes
behind. A cheerful fire burned in the grate and a bowl of out of
season flowers bloomed lavishly, dropping small, fragrant petals
onto the polished surface of the table.

Juniper and her mother were seated on elegant chairs awaiting
guests, as Juniper stared languidly towards the window, wishing
it wasn't so cold. Had it been warmer, she would have found an

excuse to stretch her legs outside, rather than endure this waiting. Young men, whom her parents deemed 'suitable', (I remember her laughing ironically as she told me this) had been arriving at the house for weeks, either with their mother or sister in tow, ostensibly for tea. She knew her parents wanted her to get married and settle down.

I could picture Juniper's angular features silhouetted against the pale afternoon sunlight as she looked towards the window and the sound of the arriving car, amusement and mild curiosity etched on her face. Her glossy, dark hair swinging, perfectly cut and styled, just above her shoulders. Her neat tailored suit, of fine, pink wool, fitted to show off her tiny waist and long legs. She told me she was accustomed to the awe she inspired in young men in those days. It had even become a bit of a game to her, watching them squirm as they struggled to be amusing, hoping to make a good impression. She told me she had rather cruelly thought of them as little fish wriggling on a hook.

I imagined Juniper's attention drifting as she became bored with the conversation; her mother carrying bravely on, recounting anecdotes of art they had seen and trips they had taken. Finally, Juniper would reward the departing young man with a warm smile and a full view of her aquamarine eyes, probably reflecting her relief at his imminent departure. As the car pulled away, Claudia would turn to her and sigh, 'That was awkward Juniper, I really do feel you could have made a bit more effort with them; your behaviour might have been interpreted as rude.' Juniper said nothing, pretending to examine her newly manicured nails. 'What exactly is it you are looking for my darling; you know that perfection doesn't exist in the real world don't you?'

'Mummy, I am quite happy as I am,' Juniper replied, and yet, as she spoke, she knew it was a lie. A deep restlessness was rising up within her; she said she wanted to stop playing Mummy and Daddy's little doll, take off her shoes and run until she was ragged and exhausted.

'Darling, I do hope that one day you will know what it is to love with all your heart and be loved in return;' said Claudia, 'it really is the greatest gift. We all need a special person to witness the triumphs and disappointments of our lives. Perhaps when you are older, you will understand.'

. 'Speaking of need Mother, there is a new Dior collection showing in Paris next week, have you received an invitation? A little trip would do me good, take my mind off things.'

'Actually I have,' said Claudia, 'it takes place on Thursday. I do need one or two new pieces for the spring, perhaps a trip would do us good.' Claudia brightened at the prospect, 'I will speak to your father in the morning.'

A few days later, Claudia and Juniper sat side by side in the luxurious Dior salon in Paris. Claudia watched as the models moved past her, the expensive fabrics rustling as they showed the drape of the cloth and the style from all angles.

Beside her, Juniper's mind wandered, she was restless, bored with her life and tired of the endless clothes. She sighed, picking at the fine wool of her skirt, admiring her long slim legs and scrutinising her elegant shoes. If only something interesting would happen; she sighed again, and this time Claudia glanced over and raised an eyebrow, her meaning clear. Her mother had briefed her about what to expect at the show and the way she expected her to behave. 'There will be some influential people attending Juniper, many of whom I have known for years. I want to feel proud of you.' Juniper straightened and began to pay attention to the models, before once more allowing her mind to drift. A ripple of clapping brought her attention back to the room as the show came to an end. Their exclusive group stood and moved to a small salon where champagne was offered and mostly declined. The collection was discussed and comparisons made, as pieces were ordered and fittings booked.

Juniper, who had been patiently waiting, saw a tall, elegant woman making her way towards them. Claudia did not see her until she was almost beside them and then, her face lit up in recognition. 'Clémence, quelle surprise! Comment allez-vous?' They leaned forward, elegantly air kissing each other's powdered cheeks. Claudia turned and with a gesture towards Juniper, introduced her. 'Je vous présente ma fille, Juniper.'

'Enchantée,' Clémence replied, pleasant but unsmiling as she reached out a gloved hand to meet Juniper's. Juniper glanced at her mother, feeling she should either curtsey or kiss the outstretched hand of this serene and rather awe inspiring woman, but in the end opted for a handshake. She continued to watch as the woman turned to speak to her mother. Her perfectly made up face was framed by a deep green velvet hat, its band of mink curling into a point just above her left ear. A matching velvet jacket fitted neatly into her waist, before flaring out over slim hips, to a narrow fur hem. Juniper recalled her mother mentioning a wealthy and important patron of charities, among those who may be present. She idly wondered if this could be the one, as her attention returned to their conversation.

'How charming,' said Clémence, 'A mother and daughter shopping expedition all the way from London.' She spent a moment in leisurely appraisal of Juniper, and finding nothing to disappoint her, nodded imperceptibly as if coming to a decision. 'Please do join me at home for a tisane this afternoon, if you have no prior engagements.'

'We would be delighted,' said Claudia, 'thank you'.

There it was, the moment that changed everything. When she told me the story, Juniper didn't try to hide the way Clémence referred to me that day, in fact, she repeated the conversation word for word.

'My son, Étienne, is staying for a few days and my sad little niece, Alice, will be with me for much longer. She recently arrived from London in very difficult circumstances.'

'Oh dear,' murmured Claudia, as Clémence continued,

'She has been very quiet since she arrived, the girl hardly leaves her room,' she paused, 'I am allowing her time to adjust before I expect too much of her. She recently lost both her parents, my younger sister Amélie and her husband, in a tragic car accident.'

'How dreadful for her,' said Claudia. 'How old is she?'

'Sixteen, it is a difficult age. She is neither child nor woman, I really don't know how I will cope,' said Clémence, 'but I am her closest family now and I must do the best I can. It is such a pity that her mother and I could not resolve our differences while there was still time.' There was a silence as Claudia considered her response, eventually nodding sympathetically. Clémence paused again, before continuing, 'There were no rules in my sister's household, no understanding of living 'comme il faut', vous comprenez Claudia?' Claudia did understand and felt rather sorry for the girl, having this formidable woman as her guardian, in such heart breaking circumstances.

The chauffeur driven car swept up in front of Clémence's home as the afternoon light was fading. A liveried doorman stepped out to open the ornate doors. 'Bonsoir Mesdames,' he said as they walked through into the large, deeply carpeted hallway. The space was dominated by an ornate marble table and a vase of extravagant blooms, illuminated by a crystal chandelier.

Once in the lift, the doors slid smoothly shut. As they emerged outside the penthouse, a maid stepped forward to greet them.

'Bonsoir Madame.'

'Bonsoir Sophie, nous allons prendre du thé au salon s'il vous plaît.'

'Oui Madame.' Sophie took their coats and they followed Clémence into a large drawing room, where a welcoming fire burned. Chinese rugs in shades of pale pink and cream were laid over light blue carpets. Beautiful sofas in a deeper shade of china blue, stood in a square around the warmth of the fire. Claudia managed not to gasp as she recognised a Monet in lilac, blue and pink hanging above it. To one side of the room, elegant floor length windows, framed by cream silk, velvet drapes, looked out onto a wide balcony with views across the twinkling city.

Juniper had fallen silent at this unexpected turn of events. She was particularly curious about 'sad leetle Alice', hoping to at least catch a glimpse of me before they left. Sophie returned with a tray bearing fine teacups, a teapot and a plate of lemon slices. She placed it on the table and waited. 'Merci Sophie, c'est tout,' said Clémence.

'Oui Madame.' She paused, 'Madame, Monsieur Étienne vient d'arriver.'

'Oh Etty is here, how marvellous.' Clémence motioned for Sophie to bring another cup and smiled for the first time, quite transforming her face, which became suddenly soft and youthful. A man in his early thirties strode into the salon, tall and broad shouldered wearing an immaculate suit and crisp shirt and tie, his face was tanned and sprinkled with unlikely freckles. His hair, although neatly cut, had a long swept back fringe that fell forward as he leaned in to greet his mother.

'Étienne, these are friends of mine from London. Je vous présente Mme de Montfort et sa fille, Juniper de Montfort.'

Étienne made a small bow and smiled, 'Enchanté Mesdames, how are you enjoying Paris?'

'Very much thank you,' replied Claudia.

Étienne sat down facing the fireplace, his large frame dwarfing the third sofa as he turned to his mother, 'How is Alice today Maman?'

'I have no idea, I will ask Sophie to check on her later.' Claudia's heart went out to the poor girl, and she wondered if there was anything she could do to help. She quickly dismissed the notion, they would only be in Paris for a few days and by the sound of it, this was a long term problem.

Juniper took everything in, watching Étienne for signs of interest in her, which were not forthcoming. She told me that from the moment he walked into the room, she fell a little in love with him. Perhaps it was the gloss of his handsome, worldly demeanour and his being more than ten years older than her, that rendered her tongue tied for the first time in her life. It also came at a time when she was desperate to break out of her gilded cage.

As well as the unexpected diversion of Étienne, she told me that she was both fascinated and curious about me, a girl younger than herself who now had the freedom she craved. Yes, Juniper knew I had lost my parents, but in spite of this, she admitted that all she could feel was an envy of my freedom and my new life in Paris.

They sipped their tea as conversation flowed. Étienne, it seemed, spent time working in both Paris and London. He was an adored only son, and to his mother's chagrin, he remained unmarried. 'I am far too busy for marriage Maman, you know that', he said, winking at her.

'Nobody is too busy to marry, Etty. The right wife is an asset, not to mention children to carry on the d'Apidae name.' Étienne smiled and sighed indulgently at his mother.

'Don't give up hope Maman, you never know, I may surprise you with a bride when you least expect it!' Claudia thought this unlikely, but could see that it was what Clémence wanted to hear and she smiled.

'Well Juniper, I think we had better make our way back to the hotel so that we are refreshed for tomorrow. Thank you for your kind hospitality, Clémence.'

'Not at all, it has been a pleasure to see you. I will have my driver take you back.' She pulled the bell for Sophie, adding, 'Perhaps you would like to join us for lunch the day after tomorrow. It will be good for Alice to meet somebody a little closer to her own age and we would be delighted to see you again, wouldn't we Étienne?'

'Of course we would, I do hope you will come,' he said to Claudia, 'you too Miss de Montfort.'

'Thank you, we would enjoy that,' replied Claudia.

'Allow me to accompany you to your car ladies,' Étienne insisted, helping them into the coats that Sophie proffered.

'How kind, thank you,' said Claudia, glancing at Juniper, whose cheeks and neck were delicately suffused with pink.

I remember hearing their conversation in the hallway that day, and I tiptoed along the corridor from my bedroom to try to catch a glimpse of them. It was then that I saw Juniper for the first time. She was tall and elegant and everything I imagined Clémence would wish me to be. She happened to turn back just for a moment and our eyes met.

Juniper remembers it too. She said she caught a fleeting glimpse of somebody tall and slim, peering from a doorway, then disappearing just as quickly when she caught her eye.

How strange, she thought, I wonder if that was Alice.

THE GALLERY

I pictured Clémence smiling as Claudia and Juniper entered the salon two days later. 'Please, come in,' I heard her say, 'and allow me to introduce Miss Lovegrove, Alice's companion from London.' Miss Lovegrove, wearing her elegant green suit, stepped forward to greet Claudia.

'Hello Miss Lovegrove, I am Claudia de Montfort and this is my daughter, Juniper.'

Juniper told me later that she glanced over Miss Lovegrove's shoulder as she greeted her, searching the room for me, disappointed that I was not already there. The truth was I hadn't been able to summon the courage to join them. I had tried on several outfits, uncertain what to wear, ultimately opting for a hand painted, Japanese top with red, silk trousers, a favourite of my mother's. I needed to feel a little of her joie de vivre that day to boost my confidence.

'You know Étienne already of course,' said Clémence, as Étienne greeted them.

'Welcome ladies, may I offer you both a glass of champagne?'

'Thank you,' said Claudia. 'How are you enjoying Paris, Miss Lovegrove?'

'Very much indeed,' she said.

'Do try to take a river boat cruise along the Seine, if you can. It really is a marvellous way to see the city,' said Claudia.

As conversation flowed, Juniper kept glancing towards the door, impatient to meet me, then Clémence stood up and said, 'Shall we go through to the dining room.'

They followed her through, chatting as they took their places at the table. Once they were seated, I walked towards the dining room and slowly opened the door. As I entered, long folds of red silk floating about my ankles and a dab of red lipstick on my mouth, Clémence let out a little gasp. Silence fell, and all eyes turned first to me and then to Clémence. I knew my outfit was not what Clémence would have chosen for me, but I had seen my mother hold a room in the palm of her hand, walking in as I had; gloriously dressed and cheered on by her friends. It was not the reception I had hoped for.

Thankfully Étienne broke the silence and did his best to hide an amused grin as he stood to greet me.

'Alice, you look lovely, come and sit here next to me? Allow me to introduce you to Mme de Montfort and her daughter Juniper de Montfort, recently arrived from England, like you.' Claudia smiled kindly.

'Hello Alice, how nice to meet you. I am so very sorry to hear of the circumstances that have brought you to live in Paris.'

'Thank you,' I said quietly as I sat down, feeling suddenly unsure of myself, my heart lurching with grief at the reference to my parents' accident. Claudia continued,

'My daughter and I are here for another week, perhaps you would like to come and join us for tea one afternoon?'

Then Étienne turned to me and said, 'Do you like art Alice? I hear there is an exhibition of the Dutch painter Van Gogh at the Orangerie.' I smiled gratefully at them both.

'Yes, very much. I would like that, and I would love to come to tea, Mrs de Montfort, thank you.'

Juniper watched our exchanges, but her face remained serene and disinterested. I know now that her mind was racing, as she took in every detail. She remembered my petite oval face and green eyes, framed by short, auburn hair but particularly my extraordinary outfit. Juniper was unaccustomed to being outshone, and she admitted that a little wedge of jealousy began to gnaw at her that day.

Clémence had not said a word since I walked into the room, and noticing, Juniper turned to her and said in perfect French, 'Mme d'Apidae the lunch is truly delicious, how kind of you to invite us.'

'You are most welcome, it is our pleasure,' Clémence replied serenely. 'Étienne I'm sure that Mme de Montfort and Juniper would enjoy the Orangerie. Perhaps you should all go for an excursion tomorrow. You too Miss Lovegrove, I understand you are a teacher of art in London?'

'Yes I am, and of French too, I would love to,' she replied. As we chatted, Sophie served elegant plates of foie gras. Once or twice I caught Juniper's eye, but she was aloof and unsmiling, so I turned to Claudia.

'How long will you be in Paris, Mrs de Montfort?'.

'Just a few days, but I know the city well. Have you seen much of Paris so far, Alice?'

'A little,' I replied. 'We are very near the Arc de Triomphe and I took some photographs from the top the other day. It was like standing at the centre of a twinkling star; the roads radiating out from it were all lit up.'

'How lovely,' said Claudia.

By the time we were finishing our salmon, Juniper's face was more animated. She was flushed and smiling as she listened to Étienne, basking in his attention. I took a deep breath, the lunch was almost over, and soon I would be able to return to my room. I still found myself overwhelmed with grief at times, often at the most unexpected moments.

The long lunch concluded with arrangements for our visit to the Orangerie, and we said goodbye. Claudia clasped my hand in both of hers as she left, smiling warmly.

'Goodbye Alice, I hope to see you again soon for tea. Perhaps you and Juniper will be company for each other at the gallery tomorrow.' Juniper glanced over at me, unsmiling, and as our eyes met, she looked quickly away towards Étienne.

'Thank you so much for your hospitality Étienne, and yours too, Mme d'Apidae. I look forward to tomorrow.'

The next day dawned clear and bright and Paris was at its radiant best. The blue sky, washed clean by overnight rain, sparkled as we stepped out to the waiting car. This time I chose purple and white culottes, paired with the neat black jacket I had worn to Brown's Hotel. I tied a purple silk scarf around my head, and the ends fluttered in the morning breeze as I stepped outside to the waiting car.

'Allow me to help you into the car Miss Lovegrove,' said Étienne, 'you too Alice. There you are ladies.' The car glided smoothly away, pulling up a short time later outside the George V to collect Juniper.

Étienne stepped inside, at first looking past the dark haired beauty sitting in the lounge. Then Juniper stood and smiled in greeting as he walked towards her,

'Good morning Miss de Montfort, how are you today?'

'I am very well, thank you,' she said, 'but please, call me Juniper.'

'Very well Juniper, are you ready to go?'

'Yes, I am.' A slight blush crept to her cheeks as she tilted her head to do up the buttons of her coat. He held out his arm, and she placed her small hand over it as they walked out to the car.

Once settled inside, the limousine pulled smoothly away. Étienne explained that we would cross the River Seine to better enjoy the sights of Paris en route. The driver turned off the leafy Avenue towards the Pont d'Alma, and as we came over the bridge, the Eiffel Tower rose up to our right. 'How marvellous!' exclaimed Miss Lovegrove, who could hardly believe she was finally seeing something that had existed only in pictures for her, until now. The driver turned along the left bank, and as we slowly cruised along the Quai d'Orsay the magnificent glass roof tops of the Grand Palais came into view over the tops of the trees. Étienne pointed out the ornate Alexandre III bridge as we approached, its four golden, winged horses shimmering in the sunlight atop great square pillars. At the foot of each, he said, stone statues represented the great institutions of France; Commerce, Industry, Science and the Arts.

As the car continued along the Quai d'Orsay the golden top of the obelisk on Place de la Concorde rose majestically into the blue sky. Just beyond it, on the other side of the river, the pale stone of the Orangerie came into view, flanked by rows of clipped, square lime trees.

'There it is,' said Étienne. 'The Tuileries Gardens surround the Orangerie along the river, as far as the next bridge.' We crossed the river, finally pulling up outside the ornate gates at the edge of the gardens. As we stepped out into the morning sunshine, I moved away from the group, holding my arms open and tilting my head up to the sky, as a deep sigh escaped my lips. How wonderful it was to feel the sunlight on my face. I took some deep breaths and smiled. Juniper straightened her coat, brushing off an imaginary piece of fluff and Miss Lovegrove stepped forward purposefully, not wanting to waste a moment of this marvellous opportunity.

There were two treasures to look forward to, first the Waterlilies paintings donated to the Orangerie by Claude Monet some 30 years before, the second was an exhibition of previously unseen works by Van Gogh. We stepped into the light filled entrance hall, deciding to save the Monet Waterlilies for last. On the lower level of the exhibition space, a guide was on hand to explain that the owner of the works, Dr Gachet, had sheltered Van Gogh during the last years of his life, along with Cezanne and Pissarro in the south of France. All had painted prolifically whilst staying with him in Auvers, and he had kept many of their paintings.

The central painting was of the church at Auvers, it was almost three feet tall and perhaps 18 inches wide. The grey and beige church was set on a hill and surrounded by a vivid blue sky. A path in shades of yellow wound to either side of it and a bell tower with a clock face, soared into the sky.

'Do you see,' said Miss Lovegrove, 'the way the shadows fall in front of the church giving way to bright, sunny green grass, but around the edges of the picture, black clouds are gathering?' We leaned in to inspect the painting more closely as she continued, 'I believe those dark clouds are said to foreshadow Van Gogh's death, a month later.'

At the mention of death, grief rose in my chest again and I breathed deeply, closing my eyes until it subsided. Could my mother have had any idea that her life would be cut short? Would there be any clues in *her* paintings, I wondered. I took another deep breath and opened my eyes, before moving to join the others.

They were standing in front of a painting of cottages at Cordeville, set against sunny fields and a blue sky. I stood back and looked carefully at it. 'Isn't it strange the way Van Gogh has created a clear, sunny day with swirling lines; it makes the sky look stormy, somehow, as if one is contradicting the other.' It made me think of the times my mother could be the life and soul of the party, yet sink into a dark depression the next day and find herself unable to paint.

Miss Lovegrove told us that the months preceding Van Gogh's death were a frenetically creative period for him. The beautiful weather in the south of France lent itself to the many hours he spent painting en plein air. As I looked at the painting, my heart was heavy at the sadness and unfairness of it all.

I looked across at Miss Lovegrove, who had become quiet and contemplative. Behind me, Juniper looked up at Étienne and suggested that they take some air and refreshment; perhaps feeling that enough time had been wasted in dismal contemplation. Étienne was happy to comply, so they strolled out of the gallery, Juniper's hand proprietorially on his arm.

When Miss Lovegrove and I joined them some twenty minutes later, they were seated together at a small table sipping coffee. Juniper's cheeks were flushed and Étienne was laughing at something she had just said. He stood up as he saw us approaching, 'Ladies do come and sit down, would you like some refreshment?'

'Thank you, yes,' said Miss Lovegrove, 'I would love a cup of coffee.'

'Lemonade for me please, thank you Étienne,' I said.

Juniper didn't look up as Étienne walked away, but continued drinking her coffee, like a cat with a saucer of cream, a small private smile on her lips. 'Did you enjoy the exhibition, Miss de Montfort?' asked Miss Lovegrove.

Juniper looked up, 'Not really, if I'm honest,' she replied, not bothering to hide her disinterest.

'You do surprise me,' countered Miss Lovegrove, 'a cultured young lady such as yourself, not interested in art?' I saw Juniper look disdainful, almost managing not to roll her eyes, as she barely suppressed a sigh.

She told me as we reminisced years later, that she had resented being lectured by the person she thought of as, 'the teacher companion of poor leetle Alice' and we laughed.

I remember thinking at the time, as I watched Juniper turn her full beam smile on the returning Étienne, that despite her apparent indifference to us both, she could be charm personified when it suited her.

MONTMARTRE

Clémence was keen for me to begin accompanying her to high profile charity events, and one morning, having failed to squeeze me into a tailored dress so that I could join her for lunch, the plan was shelved. I breathed a sigh of relief as I watched Clémence leave for the day, planning to clear my head and walk out to explore the city.

Alexandre had written to me outlining his favourite haunts, including a list of friends I should contact, *'if you need a little cheering up daahling.'* He finished the letter with illustrations of flamboyant characters in funny hats and whimsical outfits. Dear Alexandre and George, how I missed them! I folded the letter carefully into the bag that swung from my shoulder and set off.

It was a beautiful spring day, the sky was blue and the trees along the Avenue George V were showing the first signs of blossom on their otherwise bare branches. I felt a sense of freedom as I strode out into the sunshine in my blue trouser suit, a red shawl flung around my neck and my father's black beret pulled onto my head. At last I was finding my feet, settling into my life in Paris and enjoying the sense of freedom it brought me. I was inhabiting my mother's clothes now, carrying them with style rather than using them as a shield. There was a chilly wind as I crossed over the Champs-Elysées, and I paused for a moment to admire the magnificence of the Arc de Triomphe, silhouetted against the sky.

I was heading to Montmartre to look up Kiki Lagrange, Alexandre had drawn a picture of her holding a paintbrush, an artist then? I hoped so. I tried to call, but found the number disconnected, so I hoped Kiki would be at home. The last mile of the walk took me steadily uphill and I could see the white dome of the Sacré Coeur, high up ahead. Kiki's street was at the foot of the final ascent, and when I saw a café, I impulsively sat down and ordered coffee.

I watched people come and go as I sat outside, enjoying the atmosphere. A couple at the next table gazed into each other's eyes as their coffee went cold; a boy with a guitar over his shoulder brushed past me to order a beer. Then I saw a woman in a long skirt and colourful jacket walking down the hill towards me. She stopped to rummage in her bag, pulled out a huge, purple handkerchief, then bent forward to sneeze loudly. 'Christ, this effing hay fever!' she said, blowing her nose.

A girl in a knee length skirt came running down the hill after her. 'Kiki, wait!' she shouted, 'you forgot the cake!'

'Thanks Izz,' she muttered, glancing disinterestedly at the tin.

'Kiki bonjour!' said the waiter stepping out of the café, but before Kiki could reply, the younger girl stepped forward smiling and thrust the tin into his hands. 'Pour toi Marc, for your birthday last week!' Marc leaned in and kissed her on both cheeks.

'Merci Isobel, tu es très gentille !' He turned his attention to Kiki once again, 'Kiki ça va?' Kiki didn't answer at first, she was still wiping her streaming eyes. Eventually she said,

'As you see, I could be better!' She smiled and leaned in to kiss him on both cheeks, 'Et toi?' before flopping into a chair at the table next to me. 'May as well have a coffee now we're here,' she said. Isobel sat down as Marc brought out 2 steaming espressos and placed them on the table.

'Cafés pour les belles dames,' he said. Kiki lit a slim brown cigarette and inhaled deeply, turning her head to blow the smoke behind her.

I had been listening to the exchange, looking across at the women. Could this be the Kiki I had come to see? Surely that would be too much of a coincidence. Finally, I plucked up the courage to speak. 'Excuse me,' I said leaning across, 'but, are you by any chance Kiki Lagrange?'

Kiki looked up surprised, taking the cigarette out of her mouth. 'Yes I am, who's asking?'

'I am Alice, Alice Gardener, my friend Alexandre said I should get in touch. I recently moved to Paris you see. He gave me a list of a couple of his friends, and here I am.' Kiki looked me up and down before smiling and saying,

'Did he now. How is the old reprobate?'

'Pretty good when I saw him last,' I said.

'How about George, is he still tinkering with his old clocks?'

'As far as I know, yes.'

'This is Isobel' said Kiki, gesturing towards the young woman opposite.

'Not Isobel Barratt by any chance?'

'Yes! How on earth do you know that?' said Isobel, laughing, surprised.

'You can thank Alex,' I replied smiling, encouraged by her warmth. 'You are number 2 on the list. He said I should contact his friends if I needed, well,' I hesitated, not wanting to appear needy.

'Needed what?' said Isobel.

'Needed cheering up.' I said.

'And do you?' asked Isobel.

'Maybe a bit,' I said. 'I haven't met anyone in Paris so far except my aunt and my cousin. Tante Clémence keeps me on a tight rein,' I said rolling my eyes. Even Kiki managed a smile then.

'Well that settles it' said Kiki. 'We were just on our way to the Bobo Club. I'm trying to get us a gig there for tonight. Come with us if you like,' she said. So, when we had finished our coffee, we strolled together, passing small shops and another café, before turning into a narrow street. We eventually stopped outside a shabby white building with no windows, just a wooden door that had once been painted blue, now peeling and faded. Kiki rapped smartly, then pulled the old fashioned bell on the wall. We waited a minute or two, then just as Kiki raised her hand to ring the bell again, the door swung open and we were admitted by a tired looking man in shirt sleeves. We followed him along a dimly lit corridor, eventually emerging into a dingy space with a small stage at the back. Tables and chairs were arranged around it and there was a bar to the right.

'So, what've you got for me today Kiki?' called a man from behind the bar.

'How goes it Joe?' Kiki walked over and held up her hand for a palm slap, 'Izzy and I have a couple of songs for you.'

'Ok, let's have the stage lights on! Let's hear it girls.' We walked over towards the stage and Kiki and Isobel headed up the steps, as two spotlights lit up the raised floor. Kiki sat herself at the piano and Isobel stood beside her, while I sat at one of the tables, fascinated by this unexpected turn of events. After a short silence, Kiki began to play a slow haunting melody on the piano. As she started singing, her husky voice floated out into the dimly lit space, and Isobel lifted her arms up and began to sway to the music. Her hips swung gently to the rhythm, and her arms moved gracefully above her head. She closed her eyes as her flimsy chiffon skirt floated and shone under the stage lights, and holding her arms wide, she slowly turned in circles. She moved to the music as if in a dream as Kiki played, her presence ethereal, lighting the stage as a ghost might illuminate the night sky. When the piece eventually came to an end, I realised that tears were trickling down my cheeks. There was a silence and then a slow, loud clap from behind the bar. I pulled a tissue from my bag, relieved that the light was dim around the tables. Kiki stood up and Isobel became still and bowed.

'Not bad!' called Joe. 'Do you have any more stuff like that?'

'We do,' said Kiki, 'glad you liked it.'

'Ok you're on, 11 tonight,' he called. With that the stage lights went down and the two women stepped from the stage smiling. They had forgotten I was there and I felt suddenly awkward, but piped up,

'Wow, that was a surprise. I think he loved it!' They looked pleased at the compliment and beckoned me to follow them as we headed back along the dim corridor, finally pushing open the door and stepping outside into the sunshine.

I met up with Kiki and Isobel regularly after that, eventually being invited up to Kiki's small house, where she had a studio on the top floor. There was an upright piano at one end of the room, standing underneath a small roof light window. At the other end, a large, north facing window looked across the sloping gardens below the Sacré Coeur. The basilica itself was mostly obscured by bare branches, yet to come into leaf. In front of the window there was a battered sofa and next to it, an easel with a half-finished canvas propped up on it. A shabby table stood in the corner covered with tubes of paint, and a thick ceramic jar held brushes and palette knives. The palette glimmered in the light, still wet with oils and as I walked into the room, the familiar smell flooded my senses, bringing both the pain of loss and the ease of familiarity all at once. I flushed with the effort of hiding my emotion, my grief still raw. Knowing Kiki and Isobel gave me back the kind of life that had died for me with my parents, and I began to think about painting again.

Kiki said I could use her studio when I wanted to, there was plenty of room. My time in the company of my new friends made life on the Avenue George V more bearable.

Isobel was a quiet and thoughtful companion and I learned over time that she had left home a couple of years before. She told me that her parents found her in their bed with her maths teacher. 'I can laugh about it now,' said Isobel, 'but I will never forget the look on their faces as Mr Simmonds leaped out of their bed and jumped naked onto the fire escape clutching his clothes. My father closed and locked the window, knowing he would be stuck out there. You see,' she explained, 'the fire escape was being rebuilt and had no access to the ground!' We both began to laugh until tears rolled down our cheeks.

'So what happened next?' I said eventually, wiping my eyes.

'Mr Simmonds was sacked and I was expelled,' she said. 'Soon after that, my father threw me out. It was a lucky escape really,' said Isobel. 'He and my stepmother never wanted me there once they married, it gave them the excuse they had been waiting for. My father told me to pack my things and go; he handed me an envelope full of money as I left.' Her voice trailed off and despite the bravado of her words, I could see the hurt in her eyes.

'So what did you do?' I asked.

'Not a lot at first,' said Izzy. 'I stayed with a friend for a few days, then took a chance and came to Paris to look for work. I just wanted to get away and start a new life. I did the rounds of hotels, bars and cafés, hoping I might find a place that would offer me a room. That was when I met Kiki. She was sitting at the bar chatting to Joe the day I called by and when she heard my story, she offered me a room at her place for as long as I needed it. She seemed nice and I was pretty desperate by then, it was a relief to meet someone else from England. I will always be grateful to her for stepping in to help me the way she did, it has turned out well. I cook basic meals and tidy the place and now, most recently, I have been working with her at clubs, improvising dance moves to accompany her piano playing.'

'Had you danced before?' I asked.

'No, I didn't know I could dance. One day, Kiki had some music playing as she painted and I was bored. I got up, closed my eyes and started swaying to the music. I lost myself in a world of my own, I felt as if I was moving to a rhythm deep within me, a pulsing, throbbing beat. I'm not sure how much time passed, but when I finally opened my eyes, Kiki was no longer painting. She had put down her brushes and was standing staring at me, mesmerised. The next day we went looking for work as a duo and got our first gig.'

I sighed, 'I think you are really brave.' Isobel smiled,

'We do what we have to do to survive. Sometimes life can lead you a merry dance, and then one day you wake up and find,' she hesitated, staring into the distance, 'You find happiness where you least expect it,' she said, her voice trailing off. 'Come on, let's go and get something to eat.'

JUNIPER 1955

Juniper told me that in the months following her first meeting with Étienne, and encouraged by Clémence, he saw her whenever he could. He would call on the family in Richmond, inviting them out to lunch and occasionally taking Juniper out to dinner alone. He spent a lot of time in Paris too, and the long separations increased the building intensity of their feelings for one another.

When they had been seeing each other for a year, Claudia believed that an engagement must surely be imminent. She had no way of knowing that Étienne had already requested a meeting with Charles at his club in Pall Mall.

Much later, Étienne told Juniper all about his conversation with her father. After a fine lunch together, and over a glass of port, he broached the subject of marriage. 'Sir, I believe you know already that I am heir to the considerable wealth of my family. Now, I am ready to settle down and share my life with someone I love.'

He paused as Charles took another sip of his port, waiting for Étienne to continue. 'This leads me to the reason I have asked you here today. I have felt affection for Juniper from the moment I met her, and that affection has grown deeper with time. It is my hope and belief that she feels the same way towards me. Sir, I would like to ask Juniper to be my wife; I am here today to ask for your blessing.'

'I rather wondered whether this might be your purpose today Étienne, and I have been giving it some consideration. Are you aware that there is a twelve-year age difference between you?'

35

'Indeed I am sir, I hope that as I have more experience than Juniper, I will be in a position to offer her a guiding hand as she matures. Her youth will be an advantage when it comes to settling into an unfamiliar lifestyle.'

I remember Juniper laughing ironically as she told me that. 'Perhaps if Étienne had just been there in the early days of our marriage, it might have helped,' she said.

Étienne went on to explain to Charles that his parents would expect them to live in France after their marriage. This was the part that Charles had been afraid of, and he knew that Claudia would find it very difficult to accept. 'Hmm,' he replied 'I am not sure that Juniper would want to settle in France Étienne, and given her relative youth, I believe she would want to be near her mother.'

'I regret sir that I don't believe my mother will countenance the idea of her grandchildren being brought up in England, and we would hope to have children as soon as we can. However, I can promise you that if after two years of living in France, Juniper is unhappy, we will not rule out the possibility of a move to London.' Privately, Étienne thought this outcome unlikely, he knew he would have an almighty battle on his hands if he were to cross Clémence.

'I see' said Charles, disappointed. 'Well, I would like to think this over Étienne. You are a fine young man and we would be very happy to have you as our son in law. However, these considerations need further thought. Juniper is very precious to us and her happiness is of paramount importance. She has always been indulged and that has not always been in her best interest, but it is as it is. Her mother and I would hate her to be unhappy; she still has quite a lot of growing up to do.'

Étienne quietly begged to differ, his mind wandered to the last time they said goodbye after an intimate dinner, during which he knew with certainty he wanted to marry her. He remembered Juniper's small hands rubbing around his waist and up his back as she looked meaningfully into his eyes, before demurely lowering her lashes. It made him wish that there had not been gloves and a shirt, however fine, between her skin and his.

Étienne realised with a jolt that Charles was waiting for him to reply. 'Yes, of course, I understand sir, please be assured that

Juniper's happiness will be my first consideration.'

'That is good to hear,' replied Charles. 'However, may I ask you to please keep our meeting to yourself for the time being and say nothing to Juniper.'

'Of course, I understand. Thank you for seeing me today.'

'I will be in touch with you again next week with my decision.'

What to do, deliberated Charles, what to do. Juniper was an adult and Paris was not all that far away. In fact, he reasoned, it would give Claudia more opportunity to visit that confounded dressmaker of hers. He hoped over time, Claudia would come to see it as a marvellous opportunity for their daughter.

Étienne was a perfectly suitable young man with whom Juniper had, if he was to be believed, fallen in love. Privately, Charles suspected that she was more in love with the glamour of an older man and a future in Paris, than with the man himself. Always better to fly in the face of one's parents if one could get away with it, he thought, recalling his own youth and his penchant for unsuitable dalliances.

'Charles, you are grinning,' said Claudia. 'Might I be allowed in on the joke?'

Charles looked up suddenly, a sheepish look on his face.

'Just something in the paper my dear,' he closed the paper and folded it, removing his glasses and sitting back in his chair. 'As it happens Claudia, I do have some news to share with you and I think now is as good a time as any.'

A few days later, Charles telephoned Étienne in Paris to give his permission and from there, things moved swiftly. A beautiful square cut diamond ring was procured from the d'Apidae family vault, and Étienne proposed to Juniper over lunch at the Ritz. 'Yes Étienne! Yes, I will marry you!' she remembered saying. She had been on her best and most endearing behaviour for months and it had paid off. Étienne was handsome and sophisticated and now he was hers. She felt sure she must be the envy of everyone in the elegant dining room. If she had any concerns about the intimate side of their life, she pushed them to the back of her mind.

Juniper marvelled at the beautiful ring, showing only a passing interest in the fact that it had been in Étienne's family for many generations. It sparkled and shone on her finger, and she delighted in the many admiring glances that were discreetly cast their way. Champagne was brought to the table and after a toast to each other and to their future, they returned to Richmond to break the news to her parents.

'I am so happy for you my darling!' said Claudia, pulling her daughter into her arms and hugging her tightly. Juniper allowed herself to be hugged only briefly, in honour of the occasion and then pulling away, she held out her hand so that her mother could admire the ring.

'Congratulations old chap,' said Charles, shaking Étienne's hand. 'We are delighted for you both. Welcome to the family.'

The following day Claudia telephoned Clémence in Paris to say how delighted they were about the engagement. Clémence and her husband felt the same, she said. Two weeks later, Claudia received an envelope with a Paris postmark containing a thick cream and gold embossed invitation. Clémence was to host an engagement party for the couple at the Ritz in Paris.

It is sad looking back, that Juniper remembered the months leading up to the wedding as the only parts of it that filled her with joy. She told me she could see with hindsight that she had been in love with the idea of getting married. Was she to blame for the way things had turned out, she wondered. Should she have confided in Étienne from the start?

Juniper remembered that her first priority was her wedding dress. Claudia favoured the British designer Hardy Amies in Saville Row, a rising star, and designer to the new Queen Elizabeth. He suggested a pearl coloured silk satin gown, in a form fitting style, to accentuate her slim body. It would be elegant, flaring widely from the hips, with a magnificent satin train, overlaid with lace.

As Juniper talked, it was like another language to me, so far removed was it from the kind of life I could ever want; but I laughed when she told me that Hardy Amies had been an unlikely hero during the war. Apparently he worked for the Belgian resistance and spoke several languages. His flamboyant appearance actually helped him to remain undercover, it being thought so unlikely that such a man might be involved in any form of combat. As we struggled to imagine Mr Amies sneaking around in disguise and hiding in dark corners, we both laughed and then Juniper reached out for my hand and smiled. 'Thank you Alice.'

'For what?' I said.

'For listening, I haven't really had a close friend before, it is helping me to come to terms with my life,' she paused. 'I have never told anyone that during the fittings for my dress, the most awful memories came back. Memories of things that happened to me as a child.'

'What kind of things?' I asked her, but she said she couldn't talk about it, not then anyway. She would only say that as the wedding approached, it troubled her more and more. Each time she felt the couturier's hands smoothing her dress, or pressing into her waist as he went about his work, her feelings of panic increased. She hid it from him of course, as she had hidden it from everyone.

CLÉMENCE

I still remember the first time I saw the softer, more vulnerable side of Clémence. I had taken to spending the evenings in my room, having eaten with friends or at home earlier in the day. So, I was surprised when Sophie knocked on my door to say that Madame Clémence would like me to join her for dinner in the dining room. I stopped what I was doing and went to brush my hair. I had already changed into silk pyjamas and a long pink robe for the evening and although I considered dressing first, in the end, it was thus attired that I walked into the dining room to greet my aunt.

'Bonsoir Alice, what on earth are you wearing my dear? Come in.' I leaned to kiss my aunt on both cheeks, before taking my place with her at the smaller round table in the dining room. Sophie had set it with a salad, some cold meats and a cheeseboard with fruit.

'I am sorry Tante Clémence but I wasn't expecting to join you for dinner. If I had taken the time to change, I might have kept you waiting.'

'I see, well you might as well stay as you are, now you are here. It is a long time since we sat down together and talked. How are you Alice, are you happy here in Paris?'

Clémence picked at her salad, as I talked about walks and friends and art galleries. I told her about an art course I was attending and how much difference it had made to my life this past year. I wondered aloud why she had taken me away from school in London, only to leave me to myself most of the time; but she wasn't really listening. I had the feeling she didn't want to be alone this evening. Perhaps she found my voice soothing, a gentle hum in the background of her thoughts.

Clémence was much quieter than usual, her feisty spirit seemed to have left her and she looked pale and thin. Having stopped speaking some minutes before and receiving no response, I said finally, in a gentle voice, 'Are you alright Tante Clémence?'

Hearing her name, Clémence turned to me suddenly. 'Yes of course I am alright, why wouldn't I be?' she snapped, shades of her usual self quickly returning. She sat up straighter and continued eating her salad, and then she sighed and looked at me. 'I'm sorry Alice, that was unfair of me. To tell you the truth, I am exhausted and a little low in spirit this evening.' I looked sympathetically at her and waited for her to say more, reaching out to place my hand gently on her arm.

Apparently she had emerged from a steaming shower after a long day organising another fundraising dinner. When she looked into the mirror, her mascara was running in rivulets down her face and she saw that she looked haggard.

'As I rubbed my skin with cream, I closed my eyes and found my mind drifting to Simeon, to the life I might have had if we hadn't gone our separate ways. It was all such a terrible waste and now, I'm alone and exhausted. What on earth was it all for?'

I was surprised that Clémence speaking to me like this, particularly as she had been so distant up to now. I was considering how I should reply, when she continued,

'Of course I can't expect you to understand Alice, you are young and beautiful with your whole life ahead of you. I was like you once. I wish I had been kinder, and now it is too late.' She paused. 'I see so much of Amélie in you, you have that rare gift of knowing how you want to live your life. In spite of your tragedy, you have found your way in a new city and you are making friends. You are just as brave as your mother would have been. I only wish that I had possessed her courage when I was young. You asked me just now, why I took you out of school; Amélie is the reason. I wanted to try to do for you what we, as a family, failed to do for her.'

'What do you mean Tante Clémence? I know there were problems, but Maman would never talk about it.' I longed to hear more about my mother's life in Paris before she met my father and to my surprise, Clémence seemed willing to continue. She told me that she and Amélie were never close; she had frequently found fault with her younger sister as they were growing up.

'I resented Amélie, she had a careless disregard for the conventions that I had made the backbone of my life. I so badly wanted to please our parents, there was no son and Father was bitterly disappointed that his name would not live on. I told him that it would, through me. When the time came to marry, I made Simeon agree that our family would carry the d'Apidae name. You see, I tried to be everything to him. Criticising Amélie made me feel superior. I am ashamed of it now, I was jealous, she was so full of life and so beautiful. Everything came so easily to her and it didn't seem fair. I regret it,' she said. 'I can see now that it was Amélie who was the wiser of the two of us.' Clémence stared into the fire, then said, so quietly I had to strain to hear her, 'I'm not sure I would know who I am any more, if my defences were down. I might just crack open like an egg and spill onto the floor.' There was a silence, and she sighed.

'I'm so sorry for how you are feeling Tante Clémence,' I said, and I reached out and squeezed her hand. She looked up at me and smiled,

'Amélie found the courage to be true to herself, no matter what the consequences.'

'Do you mean when she ran away with my father?' I asked.

'Yes, that in particular, but even before that, she just wouldn't be tamed by our father.'

Clémence turned and looked towards the Picasso hanging on the wall behind her. 'That is my last memory of the two of us together. My father forbade Amélie to sit for the portrait in Picasso's studio, but still she did it. She said she wanted to know how it felt to live in the real world.'

I looked up at the painting properly for the first time, it depicted two young women sitting closely, side by side. I'd had no idea it was Amélie, my mother, wearing a shaped yellow bodice and Clémence a heavy red robe. Both looked demurely towards a book they were reading. Underneath was the title I had missed, 'Deux Personnages – Les Soeurs d'Apidae à la lecture'

I couldn't believe I hadn't noticed. My father often talked

about the day they met, by chance in Picasso's studio, and here was the picture! Curious now, I asked, 'How did he paint you if you didn't go to the studio Tante Clémence?'

'Oh my father was used to getting his own way, and he persuaded Picasso to come here to finish it. Amélie and I sat side by side for the longest time, and the next day, she was gone. I only saw her once more after that, it was the day we all met in London, years later. Do you remember it Alice? You were only small, maybe 6 years old.'

I did remember it, Clémence had been austere and unapproachable and my mother, nervous; I hadn't seen her like that before.

'I think I do remember it, yes.'

'Do you know that having you in the house this past year has been wonderful and yet at the same time, almost too painful to bear. I can see so much of my sister in you Alice, it has slowly chipped away at the protective shell I have built around my heart and it hurts. The pain of loss feels so great sometimes that it weakens me, I hardly recognise myself. I have so wanted to make things right, through you, but it is so much harder than I imagined. There is so much more I could have done for her, I see that now.'

I wanted to make Clémence feel better and said, 'Maman talked about you sometimes, Tante Clémence. She knew you didn't mean to be the way you were. She said you only wanted to please your parents. She loved you, I know she did.'

Clémence smiled a sad smile,

'She always could see the best in everyone.' Then, changing the subject, she said, 'Enough of that, on to brighter things. I haven't told you much about your Uncle Simeon have I? He's probably out on his boat now, off Captiva Island in Florida.'

As she began to talk about the man who was her husband and whom I had never met, Clémence closed her eyes and just for a moment it was as if she felt the ocean spray on her face and the salty wind in her hair.

She imagined Simeon sitting out on the dock listening to the waves lapping, as boats cruised slowly back to the harbour after a day out on the water. A still, bright blue sky, and birds trilling loudly above his head in the palm trees, she sighed, then said,

'Actually I phoned Simeon before dinner, I probably sounded very unlike myself. Usually on the rare occasions I call him we deal with practical matters, such as his signature on some papers, or another piece of impersonal news. This time, I think he heard a softness in my voice, a sense of vulnerability that I hadn't shown for many years. I told him all about Juniper and Étienne's plans to marry, that he had fallen in love with a charming and elegant girl from England, a girl who reminded me a little of a young version of myself. He was so pleased.'

'That is marvellous news, he said, you must be thrilled about it Clem. I know you have been trying to persuade Étienne to marry for years.'

'Yes, I know I have,' I told him, 'but now he has found someone and they are serious,' she paused, 'I'm really not sure how I feel. I mean, I like her of course, but in a strange way, I feel I am about to lose him,' she drew her breath in sharply, stifling a little cry. 'Sorry Simeon, I think I have a slight cold.' There was a pause as she blew her nose. 'He is so like you were in the early days you see, if only you knew,' she sighed.' I have been thinking about it all lately, us I mean, wondering whether things might have been different. Did we make a terrible mistake all those years ago do you think?'

Clémence told me it was her fault they had separated. Hers was no life for a free spirit like Simeon, hanging on the coat tails of her charitable dinners and other good works, but she'd refused to give it up.

'The news that Étienne was to be married brought a rush of memories for us both. We talked about the early days of our marriage; picnics at the beach in Normandy, our little boy with a bucket and spade building sand barriers against the oncoming tide. Me, young and carefree stretched out on a sun chair beside him. We used to laugh together until our sides ached in those days, we were blissfully happy. How could I have let that slip away, and for what? I was another person then and my life was full of hope for the future.'

'You still have so much to look forward to,' I said.

'I know, but it was a shock to be faced so unexpectedly with a happy, unburdened version of myself, so long gone, and so very different to the woman I have become.'

By the time Sophie had cleared away and Clémence had finished speaking, I saw her with new eyes. It was as if in sharing these intimate details of her life with me, she was finally admitting her true feelings to herself.

Eventually she rose from the table. 'My dearest Alice, thank you for listening with such a kind heart; I must go to bed now, I am exhausted. I hope you sleep well.' I gave her a quick hug and turned to go to my room.

'I hope you sleep well too Tante Clémence, see you in the morning.'

The next morning after a night of restless dreams, I woke early and walked through to the breakfast room. Clémence stood in a heavy silk robe and slippers, enjoying the sight of the plants, still dewy from the night before, through the sunny window.

She sipped her coffee, and to my surprise she turned and said quietly, 'I enjoyed our conversation last night Alice. You know, my first instinct was to apologise to you this morning for being so maudlin, but I have decided I want to be more honest from now on, not just with you, but with myself.'

I smiled at her, still not fully awake. Clémence seemed to be speaking from an almost dreamlike place, as though her thoughts were a revelation, even to her. I didn't want to break her flow, so I said nothing, and waited for her to go on. 'I'm tired of pretending I'm happy, of living the life other people expect of me. It fills me with shame when I think of Amélie, I should have taken her side, helped her to stand up to our father, but I couldn't. All I could think of at the time, was that I would be the one who found favour with him afterwards, what a fool I was. I lost my sister and my father remained distant and autocratic with me. Even then, instead of seeing him for what he was, I tried harder and harder to be what he wanted me to be. It never crossed my mind to go after Amélie, to try to make things up to her, you see I truly believed my father was right. I couldn't let my standards drop, even for the man I loved. Simmy is the most relaxed and forgiving person, but I allowed my misguided sense of duty to drive us apart. I regret that more than I can say.'

'Perhaps it isn't too late for you both,' I said, hearing the lightness in my voice. 'Do you think Simeon will come to the wedding?'

'I don't know, I hope so,' she said, 'Étienne always has been the apple of his eye. It's strange that I haven't thought of Simeon much for years and now, he keeps coming into my mind. Étienne's wedding has stirred up so much in me, I have a lot of regrets in my life.'

'Don't be so hard on yourself Clémence,' I said, pouring myself a cup of coffee. 'It is never too late,' but she continued as if I hadn't spoken.

'I failed as a wife and as a sister, but perhaps now, I have the chance to put things right. I want to be kinder to the people I care about; to you Alice, to my son and to his future wife. It is the kindness I should have shown to my sister. My father made me believe that showing emotion was a sign of weakness.' Then she looked at me earnestly, 'I wonder why has it taken me so many years to see that he was wrong.'

My relationship with Clémence improved after that, she showed more interest in my life and treated me more like the daughter she never had. For my part, I felt more relaxed around the house and gradually, even a sense of belonging.

One evening as I sat reading and Clémence flicked through a magazine, Étienne put his head around the door of the salon to greet us, 'Bonsoir Maman, Alice.'

'Etty darling, do sit down,' said Clémence putting her magazine aside, 'There is something I need to discuss with you. I will ask Sophie to bring in some cocktails.'

'Mother, I have arranged to meet a friend for dinner. I can't stay long this evening I'm afraid.'

'Darling, you are always in such a hurry! Surely you can sit down for just a few minutes, I hardly see you. We need to discuss your new home; your engagement party is imminent and these things take time to plan. I have my interior designer awaiting our decisions on fabrics and colours for your new home, it will only take a moment.' Seeing that his mother was not to be thwarted, Étienne sighed.

'I am sorry to disappoint you Mother, but we have decided that we prefer not to live in Paris after the wedding. I have already written to Jack and Rosa to ask them to open up the house in

Normandy. I am going to visit next week to look it over. We both feel that we want our children to be brought up in the countryside, as I was. I still miss it, you know.'

Clémence was speechless for a moment, taking a sharp intake of breath. She had no idea that her son hankered after their life in the country, it had been so long ago. Quietly she composed herself and after a moment said, 'Of course Étienne, if that is what you have decided, then there is little I can do about it. However, I don't believe that hiding yourself away in the country will do you any good at all. How will you manage your work? What about Juniper, does she have any idea how isolated you will both be?'

'Mother, I'm afraid I don't have time to go into this now. I am already late and I need to go out. There is nothing for you to worry about, we will talk again tomorrow.' He got up and kissed her cheek and she heard the front door close behind him; I looked at her sympathetically.

'As a matter of fact Alice,' she said, turning to me, 'I wanted to speak to you about what you will wear for the engagement party next week. I have had my dressmaker let out an evening gown of mine, I think the colour will suit you.'

'Oh I have plenty of clothes, thank you Tante Clémence, don't worry about me.'

'I don't think you understand my dear, there will be some very influential people attending and your appearance will reflect on both Étienne and myself. I would like you to wear something appropriate, and of my own choosing,' and then she added, 'If you don't mind. I have also chosen a pale yellow evening dress for you to wear to dinner with the de Montfort family the evening before.'

I didn't mind particularly and neither did I feel inclined to argue with Clémence. It was a small thing for my aunt to ask of me, but I saw that she still cared about the good opinion of others. It might be harder than she imagined to let go of the habits of a lifetime. 'No of course I don't mind, when would you like me to try the clothes on?'

JACK AND ROSA, NORMANDY 1955

The sun slanted through the autumn trees, illuminating wet leaves along the path. Ahead, Jack could see the clearing, lit up by the sunny yellow of the ginkgo tree, glorious at this time of year. He paused a moment to admire the sight. The quiet early-morning allowed his thoughts to settle as he strode along, punctuated only by the twitter of birds in the trees and his own breath, billowing mistily into the air.

Jack occupied the small cottage in the grounds of the d'Apidae estate, known as Woodman's, with his wife, Rosa. It was Mme D'Apidae who had gifted Jack the cottage when he married; the old place had been their home for the last 20 years.

A solid dependable man of few words, Jack was more at home quietly waiting for a glimpse of the Kingfisher than conversing with his fellow man. He was 30 when he first saw Rosa on a rare visit to church at Christmas time. For Jack, God was in the trees, the flowers and the sunlight, he struggled to find Him in the dark and chilly walls of the local church. That Christmas Day though, the winter sun flooded through the myriad of colours in the stained-glass window and the congregation was bathed in jewelled light. The newly arrived maid to Mme d'Apidae was seated just in front of Jack and slightly to the left. The lights illuminated her smooth complexion and long dark lashes as she looked down at her hymn book.

Rosa, free from her parents for the first time, was easily charmed by the quiet woodman. They went on walks and picnics whenever she had a free day, and a year later they were married.

Rosa became indispensable to Mme Clémence and not having been blessed with a child herself, she and Jack loved Étienne as if he was their own. When the family moved back to Paris, and a more suitable school for Étienne, the boy came to stay with them for the holidays. They took him fishing and packed picnics to eat by the stream while Clémence continued her busy life in Paris.

When eventually, Étienne considered himself too old for these trips, and the family no longer came to the country, the house was shrouded in dust sheets and closed up. The loss of the family to take care of left a gap in Rosa's life, and she felt sad to see the lovely house standing quiet and alone among the trees.

It was therefore with great excitement one day, that Rosa rushed out to Jack in the garden, cheeks flushed, holding a letter in her hand. 'Jack, I have wonderful news!' Jack put down his spade and turned towards her.

'What is it chérie?'

'It is Master Étienne! He is engaged to be married!' Jack smiled indulgently at his wife,

'That is wonderful news! Does he say who the lucky lady is?'

'Apparently she is the daughter of a friend of Madame Clémence, but that is not all. Étienne says that they are planning to come and live here in Normandy after their wedding!'

'Well, well, well' said Jack, 'after all this time. That is a surprise!'

'He asks us to open up the house, take off all the dust sheets and throw the windows open to the fresh air. He is coming next week to look it over! Oh Jacques, to think there will be a young family living here again at last!' Jack smiled, that would indeed be a blessing, especially for Rosa. Rosa hadn't seen Mme Clémence for many years, but their salaries continued to arrive, and they took care of the houses and gardens on the estate as if they were their own.

The next few days were spent in a flurry of activity. Doors and windows of the house were thrown open, curtains were washed and rehung, beds were aired and made up with fresh linen sheets and windows were polished until they shone. Rosa enlisted the help of a girl from the village and between them they swept away the cobwebs, rubbed beeswax into all the wooden surfaces, scrubbed the floors and placed flowers in all the rooms. Sunshine poured into the house and for the first time in years it was restored to its former glory.

Rosa breathed a contented sigh as she walked from room to room, remembering life as it had been in the early days of her marriage to Jack. She remembered coming to this house to meet Mme Clémence for the first time, and the warmth of her welcome. She smiled and sighed, how quickly time passes. We must enjoy every moment of this precious life, she thought. Still smiling, she hurried back to their cottage and went outside to find Jack. She put her arms around him, laying her head on his chest for no reason at all, other than that he was there and he always had been there for her. 'Je t'aime chéri,' she said looking up and planting a swift kiss on his chin. 'What would you like for lunch?'

ALICE

During the weeks leading up to the wedding, two unexpected and significant events occurred. One morning over breakfast, the doorbell rang. I heard a brief conversation and then Sophie came in holding an envelope. 'It is addressed to you Mademoiselle Alice,' she said, handing it to me. I looked at it carefully, it had a Paris postmark and an official seal on the back. I carefully sliced it open, revealing a folded letter on thick parchment paper. There was an elaborate heading at the top, Maître Séjourné, Office Notarial. I began to read;

'Chère Mademoiselle, Je vous prie de venir à l'étude le 21 Mars a 14h. Nous avons quelques documents pour vous....' and so it continued.

It was from a Notaire, asking me to go to her office on Tuesday, preferably alone, to collect some documents she had for me.

On Tuesday, I waited for Clémence to leave, before dressing carefully in the black suit I had worn to my parents' funeral. I added a colourful silk blouse and a touch of lipstick before setting out for my appointment. I arrived at the Notaire's office a few minutes early and was kept waiting in a small side office. Eventually, she appeared, introducing herself as Maître Séjourné. She shook my hand and indicated that I should follow her through to her office.

'Asseyez-vous, svp Mademoiselle.' She paused, 'Alors,' she tapped her nails on the desk as she cast her eyes over the documents in front of her. 'So, I have here the last wishes of your parents concerning your mother's property in France, as well as some financial arrangements for you.' She looked up at me over the top of her narrow glasses.

'I was not aware my mother had a property in France,' I said.

The notaire studied the papers in front of her again, 'Well Mademoiselle, it appears that she did. She and her sister, Clémence d'Apidae each own a large property on the d'Apidae estate in Normandy. There is a further small cottage on the estate, occupied I believe, by a housekeeper and gardener couple. The property stands in 8 hectares, the land being shared by both owners, the houses are within walking distance of each other. The letter accompanying your mother's wishes states that her house has been empty for many years because she chose to live in London with your father. She bequeaths it to you and I quote 'hopes you can breathe life into it again,' she says here that she loved it once, many years ago.'

'I wonder why she never told me about it,' I said, 'Tante Clémence has never mentioned it either.'

Looking back on it, I see that my mother must have needed to blank her life in France from her mind, in order to leave it behind. Leaving her family for the man she loved, must have been almost too painful to bear.

Do you have keys to the house Maître Séjourné?' I asked.

'Yes I do,' she replied briskly, 'these will be handed to you at the end of our meeting.' There was a pause as she looked at me again over her glasses, 'I also have some other news for you.' There was another pause before she continued, 'It concerns your parents' house in London. The executors did not want the house to be sold as it has been in your father's family for many years, so it was offered for long term rental. Suitable tenants have now been found and the revenue will come to you, it will provide you with a regular income.'

'Does that mean I will be financially independent?'

'Oui Mademoiselle, bien sûr! Your Tante will have the final say, as she is your guardian, but as soon as you are 18 years old you can make this decision for yourself. I see you are,' she paused as she looked at the document in front of her, 'already 17 years old and that your birthday is only two months away.' I flushed with pleasure and smiled.

'Yes,' I confirmed. Maître Séjourné nodded, and pulled some

prepared documents from a folder for me to sign. She laid them out on the desk in front of me, I was required to initial each page at the bottom and to sign my full name on the page at the end. She would witness it herself with the official Notarial seal. She explained that the documents were dated for the day of my 18th birthday, to make the legal process more straightforward.

Once all the paperwork was signed, Maître Séjourné produced a large brown envelope into which she placed copies of the documents, two sets of keys and a card giving the full address and location of the house. 'You have everything you need here. My fees have been settled by your parents' estate. Bonne chance Mademoiselle.' She smiled and shook my hand.

As I walked away from the office, the envelope in my hand, I struggled to take in the news. I was confused and surprised that neither my mother nor Tante Clémence had seen fit to mention the properties in Normandy. Nevertheless, I decided to keep the news to myself for now.

When I arrived home, there was another letter for me, this time in a blue envelope, addressed in flamboyant script. Alexandre! I thought, picking it up, delighted. Taking the letter to my room, I kicked off my shoes and tore it open;

The Hon Alexandre Fortescue,
The Mews Cottage,
Chelsea
June 1956

My dearest Alice
    George and I are on our way to Paris! We will be staying with friends in Montmartre where there is to be a party!
    The whole crowd will be there! Get your glad rags on daaahling we are going to have FUN!'
    Call me just as soon as you get this xxxx

I looked at the party invitation enclosed. It was tonight! 7pm at 15 Place des Abesses. I picked up the phone and dialled the number Alexandre had written at the bottom of the letter, he must already be in Paris!

'Oui, allo' said a gruff voice at the other end of the phone.

'Bonjour, je m'appelle Alice, je cherche mon ami Alexandre?' There was a loud cough at the other end and then a clatter as the phone was dropped.

'Alexandre, c'est pour toi,' shouted the gruff voice. A few minutes later I could hear footsteps approaching and then Alexandre's voice.

'Alex, it's me!' I said excitedly.

'Daahling! Mwah' he said, blowing kisses down the line. It was so wonderful to hear his voice.

'How are you and how is George?' I said, unable to hide the burst of happiness I felt to have this connection to home.

'We are perfectly fine daahling, how have you been enjoying Paris? Are you coming to the party tonight?'

'Yes of course I am! Who else will be there?'

'I don't know chérie! Probably Kiki and friends, Jasper, Raoul, anybody who is anybody will be partying tonight.' His enthusiasm was infectious and my heart lifted at the prospect of an evening with friends. 'Did you ever meet Jasper daahling, I'm sure I put his name on that little list I gave you when you moved to Paris, but you never mentioned him.'

'I did! It was through him that I started at the École des Beaux Arts. He teaches there, but I'm sure you know that Alex.'

'What a pair of dark horses you are,' he said. 'Well, happy days, you will know quite a few people.'

'Fabulous! See you later!' I said, smiling.

'A ce soir!' he called down the line as he hung up.

By the time I rang the doorbell, the party was in full swing. As the door opened, clouds of smoke and warmth spilled into the street. I pushed my way into the hallway, where people lounged against the walls smoking and chatting. Brightly coloured clothes glimmered in the foggy light as I made my way through to the salon and the unmistakeable laughter of George, raised against the backdrop of the party. I had almost made it through the door, when an arm shot out across the door frame and barred my way. I looked up surprised and found myself looking into the angular, tanned face of a man with dirty blonde hair and grey eyes. He stared belligerently, challenging me. There was something unsettling and brutal in his gaze, but I couldn't look away. There was a moment when I almost backed down, and then suddenly, he moved his arm and turned his back on me, as if it had never happened. Had I imagined it? Then I heard my name,

'Alice!' shouted Alexandre above the music 'in here!' I pushed my way through and he held his arms theatrically wide to greet me, 'Daaahling, we have missed you! Haven't we George.' George held his long cigarette holder up and out of the way as he leaned in to air kiss my cheeks.

'You look fabulous darling. Here, take my champagne and I will go in search of more.' He sashayed away, cigarette en l'air calling 'Gilles, où se trouve le champagne?'

I felt a tap on my shoulder and turned to find Kiki smiling down at me. 'Kiki, bonsoir!' I shouted above the din, as my eyes moved to the man beside her. He was elegant with a finely chiselled face and tightly cropped hair. 'This is Harry,' she said. His slim tattooed arm reached out from the immaculate folded back cuffs of his white shirt, and he shook my hand.

'Enchantée,' I said smiling back at them both, at which point George reappeared holding two glasses of champagne and a bottle under his arm.

'Don't want to run short do we,' he said winking at me. I turned to Kiki,

'Is Isobel here?'

Kiki waved vaguely over her head, 'She's here somewhere.' I made my way across the room to find her, reaching the far corner without success; as I turned back, I gasped. The man with the dirty blonde hair was standing over me, the same intense look in his eyes. I stepped back and met the wall as I tried to get out of his way, but before I could speak, he was gently stroking his large hand over my spiky hair and down the back of my neck. Our eyes locked as he pulled my face towards him and leaned in to kiss me. Despite the shock, the softness of his lips and the rough warmth of his skin made me momentarily dizzy with desire. He gazed into my eyes and for a long moment, it was as if I melted into them, revealing my deepest secrets. The party faded away as his lips met mine again, I tasted tobacco and honey on his mouth and I felt myself quiver at his touch. Suddenly, the music changed and I recovered myself, pulling sharply away,

'What the hell do you think you are doing!' I shouted, flustered and pushed past him to re-join my friends, smoothing my hair as I moved through the crowd. Then I felt a hand on my arm,

'Alice!' it was Isobel.

'Izzy!' I said surprised, 'I was just looking for you! How are things?'

'Not bad,' she said ' how about you?'

'Pretty good, I've really found my feet. Met some great people at the Beaux Arts, Clémence is more relaxed around me, life is good!' I said. 'Actually, I have some news. I can't tell you here though. I'll come and see you soon and we can grab a coffee.'

'Great, I'd love that, where are the others?' I led her over to the crowd on the other side of the room and on the way, we bumped into Jasper.

'Alice, bonsoir! Ça va?' I leaned in to kiss him on both cheeks and introduced Izzy. She'd been thinking of doing a course at the Beaux Arts, so we chatted for a while. When we moved on, I saw that Alexandre was talking to the blonde man. I was about to move off in the other direction when he beckoned me over.

'Alice, there is someone I want you to meet, come here!' Too late, I could feel the heat rising up my neck and face and we had no choice but to walk towards them. 'This is Xavier, our host,' said Alexandre, 'Xavier, my friend, Alice.'

'What a pleasure,' he said gruffly, his face serious, fixing me once again with his gaze. He wore a white t shirt, revealing tattoos on his tanned arms and faded, blue jeans. I reached out to shake his hand, which was splattered with paint.

'Great party,' I said. Alexandre looked at me. 'This is Isobel,' I said quickly, wanting to deflect attention from myself. Xavier lifted his hand to her in acknowledgement but didn't take his eyes off me.

'Are you ok Alice?' Alexandre said quietly.

'Of course I am, come on let's dance!' I pulled him onto the dance floor as the beats of Chuck Berry's Maybelline got everyone moving, by the time we had gyrated to some Elvis Presley and finally Be Bop a Lula, I was laughing and ready for a glass of water.

'What a night! I need some air,' I said, stepping out onto a small balcony. It overlooked the trees in the centre of the square and I took a deep breath. The cool air caressed my skin and I closed my eyes for a fleeting moment, remembering the stubble against my face and the tingling thrill of that sudden kiss. I breathed in sharply, feeling the heat rise to my face once more and stepped back inside, looking for the kitchen and a glass of water. Instead, I was handed another cold glass of champagne by George who had come to look for me. He clucked happily seeing I was safe and blew me a kiss, as he made his way back to Alexandre. As I sipped my drink, Kiki put her head around the door.

'Au revoir, we are off to the club for a gig, see you!'

'Bye Kiki, see you next week.' I called after her. I turned as I felt a large hand around my upper arm. It was Xavier, intense and serious.

'Will you come with me?' he said, his voice unexpectedly soft as he looked into my eyes again for a long moment. It was as though he could see into my soul, and I into his, and we stared at each other for a long moment. When I look back on it, I'm not sure why I went with him so willingly, but I put down my glass and followed him out of a door at the far side of the kitchen and up a flight of stairs. He walked ahead of me with a confident swagger, his boots echoing on the wooden steps. 'In here,' he said softly, as he pushed open a door at the end of a small corridor. I found myself in a huge studio with a beamed ceiling and windows across one wall, paintings were stacked in every corner. 'Why don't you lie down over there,' he said, indicating a small daybed draped in a turquoise throw and piled with cushions. 'Just relax, I need to paint you.' With my head starting to swim from the champagne, I lay back against the pillows, relieved to close my eyes for a moment, still aware of the taste of tobacco and honey on my lips. Xavier walked over to his easel and picked up a paintbrush. He watched me intently, before beginning to make marks on the canvas, as I drifted into sleep.

I awoke many hours later as the cool light of dawn seeped through the windows. Xavier put down his paintbrush and walked wordlessly over to the bed, leaning over to stroke my face before gently pulling me to my feet. He cupped my face in his large hands and began to kiss me, tenderly on the mouth at first. He began to lick the edges of my mouth, running his tongue along my lips. His rough tongue explored my cheeks and the edges of my nose and my eyelids, his stubble bringing heat to my face. He reached behind me, tugging at the zip of my dress, pulling it down so that it slid to the floor and pooled at my feet. I felt as if I was in a dream as his hands travelled down my naked back, pulling my lace pants to the floor in one fluid movement, so that I stood naked before him. He kissed my neck as his fingers drifted over my shoulders and down to my breasts, kneading and stroking as his thumbs gently played with my nipples. He finally leaned down and took my breast into his mouth, licking and sucking it, and I began to moan quietly with pleasure. I felt as if I had fallen into a gap between two worlds and sighed as I gave myself up to the sensation of it. He took off his T shirt and jeans and I put my hands into his thick blonde hair, feeling weak as his mouth travelled over my belly and down my thighs. He cupped my buttocks in his hands and guided me back towards the seat of a tall square stool behind me. My thighs fell open and he knelt and pulled me to his mouth. I gasped as his tongue made contact with my flesh and my hips began to move gently back and forth, as I moaned with pleasure. He licked me with long slow flicks of his tongue, until I climaxed with a shuddering gasp. He lifted his head and met my languid gaze as I smiled lazily into his eyes, my heart revealed to him. He stared back at me with an intensity that burned into the depths of my soul.

Xavier stood up then, and cupping my buttocks in his large hands, he lifted me up against him and gently slid himself inside me as I wrapped my legs around his waist. His gentle thrusting slowly became more powerful and his breath came deep and hot against my neck. In a final rush of heat, he cried out, looking up into my face. Kissing my mouth, he carried me over to the bed and lay down on his back, my body still straddled over his, and he pulled the throw over us both as I slid down to lie next to him. I lay my head against the side of his chest and felt the thudding of his heart gradually slow as he fell into a deep sleep.

ISOBEL

I lay by Xavier's side for more than an hour, as morning light crept into the studio. Finally, I could no longer ignore my need for the bathroom and slid quietly out of bed. I picked my clothes up from the floor and tiptoed towards the door of the studio, while Xavier slept deeply, gentle snores occasionally escaping his lips. He looked vulnerable in sleep and I felt like an intruder. While I slept, Xavier had been up all night painting, and as I was about to leave the room, I was suddenly overcome with curiosity to see what it was he had been working on. I put down my clothes and still naked, tiptoed over to the easel. The painting was illuminated by rays of early sunlight, and the canvas glowed in shades of turquoise, russet and green. He had painted me lying across the bed, my arms flung above my head, pink lips slightly parted. My russet lashes rested delicately across my lightly freckled cheeks as I lay in the complete abandonment of sleep, the fine curly spikes of my red gold hair spread around my head like a halo across the pillow. He had painted it in the style of Millais' Ophelia, as if I was floating away on a tide of flowers, drowned, as she was. It seemed prophetic now; the depth of our communion was a little like drowning, the bed our final resting place. I shuddered, tiptoeing out of the room and closing the door quietly behind me.

I washed and dressed quickly and made my way down the stairs, letting myself out of the front door and into the fresh morning air. I pulled my wrap around me and put on the sunglasses I always carried in my bag, crossing the road towards the café on the other side of the square. I stepped first into the boulangerie to buy myself a warm croissant, and then to the café, choosing one of the tables bathed in early morning sunshine. A waiter quickly appeared,

'Vous désirez Mademoiselle?'

'Un grand café crème s'il vous plait.' I sat back, and closed my eyes, listening to the sounds of Montmartre waking up; birdsong, the sound of cars starting and the clank of bin lids being lifted and closed again. I scribbled a note to Alexandre, he must have thought it strange that I disappeared without saying goodbye to them all. As for Clémence, I hoped she hadn't missed me, I would say I had been out for an early morning walk.

Place des Abesses
Montmartre
8am Sunday

Dearest Alexandre and George

*   What a marvellous party! Thank you for inviting me, I had an unexpectedly delicious and enlightening time!*

*   I have big news to tell you, I am moving to Normandy! It seems that Maman had a house in the countryside and now it is mine! I will plan a big house warming party as soon as I am settled and you are all invited! How long will you be in Paris? Long enough, I hope, to make the trip to the country and help me celebrate in my new home.*

Lots of love to you both, Alice xxxx

After my second coffee, and as I was already in Montmartre I decided to go and share the news of my windfall with Isobel and Kiki. I rang the bell several times and then knocked and waited. Receiving no answer, I walked down the hill to buy a newspaper. I was just turning to walk away when I heard an upstairs window open, and looked up to see Isobel peering out.

'Wait Alice!' she shouted. 'Don't leave, I'm coming down.' When she came to the door, her hair looked dishevelled and her eyes were red rimmed from crying.

'Izz, what is it, has something happened?' She beckoned me into the kitchen.

'Come in,' she said. 'Would you like a coffee?'

'Ok,' I said, and paused, looking at her sympathetically. 'Are you alright?' There was a silence and then she started to cry, softly at first and then as she began to speak, her cries built to sobs,

'I've been so stupid Alice, I don't know what to do.' She looked at the floor, 'I'm in a really difficult situation.'

'What is it Izzy, is there anything I can do to help?'

'No, nobody can help,' she said.

'Have you spoken to Kiki about it?'

'I can't, that's the problem.' She paused, wiping her eyes, not seeming to want to continue. She blew her nose loudly and struggling to compose herself, she filled the kettle with water and took two cups from the cupboard. Finally, she said in a quiet voice, 'You see, Kiki and I have become really good friends over the last year or so. We work together, eat together and for the last few months we have become very close.' She paused and looked at me, colouring, a tear running down her face. 'Strange as this might sound to you Alice, I love her.' As she said it, realisation dawned on me and I wondered why I hadn't seen it before. She continued, 'One day I was feeling sad about something and she pulled me to her, gently rubbing my back. She stroked my hair, then my face and neck and before I knew what was happening, she leaned in and kissed my mouth.' Her voice trailed off, 'and that was how it started.' She looked at me again as another tear rolled down her face, 'I never meant to fall in love with her.'

'Darling Izzy, I should have seen it, the two of you seemed so content in one another's company. So why are you crying?' I said, stepping towards her and taking her hands.

'So you're not,' she paused 'surprised?'

'Not at all,' I said, and smiled to myself as I remembered the frequent and unexpected faces at our breakfast table in Meard Street. It was only in the last few months of being at home with my family, that I realised our guests did not always sleep in the guest bedrooms. Apparently my parents were more adventurous than I realised. Isobel looked at me with relief and continued;

'Kiki makes me feel safe and secure, it has been so good.'

'So what happened?'

'Well, a few days ago, she came home with a man. Someone I

see at the club occasionally. When I think about it, Kiki has started going out more and more without me, but I thought nothing of it. I knew she had her own life before she met me and that it would continue, I felt secure. When they walked in, Kiki introduced me casually as a friend. She poured some wine for us all and said she'd invited Jack for dinner. It didn't cross my mind that they might be involved. We sat and chatted over wine, then shared the boeuf bourguignon. It was a good evening. We laughed a lot and then after dinner, they said they had to go out. 'See you later Izz,' she called as they left, 'don't wait up for me.'

'That doesn't mean they are involved,' I said, 'it could just be business.'

'No Alice,' she said, 'you don't understand, she didn't come back last night after the party. When she finally came in this morning to pick up a few things, I rushed at her distraught and crying, I thought she'd had an accident you see.' Isobel, put both her hands up to her face, brushing away fresh tears.

'What did she say?' I asked.

'She held me to her and told me everything would be alright. She stroked my hair, the way she did on that first day. 'Izzy,' she said, 'Nobody can be all things to all people. I need Jack sometimes too, we are close just like you and me. I never wanted to hurt you, I suppose I thought you understood.' Fresh tears began to stream down Izzy's cheeks as she said between sobs, 'I thought she loved me, we were happy Alice.' She paused adding quietly, 'I really don't know what to do.'

'Has Kiki said she wants you to move out?'

'No, of course not, but she wants Jack to move in. She thinks that everything can carry on as usual, but it can't!' She started to sob again, her face in her hands, tears dripping down her fingers and my heart went out to her. I struggled to find the right words, and decided that quiet support was what she needed now. I handed her some tissues and she dried her eyes, finally blowing her nose again. Eventually I said,

'Give it time Izzy, maybe things will settle down. Jack may not move in, and if he does, things might work out better than you think.'

'Everything will change, I know it, but maybe that's what I

need, a fresh start. Maybe it will be for the best, who knows.'

'Come on' I said, 'don't try and overthink this, let things settle down and see what happens. Why don't we go out for a walk, take your mind off it for a while?'

'Ok,' she said miserably. She went to brush her hair and wash her face, eventually emerging wearing a warm jacket and a pair of sunglasses. We stepped out into the street, and wrapped up in coats and hats, we turned up the hill towards the long flight of steps to Sacré Cœur. Despite the cold, it was a sunny morning and as we climbed the steps, the sound of birdsong filled the air and our breath rose in clouds into the chilly morning. Halfway up, we stopped for a moment and turned to admire the view below us.

'Wow, there is another whole world out here!' said Izzy smiling. 'Thanks Alice, you are a good friend.'

'Come on, let's get to the top,' I said, turning back to the upward climb. 'We're nearly there!'

Once at the top, the white basilica filled the space ahead of us, its curved domes rising majestically into the blue sky.

Isobel looked at me and smiled, 'I never tire of this, no matter how many times I see it.'

We walked across and leaned on the wall in front of the Sacré Cœur, a wide vista of the city stretching out before us. Immediately below, a long wide flight of stone steps descended through the steep gardens, where people sat chatting and smoking, some lying down in the sun.

'Come on,' I said, 'let's find a café.' We turned to walk over the cobbled square in front of the basilica, following the lane around to the side where we climbed another set of steps overhung with trees. At the top, was a busy, sunny square. A guitar player strummed as he sat on a low wall and an accordion played nearby. We found a table bathed in late morning sunshine and sat down to enjoy the atmosphere. By the time we had indulged in frothy coffees and pastries, Izzy had cheered up.

'Being up here has really given me some perspective, thanks for suggesting it Alice.'

'Chin up my friend, my father used to tell me that things have a way of working themselves out. Sometimes we need to just let go and trust that the right thing will come along. I thought I would hate Paris and expected nothing but sadness and loneliness. Instead, I woke up one morning and realised I have made a life for myself. This morning, I am happy, I feel as if a new chapter is about to begin.'

Izzy looked brighter after that, and if she expected me to elaborate on the reason for my happiness, I didn't; it was still so new and I wanted to hug it to myself.

'I'm sure your father was right,' said Izzy, 'thank you for listening Alice. I'm going to sit here for a while longer.' I gave her a hug and then stepped out into the square, turning to wave as I headed back home.

THE RITZ, PARIS

There was great excitement at de Montfort House in the days leading up to the engagement party. The family was preparing to travel to Paris. Even Juniper's brother Monty came home on leave for the occasion. It delighted Claudia that they would all be together for a few days. Juniper told me that Monty burst into the drawing room, enveloping them all in a huge bear hug. 'Mater, Pater, Juno! How goes it! Thank God I am back to civilisation for a few days. Hallelujah!' He checked the mirror, sweeping back his thick dark hair and looking at his face from all angles. 'Not at all bad,' he said, admiring his reflection, 'A little thin maybe but nothing that a slap up dinner and bottle of claret won't cure.'

'Darling how marvellous to have you home, how long have they spared you?' said Claudia, smiling, standing back to admire her son.

'Not long, but long enough!' said Monty. Charles poured them both a tumbler of whisky and handed one to his son,

'Down the hatch Montgomery, good to see you son, very good indeed!'

'Monty, I missed you,' said Juniper, putting on a little girl voice. She laid her head against his broad chest as he stroked the top of her head.

'What's this chap you're marrying like Juno, will I like him d'you think?'

'Of course you'll like him!' she said, 'won't he Mummy?'

'Only one way to find out,' said Charles, 'we have invited them to join us at the hotel for dinner tomorrow evening in Paris.

The engagement party will take place the following day.'

'Good oh,' said Monty, draining the last of the whisky from his glass. He leaned down and gave his mother a quick peck on the cheek. 'I'm going to shower and change now if you don't mind. What time is dinner?'

'In an hour darling, all your favourites are on the menu.'

Juniper couldn't have known then that her marriage to Étienne would not be the bed of roses she imagined, how could she? She was still so young. When we talked about it years later, she wondered whether she might have made different choices, if she had known then what she knows now?

'Do you think you would have done things differently?' I asked her.

Perhaps,' she said, 'who knows? I can only say that at the time, I thought my world was perfect.'

The de Montfort family arrived at the Paris Ritz the next day. Juniper told me it was Claudia's idea to invite me for dinner that evening, along with Clémence and Étienne, particularly as Charles had not yet met Clémence.

Claudia and Charles thought it unusual that Simeon wouldn't attend the dinner, but of course nothing was said. I don't know why Clémence wasn't honest about her marriage, even I was complicit when Étienne explained that his father was in America on business.

It was a chilly, winter evening when we finally arrived at the Ritz, I was relieved to step into the welcoming warmth of the Espadon restaurant. A flowering lilac tree rose up from a pedestal in the centre of the room, its pendulous blooms suggesting spring time in a beautiful garden. Large window arches topped with elaborate cornicing framed the oval room, these decorated with soft velvet swags and fine gold fringes.

I saw Charles stand up to greet us as the waiter led us to the table, he stepped forward to shake hands with Étienne smiling broadly. 'Good evening Charles,' said Étienne. 'Allow me to introduce my mother, Clémence d'Apidae and my cousin Alice Gardener.'

'Delighted to meet you both ladies!' Charles leaned in to kiss us on both cheeks. 'Of course you know Claudia and Juniper already, and this is our son, Montgomery.' Monty stood to shake hands with Étienne and leaned to kiss first Clémence and then me, lingering a little longer than he should have done at my cheek.

'What a pleasure,' said Monty, looking meaningfully at me. I looked away pretending not to notice, but it was not lost on Clémence. The frosty glare she gave Juniper's brother was also noted by Étienne, who himself seemed suddenly protective of me. I was not especially interested, but I knew I looked good in the pale yellow dress Clémence had lent me. The square neckline was encrusted with small glass beads and pearls and I wore long, butter coloured gloves coming up high around my arms, a few russet freckles visible at their edges. The spikes of my short auburn hair were tamed into a neat pixie style framing my face.

We took our seats at the table, and the waiter filled crystal flutes with champagne. Charles raised his glass, 'We are delighted that our families will be joined. Very many congratulations to you my darling Juniper, and to you Étienne, I hope you will be very happy together.'

Clémence was in buoyant mood after the success of the evening, and the glittering engagement party that followed was a triumph. This finally, emboldened me to speak to her about the house my mother had left me in Normandy. I broached the subject, expecting her easy acquiescence, but she surprised me.

'Amélie left you her house, when did this happen?' asked Clémence. 'Why did I know nothing about it?'

'I only found out myself a few weeks ago, Tante Clémence. The Notaire sent a letter asking to see me alone about a private matter. When I arrived, I learned that I had inherited my mother's house. I didn't even know that she had a house in France, she never mentioned it and we never visited it.' I looked up at my aunt and then added, 'The Notaire told me that you and Maman both have a house in Normandy within the same grounds.'

'I see,' she said, 'well, that is true, we do, or rather did. As it happens I have been thinking of signing my own property on the estate over to Étienne. He and Juniper have decided they would like to live there instead of in Paris, after their marriage.' She paused, 'Now it seems that Amélie has signed hers over to you.' She sighed looking down at her hands resting in her lap, noticing the faint age spots and the translucence of her skin. 'Time passes so quickly, and one's youth slips imperceptibly away,' she said quietly.

I pictured my aunt alone here after the wedding, and faltered, before ploughing on. I was determined to finish the conversation now I had found the courage to start it. 'The Notaire told me that I will have a regular income of my own from the rental of our London home.' I paused, unsure how to continue... 'and so, I have decided that I would like to go and live in Normandy.'

'Live in Normandy, on your own!' exclaimed Clémence. 'You are far too young to live alone and out in the middle of nowhere too!' A flashback of my night with Xavier came unbidden into my mind and I found myself blushing, I was definitely not too young.

'I am 18 now Tante Clémence, I'll be fine on my own, and anyway, you said Juniper and Étienne will be there too.'

'I'm sorry Alice, I really must put my foot down over this. I have given you such a lot of freedom, but really, this is a step too far. What about your art course? You have another two years still to do,' she added. 'You can't just abandon it.'

My heart sank, I didn't expect her to react in this way. It was true about my course, I really should stay in Paris to finish it. Clémence had been good to me and I didn't want to upset her, she seemed so fragile and sad lately. Perhaps I was just more aware of it since our evening together, but I wondered whether she was afraid of being left alone.

Finally, a compromise was reached; Clémence suggested that I drive myself to Normandy to visit my new house after the wedding, once Juniper and Étienne were back from their honeymoon. I could spend occasional weekends there and gradually get used to the house, before moving in at some unspecified time in the future. It was, she said, highly likely that when the time came, I would be married to a suitable young man; a man who would want to stay here in Paris, rather than hide himself away in the countryside, as her own son had inexplicably decided to do.

Now it was my turn to sigh. I realised that I would have to accept Clémence's vision of my future for the time being. The move to Normandy was not to be; not then anyway. Besides, I had something else to keep me in Paris now. My cheeks became hot at the thought of Xavier and of the way I had not only abandoned all sense of propriety with him, but that I was enjoying every moment of my new found sexual freedom. I began to smile.

'I'm glad you understand Alice. it is so nice to see you smiling my dear,' said Clémence.

Our lives settled back into a routine and Clémence rallied after receiving a letter from Simeon in America. For my part I continued to spend my time at the École des Beaux Arts and with my friends in Montmartre. I saw Xavier quite a lot too, and so I was surprised to hear one day that he had taken his motorbike out of Paris and headed south, something he did regularly, his friends told me. They had no idea how long he would be away.

I received a number of calls and invitations from Montgomery de Montfort after meeting him at the Paris Ritz. He was not my type, although he did seem to appeal to Tante Clémence's vision for my future, despite her frosty disapproval of him at the engagement dinner. I tried to avoid him, preferring the raw unpredictability of Xavier. When Monty did invite me for dinner or lunch, I found something important to do, which prevented me from seeing him.

As far as my move to the country was concerned, it would be almost three years before I finally drove out of Paris to move into my own home.

THE WEDDING 1956

Years later, when Juniper talked to me about her wedding day, she remembered every detail. She woke at 6.30am, the house was still quiet as she got out of bed and walked over her plush carpet to the window. Pulling the heavy floral curtains open, she leaned on the window sill and looked out at the familiar view across the park. The sky was grey and wet, although a brighter morning glimmered hopefully on the horizon. She sighed as she watched the red deer grazing, undisturbed beneath the trees. At last it was her wedding day, her honeymoon suitcase was packed and her wedding gown hung in her dressing room. She looked at her satin shoes and beautiful underwear, blushing as she realised that by the end of the day she would be married, and that Étienne would not only see her in it, but would probably be removing it as well.

Juniper told me that she was nervous about that side of things from the start, but I still didn't really understand why.

'I thought you were in love with him Juniper, that you wanted him, surely the rest should naturally follow. With Xavier, it wasn't something I gave a thought to, it just happened, it felt right and I was swept away in the moment.'

'It wasn't like that for me, I had to rely on my mother to tell me what to expect. I did try to broach it with her but we were both embarrassed and when she did finally talk to me, I didn't know what to say. I was dismissive of her, out of sheer embarrassment, I regret that. You see, there was so much I blamed her for, things we had never spoken about, so I was afraid the conversation might open up a can of worms.'

'What do you mean?' I asked.

'You'll see,' she said, continuing. 'Anyway I had already been awake for over an hour when there was a light tap on my bedroom door. I looked up to see Claudia putting her head round the door.

'Good morning Mummy.'

'Darling, you're awake, how are you feeling this morning?'

'Oh, I'm fine, a bit nervous but mostly excited. I'm thinking about how it will feel to finally be married,' I said breezily, not wanting to show my apprehension.

'You will be a beautiful bride and make a wonderful wife my darling, I'm sure of it,' said Claudia. 'Now, the hairdresser will be here in an hour, shall we go downstairs to have some breakfast first?'

Juniper said their morning passed in a flurry of activity; bouquets and buttonholes, wedding presents and cards arrived. She described the way the hairdresser arranged her hair into a beautiful French pleat with delicate flowers woven into its folds. Finally, when she put on her wedding dress, she gasped as she caught sight of herself in the cheval mirror. The dress seemed to float around her, its beautiful satin folds falling from her waist and over her hips to the floor. The dress shimmered with small crystals, each sewn on by hand, and the wide neckline gave way to short sleeves, finished with long white gloves. The veil was short and full, falling in clouds of silk tulle from the crown of her head to her shoulders. As she gazed into the mirror, it was as if somebody disguised as a bride was looking back at her childhood self. She said a sudden shiver went through her, as she realised the enormity of the step she was about to take.

Their wedding took place in a beautiful church near Juniper's home in Richmond Park. It was a glorious day. I travelled from Paris with Clémence for the occasion and it felt marvellous to be back in London. We took rooms at the Petersham Hotel, where the reception was to take place. On the morning of the wedding, we left for the church just as the sun came out and the clouds cleared. The church was full and a sense of happy anticipation filled the air as the opening bars of Pachelbel's Canon rang out. I turned to see a radiant Juniper standing serenely beside her father, ready to process down the aisle. All eyes were upon her and she blossomed suddenly, like a flower in the sunlight, gliding towards Étienne, as he turned and smiled.

After the service, flashbulbs popped as they stepped out of the church as a married couple, looking for all the world like film stars, laughing delightedly as confetti fluttered around them. Clémence was lit up with pride in her son, it was the happiest I had ever seen her.

A champagne reception, followed by the wedding breakfast, took place in the elegant dining room of the Petersham. Guests enjoyed elevated views of the meandering River Thames as they dined on French cuisine. Juniper was the object of praise and many compliments. The afternoon concluded with speeches and late sunshine sloping through the windows. She tossed her bouquet into the crowd before receiving kisses and good wishes from everyone, as she and Étienne made their way up the wide staircase to their suite.

The honeymoon suite was everything Juniper could have wished for. Étienne carried her over the threshold of their room and she smiled at the luxury of it. The vast windows looked out onto their private balcony and across the river. Étienne turned to her and said, 'Now it is time for you and me my darling. I have waited so long for you.'

That was when Juniper's problems began. The heavy, shell pink drapes were closed against the evening and after the noise of the reception, Juniper said she felt as if they were in a silent padded cocoon. She was apprehensive, so she waited, perching on the end of the enormous double bed.

'Juniper, you looked like an angel today,' Étienne said, 'my angel. I must be the luckiest man alive!' He reached out for her hands and pulled her gently to her feet, smiling down at her. Instead of reaching around his waist as she had done so often before, she felt unsure of herself and resisted. 'Don't worry my darling, I will be gentle,' Étienne murmured into her hair. She felt her body stiffen as he reached to gently unzip her wedding gown. 'We will take things very slowly.'

As her dress fell to the floor he gazed at her slim body and silk underwear, glimmering in the low light. She looked to the floor awkwardly, unsure, as Étienne put his fingers under her chin and lifted it. 'Look at me my darling.' She looked up, blushing furiously, 'I love you,' he continued, 'there is nothing to worry about.' He removed his jacket and tie, and slowly unbuttoning his shirt, he looked at her and smiled, like an indulgent uncle.

It was the realisation that she thought of him as an uncle that triggered the memories she had buried for so many years. He lifted her hand and placed her palm against his bare chest, guiding it down to his waist and the button of his trousers. 'I might need some help with the button,' he said. She looked up at him and then fumbled with the fabric before managing to undo it, hanging her hands back by her sides.

'Now, the zip,' he said smiling. He took her hand again and rubbed her open palm over the now bulging fabric. 'Not again,' she thought 'I can't do this' and silently cried out, closing her eyes. Étienne was unaware, of course, his breath heavy and warm,

'Can you feel that Juniper?' She could feel his hard flesh straining against the fabric and was mortified. She wanted to run from the room, as a low gruff voice in her head said, *That's it Juniper, up and down, no need to tell anyone about this, it is our little secret.* She ran into the bathroom, shutting the door behind her and vomited, tears sprang to her eyes as she wiped her mouth.

Juniper looked at me imploringly then, and said, 'Who cries and vomits on their wedding night Alice? You see, things happened to me as a child. My uncle,' she paused, looking up at me with tears in her eyes, 'He used to touch me, he made me do things to him, disgusting things.' I reached out for her and hugged her to me, saying simply,

'Oh Juniper, I'm so sorry. Did you tell your mother about it?'

'I tried, but I couldn't,' she replied, 'I was too ashamed. At times it seemed unreal, even to me. He made me feel dirty, I hated myself and I hated him even more, but I didn't know what to do, I was a child. So you see, that kind of revulsion was all I had ever felt when it came to sex, until much later in my life, I saw that it could be different.'

Going back to her story, she told me that she stalled for time in the bathroom,

'I'm sorry Étienne,' she called, 'I just need to have a bath. I won't be long.' When she eventually emerged, pink from the hot water and in a silk nightdress, he was lying in bed and appeared to be asleep. Juniper climbed in next to him as quietly as she could and switched off the light. She had drifted into an awkward sleep, when she became aware of his warm breath against her neck. He was kissing and licking her ear lobe, whispering, 'Darling you are exquisite, what have I done to deserve you.' As she continued to feign sleep, he slid his hand gently over the silk across her belly and along the top of her thigh until his hand found the open side of her nightdress and connected with her scented skin. She stiffened and lay rigid in the bed, opening her eyes, knowing that she must submit to his touch. She took some deep breaths as he whispered into her neck, 'Let me feel you, oh, you are an angel.' She let her thighs fall slightly apart and he probed the moist heat within, leaning over to kiss her mouth, running his tongue along her lips before kissing her deeply. She could feel the hardness of him against her thigh as he leaned towards her. 'Are you ready for me Juniper?' he said, as he lifted up her nightie and rolled on top of her. She felt him slide inside her and gasped, gripping the sheet as he moved up and down, his warm breath now covering her face as he closed his eyes in ecstasy. Much later, when he slept deeply beside her, she went back to the bathroom to wash the sticky liquid from her thighs, wiping away her silent tears.

Waking from an afternoon nap on the sofa, Juniper gazed out of the window watching rivulets of water run over the glass, remembering the morning of her wedding two years before. Then too, she had awoken to hear rain splattering against her bedroom window. That was the last time she was truly happy, she sighed, their baby was due any day now and she would be glad to have her body returned to her.

Juniper had become increasingly disillusioned with her lonely life in the country. Her beautiful clothes from London and Paris had no place in Normandy, where there was incessant rain. On a bright day a few months before, Étienne suggested that she learn to ride, to give her an interest, and although she was secretly fearful of the beasts, she told Étienne she would consider it. Her pregnancy was confirmed soon afterwards and thankfully, the idea was shelved.

Rosa and Jack were loyal and supportive; Juniper was not sure how she would have managed without Rosa. Étienne was away for much of the time and the two women had fallen into a comfortable routine. Rosa would be in the kitchen now she thought, preparing dinner for this evening. Still sleepy, Juniper pushed herself up from the sofa and walked towards the door, in search of a cup of tea. Just as she stepped into the tiled hallway, she was gripped by a sudden spasm of pain and a flood of warm liquid gushed down her thighs. 'Rosa!' she shouted in a panic, 'I think the baby is coming!'

Their daughter was born early the same evening, at the local hospital. Étienne returned from Paris just in time to see Lydia emerge red and wrinkled into the world. 'Juniper, you are so clever my darling!' he exclaimed. 'We have a beautiful daughter.' Pride shone in his eyes as he gazed down at the wizened bundle in his arms, oblivious to everything else around him. Juniper was exhausted and lay back against the pillows watching them, surprised at the immediate bond between father and daughter. She herself felt nothing but relief that her ordeal was over, and a sense of detachment from her husband and their new baby. She closed her eyes and drifted into sleep, imagining she was back in the safety of her bedroom in Richmond.

ALICE 1960

My love affair with Xavier – and it was love, I was sure of it –
became the backbone of my life in Paris. When I was not painting,
I was in Xavier's studio or in his bed. His frequent absences, often
for long periods of time, only added to the joy of our reunions.
I accepted him just as he was and he loved me for it.

My weekend visits to Normandy never materialised, such
was my life in Paris. I had worked hard over the last few months
to finish everything for the culmination of my art course, and
finally I was ready to leave. The funds from the London house had
accumulated, enabling me to buy my own car for the trip. To my
surprise, Clémence eventually gave me her blessing. She had been
so much happier since her long holiday in America, and confided
that she was planning to move there to live with Simeon again.
I was happy for her and grateful for the support she had given
me, so we parted on good terms. I loaded up my few possessions,
making sure I had the keys for my new home, and headed out of
Paris.

After three hours on the road, the countryside began to unfold
around me. I passed fields of sheep and cows, and slowing down
behind a tractor, I glanced at the instructions the Notaire had given
me. I turned off the main road into the small town of Vimoutiers,
where I stopped to buy provisions, glad to get out of the car and
stretch my legs. The square was dominated at one end by a church
with twin spires and a large, round, stained glass window. Little
cafés, a boulangerie and an épicerie stood on one side of the
square, and on the other, a pretty restaurant thronged with people

enjoying lunch in the sunshine. I took a deep breath and smiled, this would be my local town.

After lunch, I headed out of town for the short drive to my new house. I slowed the car as I recognised the entrance to the estate, just ahead. Two large hydrangea bushes bloomed at the top of the driveway beside an elaborately carved wooden sign depicting bees. I turned in and followed the narrow lane which descended sharply, before levelling out beside a lake. Ahead of me, the track wound through woodland, illuminated by shafts of sunlight filtering through the trees. I stopped the car for a moment and wound the window down, closing my eyes as I breathed deeply of the pine scented air. The sound of birdsong and the rush of flowing water ahead of me was a balm to my soul after so many months in Paris, and I realised I was smiling. Accelerating slowly along the uneven track, I rounded a corner where a small bridge crossed the stream. There, on the right was a wide wooden gate bearing the words, 'Les Lavandes'. Purple painted flowers were just visible at the corners, almost worn away with age.

I got out of the car and used my small key to release the padlock, kicking piles of leaves away with my boot. The gate moved easily, swinging wide open and coming to rest beside a tall silver birch, one of an avenue of trees flanking the lane ahead of me. I swung the car onto the leafy track and moved slowly forward until, at the far end, in a clearing, I could see the honey coloured stone of the house bathed in afternoon sunshine. I moved slowly forward, and pulling up outside, I stepped out of the car, marvelling at its beauty. How could I not have known about this place! The front door and shutters were of pale turquoise, closed over large square windows either side of the front door. At the top, there were three similar windows, their shutters open and a tall chimney rose above a mossy, tiled roof.

I took a deep breath as I turned the heavy key in the lock and the front door swung open into a large, light salon with a beamed ceiling. The wall on one side was decorated with terracotta tiles and in front of me, wide, glazed doors overlooked fields and distant hills. I pushed them open, letting fresh air and sunshine flood the house. Outside, a stone terrace ran the length of the house, and to the left, a pergola covered in wisteria offered shade to a wooden table and chairs. I stepped back into the salon, turning right through a beamed opening into a large kitchen. Two more glazed doors opened into a conservatory filled with pots of fading flowers. On one side of the room, there was a bright blue range with pale blue cupboards either side. A large scrubbed pine table took up the central space, surrounded by chairs bearing cushions in soft patterns of blue, turquoise and green. The walls were painted a bright yellow and these formed the backdrop to numerous paintings.

The sudden, unexpected joy of being in a space that my mother had created, and so resonant of our London home, suddenly overwhelmed me. The build-up of excitement and anticipation gave way to a wave of grief and I sat down at the pine table and put my head in my hands. Tears sprang to my eyes and began to leak through my fingers, as I reached into my handbag, searching for a tissue. Finally, I wiped my eyes and headed to the kitchen to get some water. The cold tap spluttered on, eventually delivering a cool stream into my glass. I gulped it down before splashing my face, then made my way slowly up the narrow, oak staircase to a small landing. The door to my right opened into a sunny bedroom overlooking the garden. A thick, bright rug covered the old, terracotta tiles and a set of glass doors at one end led into a tiled bathroom. From here, more glass doors opened onto a large sunny balcony. There were two further bedrooms, both a little smaller, and another bathroom.

'I'm finally here and this house is mine!' I said incredulously, smiling as I headed down the stairs to unload the car.

Two weeks later, Xavier came to stay for the first time. Usually pacing and distracted when he was away from his easel, or primed for his next adventure, I saw a different side of him. He leaned his motorbike onto its stand among the fallen leaves, and paused to look up into the canopy of trees over his head. I watched his shoulders relax and a smile form on his lips. The brooding energy and intense eye gazing that was typical of him faded away as he took time to slowly look around him and breathe in the fresh air. Finally, he walked towards me and swept me up into his arms. He carried me into the house and kissed me deeply, before strolling around and familiarising himself with the space. 'I love it,' he said simply.

'Do you want to look outside?' I watched the blonde hairs on the backs of his tanned arms, as he lifted a glass of water to his lips. I studied his hands, remembering the way they moved over my body, saw the way his gold signet ring was catching the light and the traces of paint under his nails.

'Show me,' he said. So we walked in the garden and then across the small paddock to the barn.

'I was thinking of making an art studio in here, if you want to paint,' I said.

He slid the door closed behind us, and pulled me into his arms, kissing me again as we fell onto an old sofa. Dust motes rose up into the shaft of sunlight as it sliced through the wide, high windows, cocooning us from the world as we lost ourselves in each other.

In the months following, Xavier came to love spending time in the countryside with me. He would arrive on his motorbike without warning and stay, sometimes for long periods, before disappearing again without explanation. He was moody and unpredictable at times, but I accepted him just as he was, giving him space when he needed it and submitting to his, and my own desire, whenever we felt like it. We created our studio in the barn, and Xavier began another canvas in his 'bed as a river' series. This time, he depicted the two of us together, raw desire on his face and me lying indifferent to him among the flowers, my halo of hair floating about the pillows. We lived for weeks at a time, oblivious to the outside world, content in our bubble of happiness. It seemed almost too good to be true.

JUNIPER

Soon after Lydia's second birthday, Juniper learned that the other house on the estate belonged to me and that I had recently moved from Paris. She was often away, leaving baby Lydia in the care of Rosa and Jack, thinking nothing of being absent for up to a week at time. She had come to despise the countryside, and later told me she was about to admit to Étienne that moving here had been a terrible mistake, when I arrived and became her neighbour. I had been in residence for just over a month when Juniper came to see me.

It was bright and sunny when she set off along the lane, carrying a basket of fruit and a pot of Rosa's jam. She strolled along the path through the trees, the sound of rushing water and birdsong breaking into the quiet of the morning. She stepped off the path for a moment, towards the sound of the stream, watching it tumbling over the stones. The water shone like diamonds in the sunshine and blue damsel flies hovered. She took some deep breaths as she watched them dart and dive over the water, feeling more relaxed than she had for a long time. A smile played about her lips as the joy of the moment caught her off guard, and she wondered why she had never thought of walking in the garden before. Rosa had often suggested she get out for some fresh air and that day, it was as if her eyes had opened for the first time to the beauty of the natural world around her.

Juniper continued along the lane, and when she eventually arrived at Les Lavandes, she tapped smartly on the door. I heard her call out, 'Hello, is there anybody at home?' I opened the upstairs window and leaned out, my hair dishevelled from sleep.

'Oh, Juniper, what a surprise! Hold on, I'm coming down.' I closed the window and went down to find her standing awkwardly at the door. It obviously hadn't occurred to her that I might still be in bed at half past nine in the morning.

'Come on in!' I said, smiling. Juniper followed me into the room filled with morning sunshine and I opened the doors to the sunny terrace. We stepped outside onto the already warm tiles, 'What a surprise,' I said again, tying my floral dressing gown at the waist.

'I just wanted to say hello, and to welcome you,' said Juniper, handing me the basket. 'I didn't mean to wake you, I should have thought. I've brought you some fruit and a pot of apricot jam.'

'Ooh thank you, how delicious!' I said. 'Let's sit down out here, I'll put some coffee on.' Juniper sat in a chair beneath the wisteria, and I saw her taking in the tranquillity and the distant view of the hills as she waited. I put the coffee pot and cups onto a tray, added a crusty baguette to go with the jam and set it on the table. As I enjoyed a hearty breakfast, spreading hunks of soft bread with butter and the apricot jam, Juniper sat up straight, carefully sipping her coffee. 'This is absolutely delicious! Are you sure you won't have anything to eat Juniper?' I said, wiping the crumbs from my chin.

'I'm sure, thank you,' said Juniper, as she watched me.

'That was just what I needed!' I said finally, sitting back in my seat. 'Thank you so much for the jam.'

'Rosa made it actually,' said Juniper. 'Our housekeeper,' she clarified. 'So, how are you settling into life in the country?'

'Oh I love it.' I said, sighing contentedly as I leaned back, basking in the sun. 'How do you like it Juniper? You are living the dream aren't you. The envy of every Parisian wanting to escape the rat race,' I said smiling.

'I suppose to some, I am,' she said, and to my surprise she added, 'To be honest I'm not sure I like the countryside. It's the sense of isolation and the incessant rain, I find it unbearable at times. My trips away keep me sane, I am actually away quite often.'

'What about your little girl, Lydia isn't it?'

'Oh, she and Rosa are as thick as thieves, she hardly notices whether I am there or not. It's a good thing really, she needs the stability.' I was surprised, I naively imagined Juniper living in a maternal idyll.

'Where do you travel to?' I asked.

'Oh, you know, here and there. Mostly London, my parents expect me to keep in touch and I don't like to unsettle Lydia by uprooting her too often'

'What about Etty, does he mind your being away?'

'He doesn't really know,' said Juniper. 'He's always travelling on business and when he's home, I make sure I'm there.' She didn't tell me then of their separate bedrooms, their increasingly separate lives, and how she often wondered whether her being there actually made any difference to him. The conversation petered out, both of us reflecting on our words as we gazed towards the hills.

'More coffee?' I said, to break the silence.

'No thank you, I really must get back,' said Juniper, getting up to leave.

'Of course,' I said. 'I'm planning a house warming party, a few friends are coming down from Paris and some from London. You and Etty should come.'

'Thank you, maybe we will,' said Juniper. Then she left, closing the door quietly behind her.

I learned years later that Juniper's visit to see me that day stirred up an inexplicable discontent in her. She struggled to understand that despite my sad story, I was so happy, relaxed and well adjusted. She commented on the way I had 'stuffed myself with bread' that morning, as if I hadn't a care in the world. She was resentful of my sitting in the garden, admiring the view, and sleeping late when there was so much to be done. My garden was a mess, the overflowing pots of lavender needed trimming back and for some reason, it made her angry; at the time, she didn't know why. She made odious comparisons around our values and lifestyles and found me wanting. She told me that as her anger towards me grew, she resolved to offer me some timely advice and the benefit of her experience.

Thankfully I knew nothing of her thoughts back then, nor of what she would see when she did come back a few days later. I could not have known that the repercussions from that day would affect the rest our lives.

A few days later, bored after lunch, Juniper decided to stroll out towards Les Lavandes. She wouldn't disturb me, she decided, but if she happened to see me, she would casually mention her thoughts on household and garden maintenance. That way, I would have time to put everything right before my party, and would later thank her for her intervention.

As she approached the house, Juniper saw a motorbike parked outside, half hidden in the trees. There was no sign of anybody outside, so she slowed her pace, deciding to walk around the side of the house to the patio at the back. Still nobody.

She decided that I must be out walking and was just about to turn away, when she heard the sound of laughter coming from the barn behind the house. Her curiosity piqued and having nothing better to do, she let herself through the gate and walked across the grass towards the barn. If she was seen, she would simply say that she wanted to make sure I was alright, in the light of the motorbike and the possibilty of a stranger roaming the estate.

As Juniper approached the barn, the laughter stopped and she wondered whether she had imagined it. The barn doors were pulled closed and she peered through a gap between the planks. She could see an old trestle table set up with paints and brushes and an easel, on which stood a large canvas. In front of it, and illuminated by light flooding into the barn from the far side, she saw a scruffy looking man with blonde hair. He held a paintbrush in one hand and a fat rolled up cigarette in the other. He leaned back to put his brush to the canvas and then to scrutinise whatever it was he was painting. Juniper said she couldn't quite see. He took a drag of the cigarette and then put the paintbrush down, stepping forward out of her sight. 'Who is that,' she thought, 'and what is he doing here?'

Frustrated that she couldn't see, and intrigued, Juniper walked around to the far end of the barn, hoping to get a better view. There was a small window but it was too high for her to reach. Then, she noticed a gap in the wood, quite low down, where one of the planks had warped away from its neighbour. She knelt down on the grass to peer inside and gasped. At the far end, I was reclined on an old chaise longue, naked but for a garland of fresh flowers around my neck, my legs outstretched along the bench. The man was standing over me, his face out of her sight as he straddled the chaise longue, his old denim jeans low on his waist. She said she thought I might be in danger, and panicked for a moment as she considered getting ready to run for help. When she looked through the gap again, she said the man was sitting. She watched him lift my legs up onto his shoulders and take one of my feet to his mouth as he began to lick and suck my toes. I giggled as he began to kiss my ankle, slowly moving his mouth down the inside of my thigh. She heard me make soft whimpering noises. My halo of auburn pixie cut hair and closed eyes, were illuminated by a slice of sunlight as I moaned with pleasure, my lips parted and my head tilted back.

Astonished Juniper was telling me this and mortified that she had witnessed such a private moment, I was lost for words. Apparently I looked as if I had been transported to another world and Juniper said she was mesmerised. She said she knew she should look away, but she couldn't take her eyes off us.

Suddenly I gave a loud gasp and began to laugh. She said it was a long languorous chuckle of pleasure. The man smiled then, and took a lazy drag of his roll up, not taking his eyes off me. She watched as I too inhaled the aromatic smoke, before sitting up to pull a pillow behind my back as the man stood, still astride the bench.

She watched me place my hands either side of his hips and lean forward to kiss his flat, muscular stomach, as I slowly undid the buttons of his jeans.

'I won't say more,' said Juniper years later, 'you know what happened next, you were there.' I did know. It had happened on that day and on many others, but still, I blushed as I saw myself through Juniper's eyes.

Juniper told me that after witnessing the scene, she closed her eyes to block the terrible wail of pain and sadness that rose up from the pit of her stomach. She stood up and not bothering to brush the grass off her clothes, ran as fast as she could back to the lane, tears pouring down her face. She ran off the path towards the stream and when she reached it, threw herself down on the grass beside it, finally giving way to the flood of grief she had carried for so many years.

THE PARTY

The next few weeks passed quickly, Juniper was away a lot and when she was at home, she took care not to come down to Les Lavandes again. My party was to take place at the weekend but when Juniper mentioned it to Étienne, he told her he had business in Paris and could not be there. 'Well one of us needs to be there Etty, Alice is your cousin after all,' she said. Eventually she told him not to worry, she would go to the party on behalf of them both, for appearances sake. 'We need to fly the family flag, and welcome Alice,' she told him, 'I can't believe you don't see that Étienne.'

'That is good of you darling, but I'm sure she won't expect it. I have to travel to America next week to sort out some business with my father. I'll be away about a month,' he said matter of factly. 'Will you be alright?'

'Of course I will,' she said, swallowing her disappointment, 'Lydia and I will be fine.'

'How is my girl?' he asked. 'Is Lydia behaving herself?'

'Of course she is, I'm so thankful for Rosa. Lydia adores her and we would both be lost without her.'

'I'm glad you have her there to keep you company,' he said. 'It won't be for much longer now, all this travelling I mean.'

Juniper said nothing, it hardly mattered any more. She couldn't face the possibility that he was seeing someone else, so she pushed her concerns to the back of her mind. 'Enjoy your trip Etty and give my love to your father, won't you,' she said, as she replaced the receiver.

That was the moment Juniper decided to come to my party

and throw caution to the wind. She was tired of being alone and weary of making excuses for her husband. She remembered exactly what she wore and the heady sense of possibility she felt. She dressed carefully in a black, sequinned dress that fell just above her knee and pinned the sides of her hair up, letting the rest fall to her shoulders. She felt young again, carefree and beautiful for the first time in a very long time.

Juniper drove herself along the lane and when she arrived at Les Lavandes, she pressed the doorbell. When nobody answered, she pushed the door open and stepped inside. She said the scene took her breath away.

The fairy lights I had woven through the room and over the pergola outside, and the candles decorating the interior of the house were magical. Guests stood outside under the stars sipping drinks and smoking. People were gathered in the kitchen and others spilled into the conservatory. Music pulsed through the room and despite the open doors across the back of the house, a pall of aromatic smoke floated in the air. The kitchen table was pushed to one side and some people danced, swaying together, their arms draped around each other's necks. Long skirts skimmed the ground and frayed jeans encircled bare feet and ankles. Others showed their legs in mini-skirts and boots, adorned with tassels.

'Juniper, you made it!' I called, seeing her come in. I put a glass of wine into her hand and introduced her to the people closest to the door. 'Kiki, this is Juniper, my cousin's wife and also my neighbour. Juniper, this is Kiki and her friend Jack, from Paris. Kiki is an artist.'

'Hello' said Juniper, a little tongue tied. She told me later that it was unlike any party she had ever been to. Kiki wore a long faded batik skirt and Jack an old t-shirt and faded jeans. Another young woman joined them, and Kiki introduced her as their friend Isobel. She wore a loose silk shift with spaghetti straps and apparently little else.

As she stood there, Kiki put her hand around the girls back and briefly drew her closer to say something into her ear. Isobel flushed and stood back, as a cheery man with unkempt hair, reached into their circle to top up their wine glasses. She said she was surprised how quickly she drained her glass, and as she began to sip the next, she felt a heady freedom among these people she hardly knew, and it emboldened her.

'Who's this?' said a tall lanky man as he approached, winking at Juniper.

'I'm Juniper, Alice's neighbour,' she said.

'Good to meet you Juniper, I'm Simon, do you fancy a dance?' The wine had made her brave and placing her empty glass on a nearby table, she answered,

'Yes, why not?' 'Teenager in Love' was playing as they began to dance, and the sequins on the short dress she had chosen caught the light as she moved. When the tempo slowed, I saw Simon pulled her to him as, 'I only have eyes for you' filled the room.

I watched them for a moment. Her face was level with the pockets of his shirt and she struggled to position her head, eventually giving up, and resting her cheek against his chest as they moved to the music. She told me later that she was enjoying the warmth and comfort of being held, forgetting for a moment where she was.

I walked back into the kitchen to find Xavier and Alex, their backs to me, deep in conversation. 'Is that want you think I am?' said Xavier, 'A rolling stone.'

'I just wonder what compels you to keep moving,' said Alex. 'Just thinking about your nomadic life exhausts me.' I was arranging more food on large platters, curious to hear Xavier's reply, I had often wondered the same thing.

'I guess I just have a restless spirit, always looking for something new, it must be in my blood.' There was a silence as Alex topped up their glasses,

'Perhaps you haven't met anyone yet who makes you want to settle down,' said Alex. 'I know when I met George, it was enough just to be with him. Our home in London is our sanctuary, along with George's clocks.' They both laughed and I waited, wanting and yet afraid to hear Xavier's reply.

'I guess I'm just a player,' he said laughing as he took a long sip of his wine. I noticed his jaw twitch in the candle light as he said more seriously, 'My father always said I would come to nothing and maybe he was right.'

'Christ, I wouldn't say that' said Alex. 'You're a legend in the art world.'

'Meaningless,' said Xavier, 'as far as he was concerned I was a failure, in every traditional sense. The only time I felt free of him was when I was on the open road on my Harley, the wind in my hair, heading for pastures new. The need to recreate that feeling is like a drug.'

I walked slowly out of the kitchen, carrying the plates of food, offering them around before putting them on the table. Kiki and Isobel beckoned me over and I picked up a bottle of wine to top up our glasses. 'I love the house,' said Kiki, 'what a sanctuary.'

'I know,' I said, 'I love it. I had no idea my mother had this place, or why she never told me about it.'

'What does Xavier think of it?' asked Isobel.

'I don't know,' I said honestly. 'He seems content when he's here but he comes and goes, you know.'

'He always looks so moody,' said Kiki, 'I don't think I've ever seen him laugh.' She looked at me expectantly, sympathy in her eyes, as Isobel interjected,

'Kiki, have you seen his eyes? They are like two pale grey pools,' she said. 'Looking into them is like being hypnotised.'

'Is it now?' said Kiki, 'and when exactly did you have occasion to gaze into them I wonder?' she said smiling.

'Come on you two,' I said, 'enough of this. Let's dance!' We threw ourselves into the music, flailing our limbs and swirling our skirts, until finally, exhausted, I went in search of some water.

Xavier appeared behind me as if from nowhere and pulled me into him, leaning over my shoulder to take a sip from my glass. For some reason I held back, his words earlier had stung me and I stepped towards the sink to refill the glass. I realised suddenly that I hadn't seen Juniper for a while. I was about to go and look for her when I saw her in the garden, walking slowly back towards the house. She had obviously been out to get some air, or at least that's what I thought at the time. As she approached I called,

'Juniper, there you are. Do you want a drink?'

'No thanks,' she said. 'I need to go actually.'

'Don't go yet, come and say hello to Xavier,' I said. As she looked up, he winked at her, but she seemed distracted.

'Actually Alice, I really must go,' she said quickly. 'I promised Rosa I wouldn't be late.'

'Are you sure you're ok?' I asked. ' You look a bit flushed. Hold on you've got some grass in your hair,' I added, reaching across to brush it out.

'Of course, I'm fine,' she said,' it must be the wine. I ought to go, thanks for the party.'

'It was my pleasure,' said Xavier, interrupting, and looking straight at her as he spoke.

'Shut up Xavier this isn't your party, it's mine!' I said, nudging him in the ribs. 'Bye Juniper, take care!' I walked over to the door to see her out and was thankful she had had the foresight to turn her car around in the lane. She got behind the wheel, turned on the lights and started the car, before turning to give me a quick wave as she set off slowly towards home.

She told me later that the party had both exhilarated and exhausted her, and after quietly climbing the stairs, she sank gratefully into her bed and slept the sleep of the dead. The next morning, she said, it was as if the events of the night before had happened to somebody else, in a dream. I didn't really know what she meant then, but I didn't know the full story

LONDON

Five weeks later, Juniper was at her wits' end looking after Lydia alone. Rosa had asked for some time off to look after Jack, who had fallen in the woods and hurt his leg. She'd really had no idea up to now, quite how much Rosa did for her. She decided to telephone her mother in Richmond. The phone rang for quite some time before Claudia eventually answered.

'Hello de Montfort House.'

'Mummy, it's me,' said Juniper.

'Hello darling, what a lovely surprise. How are you and my little Lydia?'

'Oh Mummy, Lydia is fine but she just won't give me a moment's peace. I had no idea how time consuming she could be. I'm at my wits' end. Rosa has not been at work and I'm exhausted.' Lydia began to cry in the background. 'Just a minute Mummy, Lydia has got her finger caught in something, you know what three year olds are like.' Juniper put the receiver down and went to extract Lydia's finger from the window of a toy car, before picking her up and sitting her on her knee. She picked up the receiver again. 'Mummy, would you mind if I bring Lydia with me and stay with you for a few days? The house is so lonely without Rosa and I really do need some help.'

'Of course you can darling, when is Étienne back from America?'

'He was due back last week actually but has been delayed. He said he will be arriving in Paris next week.' She paused, 'Mummy, if you are sure about us coming to stay, we will fly to London later this afternoon.'

'My goodness, so soon? Of course darling, that's fine. Just let me know what time your flight arrives and I'll send the car for you. Have a safe journey and I look forward to seeing you both later.'

Juniper told me that as she boarded the plane, she felt nothing but relief to be heading back to the civilised world after life in the 'muddy backwaters of Normandy'. 'Perhaps it was your party that opened my eyes Alice. I suddenly saw the emptiness of the life I had been leading, it made me angry and jealous. My life seemed to be passing me by, while you were surrounded by friends and apparently finding it all so easy. How much longer could I go on pretending it was the life I wanted.'

The journey to London was tiring and difficult because of Lydia, and Juniper breathed a sigh of relief when they finally arrived in Richmond. Claudia was thrilled to see them and picked Lydia up for a hug.

'Hello my darling girl, haven't you grown!' she kissed Lydia's cheek, but the toddler squirmed in her arms, wanting to be put down. She didn't recognise her grandmother and was already missing Rosa. The de Montfort housekeeper, Bridget, offered to take Lydia upstairs for her bath and then give her supper in the nursery.

'Thank you Bridget, how kind,' said Juniper relieved, handing Lydia over, then following her mother into the drawing room. They could hear Bridget chatting away to Lydia as she carried her upstairs to the nursery and smiled at one another.

Finally, mother and daughter sat down together to enjoy a glass of wine.

'I'm so relieved to be back in London,' said Juniper.

'It is so good to have you here again darling, but I can't remember the last time I saw Lydia, hasn't she grown. Darling, why do you say relieved, is everything alright?' asked Claudia, concerned. When Juniper did not reply, and appeared to be examining the rug at her feet, she continued, 'I thought you liked your life in the country, it's what you said you wanted when you married.'

'I know, but it's not at all the way I thought it would be, I'm bored out of my mind at times. To be honest I really wish I could move back to England. Etty is always travelling and when he is home, he seems tired and distracted. I have no idea how to tell him, he thinks I'm happy.'

'Where would you live?' said Claudia.

'I don't know, but I can't go on as I am.'

'Has something happened darling? You have never mentioned that you are unhappy.'

'Things aren't good between Etty and me,' Juniper paused, and to Claudia's dismay, she put her face in her hands and began to cry.

'Whatever is the matter? Is there anything I can do to help?'

'There is nothing anyone can do,' she paused to wipe tears from under her eyes. 'I feel as if I'm losing him.' Claudia got up from her chair, pressing a small handkerchief into Juniper's hand.

'Darling, it can't be that bad.'

'It is, I've done something really stupid, and now,' she paused again and her face crumpled. 'There is so much you don't know Mummy, things that happened to me when I was younger, things that have affected my life with Étienne.'

'What do you mean?' said Claudia looking at her daughter with dismay. 'Tell me.'

Juniper finally needed to talk about it, to lash out and blame someone for what happened all those years ago. She had been only a few years older than Lydia was now when it had started, and as Lydia got older, the memories came back to haunt her. They blocked the joy she should have found with her child, instead bringing anger and pain, it was too much to bear. Juniper took a deep breath, looked at Claudia and said angrily through her tears, 'I'm talking about Uncle Leonard Mummy, when he used to come into my room to read to me. He did things he should never have done and you just let him!'

'Oh my darling.' Claudia looked down at her hands, a distraught expression on her face. 'You don't mean, he didn't...' she said, almost in a whisper.

Claudia's face changed with a dawning comprehension and she prayed that she was wrong. As Juniper nodded through her tears, Claudia began to weep.

The two women talked late into the night. Claudia listened

as her daughter described events that no child should ever have to experience. 'I am so sorry Juniper, if only I had known, if only you had come to me.' But she knew now, with terrible clarity, that deep down, in some way she had suspected and done nothing. 'I'm so sorry my darling, so very sorry that this happened to you. I didn't want to believe it, I couldn't. Oh my God, what have I done.'

Afterwards, Juniper went on to tell Claudia the truth about her marriage. She told her that she and Étienne had been living separate lives and that she had long suspected him of having affairs. Finally, she talked about what she had seen that day in the barn and the unexpected outpouring of grief it caused her.

'When I saw them together, I suddenly saw what love could, and should have been for me. I felt angry and bitter and jealous that these things would never be mine.' Claudia's heart went out to her daughter and she walked across the room to put her arms around her.

'Darling, I am so, so sorry,' she said quietly. Finally, Juniper told her mother about the party and the way she had behaved, having drunk far too much wine. Exhausted and defeated, she said, 'So you see, I really have made a mess of my life, I just don't know how I can carry on.' Claudia struggled to comprehend the ways of the modern world, and felt ill equipped to deal with it all. She pulled Juniper to her, hugging her. 'Don't worry my darling, everything will be alright, you'll see. First, you need a good night's sleep, we will talk again in the morning.'

The following day, Claudia rallied. She looked at her exhausted daughter and said, 'Juniper, I have a plan.' Claudia suggested that Juniper pay a surprise visit to Étienne in Paris, so that the two of them could spend some time together in that most romantic of cities. 'Darling you need to remind him why he married you. Go to Paris looking your best and do everything you can to repair your marriage. Lydia will be fine here with us for a few days.'

Claudia had a way of making everything alright, and Juniper wondered why it had taken her so long to feel this new closeness and appreciation for her mother.

PARIS

When Juniper told me what she did next, I marvelled at her ability to switch from distraught child to manipulative adult. She sat up straighter in her chair with a gleam in her eye and the shadow of a smile on her face, as she began to tell me more.

'A few days later, I was on my way to Paris. When I arrived, I let myself into our apartment, and set about preparing everything for Étienne's return the following day. I put fresh sheets on the bed, a vase of flowers in the hallway and set the table for a romantic dinner. I rang a local restaurant and asked for dinner to be delivered early the following evening. The next day I went shopping for a new dress, silk underwear and a flimsy nightdress, finally visiting the beauty salon to have my hair and nails done. As a matter of fact Alice, I began to enjoy it.

When I got back to the apartment, I took a long leisurely bath pouring in a generous quantity of rose scented bath oil. I lay back in the water to contemplate the evening ahead. Étienne was due back at 7.30pm, the food would arrive at 7, so I would need to be ready just before that. I knew it was essential that I play my part well after dinner, in order to pull this off.'

I wasn't sure what Juniper meant by playing her part, but guessed that it would soon become clear.

'Soon after 7.30,' she continued, 'I heard Étienne's key in the lock, I also heard a woman laughing, and realised with a shock that he was not alone. I walked from the bedroom into the salon in my new, figure skimming red dress, its satin folds draped elegantly at my neckline. My dark hair shone and I hoped my pale eyes were offset by just the right amount of red lipstick. I waited for Étienne to come in, wondering who could be with him, a colleague perhaps, or worse, a mistress? My heart sank. At that moment the door opened, and a tall elegant woman with blonde hair strode proprietorially into the room.

'Who on earth are you?' she demanded, stopping in her tracks at the sight of me.

'If I'm not mistaken, it is I who should be asking that question,' I replied coolly. 'Who are you and what are you doing in my apartment?' Just then Étienne appeared.

'Juniper, darling, what a surprise, you look absolutely stunning.' He put his arms around me and hugged me to him. 'Juniper, this is Catherine, a friend of my father's. She wanted to see Paris and so I invited her to use our apartment. Catherine, this is my wife, Juniper.'

'In that case, you are welcome!' I said, forcing a smile.

'Gee I'm so sorry Juniper, you gave me such a shock. Etty didn't mention that his wife would be here.' Then she added, 'I thought you lived out in the country.'

Juniper stopped for a moment and said to me, 'When I heard her call him Etty, a flash of anger rose up in me. Can you understand that Alice? That is our private family name for him, and she had no right. That night, a battle line was imperceptibly drawn.'

'Did she realise she had angered you?' I asked.

'Oh no, I hid it. I'm good at that,' she said sadly, 'but I was not friendly.'

'How did you reply?'

I just said calmly, 'Well, I'm sorry to disappoint you, but as you see, today I am in Paris. I came to surprise my husband.'

'You certainly did that,' she said, looking across at Étienne. 'You know, I think I'll get a hotel,' said Catherine. 'I really don't want to intrude.'

'There is no need for that,' said Étienne.

'No really, I insist,' she said, 'I'll take a cab.'

'Well if you insist,' said Étienne awkwardly. 'We will be leaving the day after tomorrow, you are welcome to make it your home for a few days after that.'

'Thank you,' she said.

'Enjoy our beautiful city while you are here and call me if you need anything.'

'Thank you, I will,' she said, picking up her small suitcase. 'Goodbye Juniper, I hope you both have a nice evening. Thanks for offering to put me up Etty, I'll take good care of everything,' and she walked out of the apartment, closing the door quietly behind her.

I interrupted Juniper's story again to ask, 'Did you believe him, that she was a friend of his father's, I mean?'

Juniper looked at me sadly, 'I wanted to, I really did, but finding her there with Etty, hearing how easy they were with one another, I came face to face with my worst fears. I think I knew deep down, yet still I made excuses for him. I was in Paris for a reason and the show had to go on.'

Étienne looked at me, 'Come here darling, I am so happy to see you.' He leaned in and kissed my mouth. Instead of pulling away, I closed my eyes and kissed him back, lingering in his embrace. Despite my anguish, I managed to say, 'I have missed you so much Etty, I wanted to surprise you by coming to Paris to welcome you home.'

'Darling, I can't remember the last time you looked this beautiful or kissed me the way you just did. I am so happy to see you; you must know that I adore you and tonight, you fill my heart with hope.'

Over dinner, Étienne couldn't keep his eyes off me, it was as if he was seeing me for the first time. My confidence grew as I realised I had the upper hand. I was sure I had caught him red handed with his mistress, but now, it was me he wanted. After dinner, in the bedroom, he smoothly undid the zip of my dress and it fell to the floor. I was naked beneath it and he ran his hands over my silky skin, barely able to contain his lust for me.

'Juniper,' he said hoarsely, 'Is this really you? You are a goddess tonight.' I closed my eyes and, picturing the scene in the barn, I began to enjoy it. Etty, now naked himself, pulled me roughly onto the bed, kissing my throat and shoulders. He began to lick the warm skin between my breasts, running his tongue over me as I felt him hard against my thigh. I imagined myself on that sofa in the barn as he slid into me, his hot breath against my neck and face; then anger began to rise up in me again. I dug my nails into his buttocks and began to lift my hips angrily towards him, but he loved it. He reached up and held my wrists against the pillows, laughing as he looked briefly into my eyes, assuming my complicity. Then he buried his face between my breasts as he came.

'My god Juno, you are a little minx,' he said breathlessly, 'and I love you!' I smiled into his hair, flooded with relief. It didn't occur to Étienne then to wonder what had brought about the change in me.

We made love not once but twice that night. Etty told me that now he had me all to himself, he wanted to make up for lost time, he was putty in my hands.

To my surprise, the next morning Étienne announced that he was taking the day off. 'Darling, I'm going to take you on a river cruise. It's a beautiful day to enjoy the sights of Paris and we can have lunch at a little restaurant I know beside the Seine.' I was thrilled. I felt like a honeymooner again as we boarded the Bateau Mouche, finding seats together in the sun. When the engines started and the boat pulled away, I reached over to hold Étienne's hand. The circular route took in the Grand Palais, and the Pont Alexandre III; as we passed the Tuileries gardens, Étienne put his arm around me and held me close. 'Do you remember the very first time we went out together?' he said, 'You, me, Alice and her teacher from London?' I nodded thinking how much had changed since that day. As the boat slid over the water, the Eiffel Tower rose into a clear blue sky ahead of us, and I pulled out my camera to take some pictures. We disembarked at the Île de la Cité, marvelling at the majesty of Notre Dame rising high above the river, as we strolled over the bridge to the Île de St Louis.

Étienne had reserved a table outside in the sunshine under a bright red awning, its edges fluttering in the sun. A waiter stepped forward to greet us, shaking Étienne's hand like an old friend. We enjoyed a crisp salade verte and moules à la crème, blotting up creamy sauce with chunks of crusty bread and laughing together in a way we had not done since before our wedding. Étienne ordered coffee and it was only after our leisurely lunch in the sun, when I was at my most relaxed, that he broke the news that he would not be able to return with me the following morning after all. Business would keep him in Paris for the rest of the week.

'Of course Etty,' I said, 'we've had a marvellous day together and I know you have neglected your work to make it possible. Come home when you are ready darling, and I will see you soon.' Étienne dropped me at the Gare St. Lazare the next morning, kissing me and telling me he would see me at the weekend. As soon as his car was out of sight, I took a taxi to the airport and returned to London.

LONDON 1960

Juniper told me that the trip to Paris was a great success and although she still had her doubts about Catherine, she was bright eyed and hopeful for the future. Étienne was her husband and she would do everything in her power to bring him back to her. She would fight for him, show him that she could be the confident woman she had been in Paris. She had taken control of the situation because she had to, and the experience brought out a side of her she didn't know she possessed. Étienne responded like a puppy coming to heel, hardly able to believe his luck. Was it because he had almost been caught out or because this was how he had always wanted her to be? She smiled at the memory of it and the power it had given her. At last, she could see the way forward, the success of her marriage was in her own hands.

Étienne was to return to Normandy the following week, so she stayed on in London for another couple of days to talk things through with her mother. On the morning of her return to France, Claudia said, 'Darling, I have something to tell you before you leave. I have spoken to your father and we have both agreed that we would like you all to come and live here, back home in Richmond. We are ready for a change ourselves, and we are going to redecorate the old family apartment in town and move closer to the theatres and the buzz of the city. Your father was surprisingly keen when I made the suggestion.'

'Mummy!' cried Juniper, 'Do you mean it?'

'Of course I mean it darling, all we want is for you to be happy. This house is too big for us now and it is, after all, your family home. I think it will be perfect for you all. You have given life in France a fair try and in the circumstances, I think it would be churlish of Étienne to refuse you. Oh darling, it would be so wonderful to have you living nearby again.'

When Étienne returned to Normandy, Juniper was ready for him; she lit candles and prepared a special dinner. They talked for the first time as adults and equals. Gone was the childlike bride Juniper had once been and in her place, a confident woman looked back at her husband, determined to show him that she was a match for any woman he might have taken to his bed in Paris. Things would be different from now on, there was too much at stake for it to be otherwise. Later, entwined in each other's arms, clothes scattered over the bedroom floor, Juniper smiled into his face.

'Etty, I love you,' she said simply.

'Are you happy Juno?'

'Mmm,' she replied, 'I have almost everything I could possibly wish for.'

'Almost?' he asked, nuzzling her neck.

'There is just one more thing Etty,' she whispered into his ear.

'Anything my darling, what is it you want?'

'I want us to live in London again.'

I wish I had known then, how difficult Juniper had found her life in Normandy; perhaps we could have been friends much sooner. Her self-contained demeanour and apparent control of her life, seemed to leave room for little else. I can see now that she did it to protect herself, to hide her unhappiness.

It took me by surprise when, the following spring, Juniper and Étienne moved with Lydia to de Montfort House in Richmond. She told me things improved markedly between them as she began to inhabit her new found strength as a wife and mother, and Étienne started to spend more time at home.

When Charles had a quiet word with Étienne about his long absences from the family, and the effect it was having on Juniper, he assured him that things would be different from now on. He and Juniper had reached an understanding, he said, and were looking forward to their new lives in London.

'How do your parents feel about the move?' asked Charles.

'Well sir, my father has been based in Florida for some time now and my mother has decided to move over there, so that they can spend more time together. I think hearing about our move to London helped her to make up her mind. She was tired of Paris. Much has always been expected of her on the charity circuit and I think she felt ready to hand the responsibility over to others. She has certainly earned a quieter life and I will be pleased to see them together again.' Charles nodded as he spoke and then stood up and patted his son in law affectionately on the shoulder.

'Good news old chap, I'm glad we understand one another.'

Soon afterwards, Juniper announced the news that their second child would be born in the autumn, to great delight in the family. Claudia ordered the redecoration of the old nursery, a beautiful crib and new curtains as their gift to the couple.

Juniper gave birth to a beautiful baby boy as the yellow and russet leaves fell from the trees in Richmond Park. He arrived a little earlier than expected, but Juniper's doctor put this down to the stress of their move, reassuring her that the baby was a good size as well as fit and healthy. With some difficulty, Juniper persuaded Rosa and Jack to come and live with them in London, offering them an apartment annexed to the house and a generous salary. It was the news that a new baby was on the way, that finally convinced them.

Baby Roger was the apple of Étienne's eye, and as he began to spend more and more time at home, the family settled into their lives in London. For the first few months Juniper told me she was ecstatically happy and relieved to be back on her home ground. There were times when she felt like a nesting mother hen, but it was short lived. Motherhood was not only tiring, she said, but very limiting for her, and soon she began to hand more and more responsibility over to Rosa.

Juniper involved herself in small charity events to start with, gradually increasing her work load. Étienne began to travel again and it was left to Rosa and Jack to organise the children. One by one, they started at the little prep school nearby, growing in stature as well as confidence as the years passed.

One day, after a rare quiet afternoon, Juniper looked up from her Vogue magazine to see Étienne standing in the drawing room.

'Étienne, where did you spring from?' she said surprised. 'I thought you were in Paris.'

'Well I was, I thought I would surprise you and come home early. How are the children?'

'I've no idea,' she said. 'They have been at school all day and I expect Rosa has collected them as usual. They are probably down in the kitchen having their supper.' Étienne looked coldly at his wife for a moment and then walked out of the room. Juniper went back to her magazine, as she heard his footsteps retreating across the marble hallway towards the kitchen stairs. The children's shrieks of delight echoed up the stairs and into the drawing room, where Juniper suddenly felt a stab of remorse. She had not thought to go down to the kitchen and see the children herself; she knew she ought to make more effort with them. Étienne's coldness towards her had not gone unnoticed and she sighed. She would take Lydia clothes shopping to make up for it; perhaps one of the pretty party dresses she had seen in Vogue. She brightened at the thought, she and Lydia would go to Harrods at the weekend, Roger would be happy here with Jack.

After a light supper with Juniper, Étienne climbed the stairs to look in on the children. Lydia was reading when he put his head round the door and he sat on her bed for a while, listening to her talk about her riding lessons in the park and their games of cricket with Jack in the garden. 'Rosa let me help her with some baking today too,' she said, her eyes shining. He smiled to himself, remembering what a comforting presence Rosa and Jack had been to him when he was young. Yet, one day he had moved on with his life without a backward glance. He would make a point of thanking them, he decided, and perhaps give them an extra bonus for Christmas.

'Time to sleep now Lydia darling,' said Étienne. She put her book down and snuggled under her covers. 'I'm so glad you're home Daddy, night-night,' she said, as he kissed her forehead.

He turned out the light and left the room, leaving her door ajar as she liked it. When he stepped quietly into Roger's room he was already asleep, lying pink cheeked, lips slightly parted with his arms flung above his head as he slept.

PART 2

ROGER 1971

By the time Roger was 11, he was tall and lanky with thin white legs and bulbous knees, absurd in the shorts Juniper insisted he wore much of the time. Étienne tried to intervene on his son's behalf, 'Juniper, the boy is miserable, the constant butt of jokes and teasing among his peers. I say we should relax the rules and let him grow up for heaven's sake. It can hardly matter to you one way or the other, you never even see him.'

Juniper looked up from her magazine, bored, 'Boys under the age of 10 do not wear long trousers Étienne.'

'He is nearly twelve Juniper, you can't keep him a baby forever. Anyway it is eight, boys under eight.'

'Oh for heaven's sake Etty, must you argue with me over everything!' Juniper sighed as he left the room, closing the door quietly behind him.

Roger took cover under the stairs as his father strode out into the hall. He couldn't wait to get away from his mother's indifference and the taunting of the boys at school. 'Knobby legs! Mummy's boy!' He was embarrassed by his French surname too. Why couldn't he just be called Brown or Jones so that he blended in. Instead, his name had become Dippy Day, but he no longer cared. He hoped he would soon be leaving it all behind for boarding school. It was alright for Lydia, what did she know of misery, she was their mother's favourite, always had been.

No, boarding school couldn't be any worse than his current situation and there was every chance it would be much better.

He sauntered out from under the stairs as soon as the coast

was clear and headed down to the kitchen. Rosa could always be relied on for a biscuit or some cake. He wasn't really allowed down there to bother her, but who cared, he certainly didn't. His mother would never dream of coming as far as the kitchen and would assume he was in his room doing his homework.

'Hello young man,' said Rosa, in her French accent, looking up from the dish she was stirring. 'What have you been up to this afternoon?'

'Not much,' said Roger shrugging his shoulders. He slumped down on a chair by the Aga and stretched his long white legs out in front of him, his grey woollen socks sagging around his ankles.

'Mr Jack will be coming in soon for a cup of tea and some cake, would you like some too?' Roger's face lit up,

'Yes please! Don't tell Mother though.'

'A young man like you needs plenty of food inside you. Don't you worry, I won't say a word,' she said and winked at him. The door opened and Jack walked in, carrying a rabbit swinging from a stick on his shoulder. Roger jumped up,

'Mr Jack! You've got a rabbit!'

'Right I have, it was caught in a trap. I expect Mrs Rosa will find something to do with it, won't you, ma chérie?' He dropped it onto the side table and Roger saw its baleful, lifeless eyes staring back at him.

'Poor thing, I wish things didn't have to die so that we can eat, it seems so unfair.'

'That's just the way of the world,' said Rosa, 'Nothing you or I can do about it. Now come on Mr Roger, up you get, go and wash your 'ands over there at the sink and then sit down, while I cut you and Mr Jack a nice piece of cake.'

When he was back in his room, Roger thought about Mr Nightingale, his form teacher. He tried to imagine what Mr Nightingale would do if he had a mother like his. Mr Nightingale would stand up for himself and make his mother, at the very least, look up from what she was doing when he entered the room. Mr Nightingale would probably make her listen to him and make her care about him.

Mr Nightingale had made Roger's school life more bearable this year. He alone noticed how mercilessly Roger was teased, and did his best to intervene whenever he could, without making things more difficult than they already were. He suggested at the last parents' meeting that the best thing for Roger would be a complete change and a new school. It was his father who had shared this with Roger, when he had broken the news that they were considering his own alma mater, The Park School in Kent, for Roger's continuing education. It would be tough at times, his father told him, but he would make lots of new friends and become a young man with a string of qualifications to his name. He just needed to work hard and make them proud.

His father didn't mention what his mother thought of the plan, and Roger didn't ask. He assumed she would be glad to be rid of him. He certainly hoped she would not put a stop to his going, which he saw as an escape route from his current life of misery.

The matter of school was not mentioned again and the summer term at Forest Prep dragged on. Roger counted the days until the start of the holidays and now, in mid-June, the end was in sight. His only friend, Ashcroft, a ginger haired boy with freckles and a recent eruption of spots, invited him to go down to Cornwall with his family for the summer. His mother wanted to paint the sea, Ashcroft explained, as if there was nothing unusual in a person's mother wanting to paint a patch of grey water. 'What does your father say about it?' asked Roger. 'Nothing much, why should he? Mummy does what she likes and Daddy plays golf. We'll be able to do pretty much whatever we want Dippy.' Roger thought this unlikely, but whatever the truth of it turned out to be, he wanted to go! The only question was how to broach the subject with his parents, he would have to plan it carefully. He decided to ask his father first in the hope that he would be able to get his mother's agreement, he just had to wait for the right moment.

The following Monday, Roger was listening as usual at the door of the drawing room. His mother was making a telephone call, 'Good afternoon, am I speaking to Harrods? Good. Yes, you can, I wish to place an order for school uniform please.' Roger was straining to hear more, when he became aware of footsteps approaching. He turned to find his father standing in the hall behind him.

'Roger! What are you doing! You know you are not allowed to eavesdrop on private conversations. Come to my study before your mother catches you.'

'Sorry sir,' said Roger, hanging his head.

'Sorry you listened or sorry you were caught?' said Étienne, hiding a smile.

The study was a small room with two green, well-worn leather chairs either side of a walnut desk and a long glass door facing the garden. There was a large painting on the wall showing their home in France, on a perfect summer's day, the place where his father had grown up. The house was built of pale beige stone which, in the painting, had taken on a golden glow in the afternoon sunshine. Roses and clematis climbed the walls and for a moment, Roger forgot himself as he gazed at the house where they had enjoyed so many summers. His father's voice was soft when he spoke, as he too looked at the painting. 'Des jours heureux, Rojay, happy days, mon petit brave.' A tear spilled out of the corner of Roger's eye and he quickly grabbed the hankie from his pocket, pretending to blow his nose. He hoped his father hadn't seen it.

'I'm sorry Father, for listening at the door. I was only trying to find out if I'm going away to school next term. I thought I heard mother ordering school uniform'. Étienne's heart went out to his son, the poor chap had been left in the dark over this, it really was too bad. Juniper promised she would tell him of their decision weeks ago and apparently she had not. His momentary drift into reminiscence forgotten, Étienne turned to his son. 'Would you like to go away to a new school Roger?'

'Yes sir, I would.'

'In that case you shall go, I think you will like it there. You will follow in my footsteps to a school where I had some very happy times. One day you will understand that your school days are the best of your life. You have all that ahead of you and you are a very lucky boy.' Roger looked at his father, struggling to imagine a time when he would look back on his school days as anything other than misery. His father sighed, gazing again at the French idyll hanging on the wall. Seizing the moment, Roger said,

'Nigel Ashcroft from school has invited me to stay with his family in Cornwall this summer, may I go Father?'

'You know we will be in France for most of the summer Roger, but I will discuss it with your mother, and see what I can do.'

'Thank you sir.'

'Now, no more listening at doors, do you understand? Those who eavesdrop never hear any good of themselves.'

'No sir,' Roger waited, hoping that the lecture was over.

'Alright then, off you go.'

'Thank you sir,' Roger walked out of the study and turned left along the corridor, walking to the end where there was a side door into the garden.

Their home was on the edge of Richmond Park, so although the garden was not large, it backed onto many acres of parkland where deer grazed, and the bracken took on a glorious russet colour. There was a summer house at the far end of the garden, and it was here that Roger would hide out when he needed to be alone. He pulled open the doors at the back so that he could see out across the park, then flung himself down on a beanbag to contemplate his new life. He would finally be going away to school! He had wanted this more than anything, but now it was a reality, his anxiety began to build. What if he couldn't do the work? What if he didn't make friends?

Checking that there was nobody around, Roger reached under some old cushions in the corner of the shed for the magazine that Ashcroft had given him for safe keeping. The bright yellow cover looked innocent enough, a woman in a red jumpsuit holding up a blackboard. Even the word 'Playboy' on the front had not alerted him to what was inside the magazine. The pair of them smirked guiltily in the playground, hidden by the branches of a willow tree, as they pored over pictures of women wearing hardly any clothes. Finally, Ashcroft proudly opened the centre fold showing a completely naked woman lounging across the page, and looking them straight in the eyes! Roger was hardly able to believe it and quickly looked around to make sure there were no teachers in sight. Suddenly the bell rang for the end of break and Ashcroft turned urgently to him, 'Dippy, you need to take this home and hide it for me, Dad will kill me if he finds out I've taken it.' In horrified awe, Roger quickly stuffed the magazine into his satchel and followed Ashcroft back inside.

The shed was the only place he could think of to hide the magazine, and since then, he made regular trips there to have another look at the pictures, finding he quite enjoyed the feeling they gave him. He wasn't sure why, but when he looked, he felt a strange heat come over him and flush his cheeks. The first time his thing had started to move in his trousers, he was confused, unzipping his fly to check, fascinated that it had grown so large and had a life of its own. Now, he gripped it in his hand, slowly sliding his fingers up and down, his cheeks flushing as he gazed at the naked woman looking back at him. His breath quickened and his lips fell slack, as with a jolt he felt the release of hot sticky liquid. He grabbed his hanky and wiped up the mess, before lying back on the bean bag. A laugh escaped him and a sense of freedom, there was nothing his mother could do about this! At the thought of her icy face glaring at him, however, he quickly pushed the magazine back under the cushions in the corner.

As it turned out, his mother had been indifferent to his summer holiday plans. Her attention was focused on 14 year-old Lydia, her new holiday wardrobe and an outfit for her next horse riding event.

'Roger can do whatever he wants darling,' Juniper told her husband, 'It's fine by me,' and she returned to choosing Lydia's clothes.

Roger couldn't wait to tell Ashcroft that he would be allowed to spend the whole summer with him and his family. How spiffing to get away from dreary old Lydia and his mother for weeks on end. He could hardly wait!

CORNWALL

Roger had been awake since first light and heard his parents leaving the house very early to drive Lydia to her event. They said their goodbyes the evening before, and he felt a sense of relief that there was nothing now standing between him and his holiday in Cornwall. He had packed and unpacked his bag over the previous days not wanting to forget anything. He and Ashcroft spoke regularly on the phone to discuss the trip, Roger asking about the house and the beach, trying to imagine how they would spend their days. This morning, the sun shone brightly in a clear blue sky, and Rosa was there to make sure he went safely on his way. He could hardly believe he would be away for five whole weeks!

Rosa had fussed the whole of the previous day, making sure he had everything packed. As far as he was concerned he would only need his swimming trunks and change of clothes. He had no plans to wear anything that his parents would deem suitable. Freedom was calling him and he felt the first fluttering of independence.

He washed swiftly, brushed his teeth and packed the last of his things before grabbing his bag and clattering down the stairs. It was a good hour before he was due to be collected, so he threw his bag down in the hall and went downstairs to the kitchen and the smell of buttered toast. Today was the beginning of his new life, first the holiday in Cornwall and then a new school in September.

Good old Rosa had made his favourite, poached eggs and bacon, he was starving! After breakfast he rushed upstairs to the drawing room, where the window would give him a good view of the driveway. He stood sipping his orange juice, peering out to try and catch a glimpse of the car as it approached. This time tomorrow he would be in Cornwall. Finally, he saw the long sporty bonnet of the Ashcroft car, a red e-type Jaguar making its way along the drive. It pulled up outside the house, emitting a throaty roar and a spray of gravel before coming to a halt.

Roger hadn't met Ashcroft's parents before and had definitely never seen his car. He was expecting a couple not unlike his own mother and father, driving a staid old Daimler. Instead, a petite woman with long blonde hair and a floppy brimmed hat, emerged from the car. She wore bright red lipstick and a mini skirt with flowers on it. Her square heeled boots were knee high, and she wore her hair loose and long with a flowing chiffon scarf tied around her neck. Roger almost choked on his orange juice at this unexpected turn of events, and watched as she walked confidently to the front door, her heels tapping on the path. Thank goodness his parents had gone out, he feared that had they had been here to meet Mrs Ashcroft, they might have put a stop to the trip.

The doorbell rang and Roger heard Rosa answering the door, he stifled a laugh as he heard Mrs Ashcroft mistake her for his mother. 'Unfortunately Mrs d'Apidae is not at home but please, do come inside,' he heard Rosa say, 'I will go and find Rojay.' By then, Roger had recovered his composure, he opened the door of the drawing room and stepped into the hallway, ready to shake hands with Mrs Ashcroft. Instead, she rushed forward, put her arms around him and kissed him firmly on both cheeks, 'Roger darling, welcome to our family for the summer! Are you ready to go?' Roger felt the blood rush to his cheeks, first at the unexpected kisses and then at her casual warmth towards him. He felt his cheeks redden, but she seemed not to notice.

'Yes Mrs Ashcroft, I'm ready, thank you.'

'Oh darling do call me Caro, no need for formalities, you will be doing me a favour actually. Mrs Ashcroft makes me feel like my mother in law, so very old!' Her tinkling laugh filled the hallway as he bent to pick up his bag and coat.

'Yes Mrs Ash, I mean… Caro,' using her Christian name made him feel grown up and a bit subversive. He looked over his shoulder as if expecting his parents to appear, then he called goodbye to Rosa, and followed Caro out of the door in a cloud of chiffon and musky perfume.

As they stepped out of the house Mr Ashcroft got out of the car, seeming to unfold as he did so. A tall man in an open necked shirt smiled broadly at him, 'Hello young man, let's get your bag into the back.' He took Roger's small holdall from him as Ashcroft peered through the window, giving him a quick wave and a grin.

'Come on Dippy, get in!' his father's seat tipped forward and Roger clambered in next to his friend.

'Cool car Ashcroft, you never said!' The curls on top of Roger's head almost touched the roof of the car, as he leaned back in his seat. He flushed with excitement, hardly believing that they would be travelling all the way down to Cornwall in this red sports car!

As the car made its way out onto the road, the sound of the engine almost drowned out Caro's voice as she called out, 'Ready boys, we are on our way!' At first their progress was slow as they made their way out of London, but once on the main road, the engine roared into life as they sped along. Fields and trees flashed past in a blur, as they slid further down into their seats. After a while Caro switched the radio on and the sound of the Beatles' 'Eleanor Rigby' filled the car. She lowered her window a little and her chiffon scarf lifted and fluttered towards them as cool wind rushed into the back. Roger began to feel sleepy, as if he was in another world, where faces could be kept in jars by the door and he was alone, with all the lonely people. The words of the song filled his head, as he drifted into sleep.

It was much later when he awoke, the music softer now, barely audible above the steady hum of the engine as they cruised along. He watched as Caro reached for what looked like a lipstick case, from the console of the car. She held it to the end of the cigarette she had just put between her lips, and almost immediately, a ribbon of smoke began to drift upwards and a rich woody smell wafted into the back of the car. Every now and again she passed the cigarette to her husband so that he could share it, resting her hand lightly on his thigh as they rushed along. Roger glanced at Ashcroft to see if he had noticed, but he was asleep. Roger closed his eyes again and the next time he awoke, it was to the sound of lemonade being poured and packets of sandwiches rustling. They had pulled over in a country lane for a late lunch. 'Come on boys!'

called Caro, 'We are having a picnic!' He and Ashcroft clambered out of the car stretching and yawning. 'If you want to have a pee, go over there', she gestured vaguely in the direction of the edge of the field. 'You can wash your hands in the stream.'

Several hours later, the car finally bumped along the unmade road to their home for the summer. The light was fading as they approached, and soon the cottage came into view. When they clambered out of the car, their legs were stiff and they were tired and hungry.

'Grab your bags out of the back boys, let's get inside.' Caro unlocked the door, flicked the switch and a low hanging metal light above a scrubbed pine table brightened the room. 'At last!' she said, 'I thought the journey would never end!' They dropped their bags to the floor and Caro walked over to the fridge to look inside. 'Oh good, Mrs B has left us a shepherd's pie for supper!' She opened the door of the already warm Aga and slid the dish into the oven. There was a bottle of red wine on the table and a note welcoming them back to Cornwall. 'How lovely!' said Caro. 'Come on boys, let's get our things upstairs.' The boys raced up a flight of stairs in the centre of the hallway, onto a galleried landing. There were three bedrooms, the largest of which was directly in front of them. 'Obviously the parents' room,' thought Roger, as he ran to the right, only to discover that the right side of the house consisted of an art studio with a small kitchen and bathroom leading off it. He quickly ran back to join Ashcroft on the left side of the house. His was a twin bedded room overlooking the garden, which was just visible in the dusky moonlight. 'This my bed', said Ashcroft, 'yours is under the eaves.' They threw their bags onto their beds before rushing along the landing to explore. 'That's our bathroom,' said Ashcroft 'and there's a spare bedroom there.' They could hear Mr Ashcroft slowly mounting the stairs with Caro's oversized suitcase as she called out to him, 'Darling, I'm in here.'

'God I'm dying for a pee,' said Ashcroft diving into the bathroom and slamming the door behind him.

'Hurry up Ashcroft, so am I,' said Roger under his breath, as Mr Ashcroft's voice drifted up the stairs.

'I thought you said you would travel light this time Caro,' he said, giving a final heave of the case as he reached the top, slightly out of breath. 'Dear Lord, I made it,' he gasped as he lifted the case onto the wooden blanket box at the bottom of their bed. Then he walked over to join his wife at the window.

'I never tire of that view,' Roger heard her say, as they took in the sight of the shimmering water lit by the moon.

'Everything looks lovely darling, Mrs B never lets us down does she?' He pulled Caro to him, her long hair fanning out over his chest as he kissed the top of her head.

'Come on Dippy, let's go down,' said Ashcroft, and they clattered downstairs in search of food.

'What are you up to boys?' he called, releasing Caro and stepping out onto the landing.

'We're down here, in the kitchen!'

'Good for you,' called his father. 'Now you are down there, why don't you look for some knives and forks and lay the table for supper.'

'Ok Dad.'

Twenty minutes later they were sitting around the pine table, a steaming dish of shepherd's pie in front of Caro as she began to serve. She had lit a large, well-used candle which cast a warm glow about the kitchen and she had put the fruit left over from their journey, into a small bowl beside it.

'There you are boys,' she said as she placed steaming plates of food in front of them.

'Thanks Mrs Ashcroft!' said Roger, his face lighting up at the sight of the food. Caro smiled.

'Thanks Mum, I'm famished!' added her son. Michael poured the wine and Caro put a jug of water on the table for the boys. 'There you are Mike,' she said as she passed her husband his plate.

'Here's to us and a wonderful summer,' he said, clinking his glass with Caro's.

Roger put his head down, and concentrated on his food. When they had finished, he looked up, 'That was delicious Mrs Ashcroft, I mean, Caro,' He mumbled awkwardly, as he put his knife and fork neatly together on the plate. 'Thank you for inviting me to come with you.'

'You are very welcome young man,' said Michael. 'We will go exploring tomorrow after a good night's sleep.'

After the boys enjoyed apples and tangerines, they made their way upstairs.

'Don't forget to brush your teeth,' called Caro after them. 'Sleep well, see you both in the morning.' Ashcroft ran ahead and Roger lingered on the stairs, half listening to the conversation in the kitchen.

Caro turned to look at Michael as he refilled their glasses. 'We are finally here,' she sighed. 'I have so looked forward to this time together in Cornwall,' she leaned in to him and he put his arm around her shoulders.

'The time is ours,' he said. 'You can paint to your heart's content and the boys can run free on the beach. We can all relax for a few weeks.'

'I feel quite sorry for Roger,' she said quietly. 'The boy seems frightened of his own shadow.' Hearing his name, Roger strained to hear more from the top of the stairs.

'Give him time' said Michael, 'I'm sure this place will work its magic, but now,' he paused and said quietly into her ear, 'I'm going to work my magic on you.' Caro flushed with pleasure as he leaned in and grazed her neck with his lips, and the tip of his tongue.

The boys fell into their beds, tired but longing for morning and the start of their holiday. Ashcroft switched off the light. 'Wait 'till you see the beach,' he whispered, 'we'll probably take a picnic.'

'Can't wait,' said Roger trying to get comfortable, hiding the old teddy that Rosa had embarrassingly packed in his case, under the duvet. He got up to use the bathroom one last time, and as he stepped back into the hall, he heard the parents' bedroom door click quietly closed. The faint sound of Caro laughing was followed by a gentle thud against the door, as her laughter became a sigh. Roger stopped to listen, the quiet creaks of the door and the rough sound of fabric moving against it was broken by little high moans. He stood rooted to the spot and to his mortification realised that the front his pyjama bottoms had begun to move outwards, as he tried to imagine what might be going on in the Ashcrofts' bedroom.

'Dippy, what are you doing out there,' called Ashcroft. Roger said nothing for fear of being heard, but blushing furiously, he pulled his dressing gown around himself and tiptoed back to the bedroom, thankful that the room was in darkness.

'Needed a pee,' he said, and getting into bed, he turned onto his side and put his arms round his teddy. As he lay there, he tried to imagine what might be happening in the parents' bedroom, but soon, exhausted from the journey, he fell asleep.

The next morning, sun poured in through their bedroom window throwing a bright shaft of light across the floorboards.

Roger got out of bed to pull back the curtains. 'Look at that!' he said. Ashcroft felt for his glasses on his bedside table and putting them on, he joined his friend at the window.

'What's going on down there,' he said, as he looked out. The small garden below was surrounded by a wire fence that barely contained a field full of sheep, all pressing up against it. They were trying to get at the longer grass growing in the garden of the cottage. The door opened below and they watched as Caro walked towards the sheep in a flowing pink dressing gown, reaching out to try and stroke their heads. The sheep ran in fear as she approached, leaving behind a hapless lamb, whose fur had become caught in the fence. 'There, there,' she crooned, as she bent down to try to release the animal, her presence causing it to struggle and pull even more. Michael stepped out of the back door to try to help, but she held her hand up to stop him. All of a sudden, the lamb broke free and raced across the field to join its mother, who had been standing a safe distance away, and Caro turned and broke into a smile.

'Come on let's go down and get some food,' said Ashcroft. The boys clattered down the main staircase and into the kitchen, just as Caro walked back inside.

'You won't believe what just happened!' she said.

'We saw it Mum,' said Ashcroft. 'Is there anything to eat?'

'Dad went shopping early this morning, so we have cereal, fresh bread and milk and some other groceries from the local shop. So, help yourselves,' she said, drifting out of the kitchen. 'I'm going to get bathed and dressed now, see you in a little while.' Roger coloured, heading over to the fridge to have a look inside, while Ashcroft grabbed two bowls from the cupboard and put them onto the table with a full packet of cereal.

'Pass the milk Dippy,' he said. 'Is there anything to drink?'

Roger looked, but couldn't see anything other than some pink liquid in a jug.

'No, just some pink stuff,' he said.

'Oh that's just Mum's grapefruit and strawberry drink,' he said. 'Yuk, don't bother with that.' Instead, Ashcroft got two glasses out of the cupboard and poured water from last night's jug into them, pushing one across to his friend.

By the time Caro came downstairs again, the boys were outside playing a makeshift game of cricket with an ancient bat and some old stumps they had found beside the garden shed. She called to them, 'Boys, I'm heading down to the cove to do some painting, see you later.'

'Ok,' they shouted in unison. When Michael eventually appeared, the game was over and the boys were having another look in the fridge.

'Who wants a swim?' said Michael.

'Yes please!' they chorused.

'Ok, go upstairs, get your swim things on and find a beach towel each. I'm going to pack some sandwiches and drinks and we'll go down to the cove to join Caro for a picnic.

CÔTE D'AZUR,

ALICE 1971

I didn't imagine that I was the only woman in Xavier's life over the years we were together, but I knew I was the one who was his constant, his touch point and his home. We became like a long married couple when we were together, even though marriage could not have been further from our minds. We enjoyed our individual lives for weeks at a time, becoming one again when we were together. There were times when Xavier needed the buzz of Paris, and others when he wanted to soak up the colours and warmth of the Côte d'Azur. I understood his need for freedom and enjoyed the sense of balance his absences gave me.

One summer, to my surprise, Xavier suggested that I join him on the Côte d'Azur; he wanted to spend the whole season painting and introduce me to some friends. I discovered he had a stone cottage in the hills above Grasse, where I would be able to swim in the small pool and visit the perfume makers nearby. 'Yes,' I said, 'I'll come,' realising how little I knew of his life when he was away from me.

Just a few days later, I was stretched out on a sun chair enjoying distant views of the sea and mountains from the stone terrace. Terracotta pots of bright geraniums trailed their foliage and flowers over the warm ground, and I breathed in the glorious beauty of it. Xavier wasted no time settling into his studio, he was working on a new painting, and I was alone. I lay back against the beige cushion and sighed, it was a perfect day. I closed my eyes for a moment and allowed my thoughts to drift.

I must have fallen asleep because I was woken by the sound of a car pulling up on the gravel outside. I reached for my robe, but before I could get up and put it on, I heard footsteps and a woman's voice calling out, 'Zav darling, are you out here?' A tall, elegant woman wearing white linen shorts, a cutaway sun top and espadrilles appeared by the pool, blonde hair tucked behind her ears and bright pink lips stretching into a smile as she saw me. 'Bonjour darling, you must be Alice. Zav has told me all about you.' She walked towards the pool and crouched down, trailing her fingers in the water. 'Ooh perfect,' she said, walking to the chair next to mine and dropping her bag onto it. She slid her shorts off, revealing long tanned legs and a barely-there bikini bottom. Her top quickly followed and within moments she plunged almost naked into the pool. I was speechless, still lying back on my chair as she surfaced, blonde hair clinging to her head and droplets of water running over her freckled face. 'Wow that feels good,' she said smiling at me. 'I'm Lara by the way,' before stretching out in the water, face turned up to the blue sky as she floated on her back, nipples intermittently breaking the surface.

Just then Xavier came out with a bottle of chilled rosé and three glasses, 'Hey Lara, Alice, I see you two have met.'

'Yes, we have,' I said, finding my voice, looking first at him and then at Lara, who was now making her way up the steps and out of the pool. She walked towards Xavier trailing water and leaned in to give him a quick, familiar kiss.

'Good to meet you Lara,' I said. As I watched their familiarity, some of the pieces of the puzzle that were Xavier, fell into place and my heart squeezed.

'Isn't it beautiful?' she said simply, looking out at the view.

'Glorious,' I replied, without missing a beat, donning my sunglasses for cover. Xavier handed us each a glass of wine and we raised our glasses.

'To new friends,' she said, raising her glass in my direction. Her skin already dry, Lara pulled a bottle of Ambre Solaire from her bag and began to rub it along her arms and shoulders. As she slowly moved to her stomach and breasts, I looked away.

'How about some lunch?' I said, getting up and wrapping a

sarong around my waist.

'Yes please,' said Lara without looking up, adding, 'I picked up some baguettes on the way, I'll bring them up from the car in a minute.'

'Great, thanks,' I said. Xavier smiled gratefully at me. He gave me a little wink before looking back at Lara, apparently unable to tear his gaze away as she rubbed in her sun oil. By the time I had climbed the stone steps to the terrace, and glanced over my shoulder, he was rubbing oil into her back.

I stepped into the cool of the house and took off my sunglasses. My heart was hammering at this unexpected turn of events, and I wondered why Xavier hadn't at least prepared me for the possibility of Lara joining us. I decided to see how the day would unfold and do my best to take this in my stride. I opened the fridge and pulled out a lettuce, gave my hands a rinse and began to peel off and wash the leaves one at a time. As I was tossing the leaves into a large wooden bowl, Xavier came up behind me and pulled me into an embrace, my back against his chest. I let the salad spoons fall and turned to face him,

'Hey,' I said, kissing him, 'Lara seems nice.'

'She's my neighbour,' he said, 'lives in the villa just along the lane. She keeps an eye on things for me when I'm not around.'

I'll bet she does, I thought. 'Does she live out here alone?'

'Mostly,' said Xavier, 'her husband spends a lot of time in Paris. It was Lara who found me this house a few years ago.'

'Ah, I see.' Xavier was about to reply, when we heard a car pull up and the beep of a horn. 'That'll be Marc,' said Xavier, stepping out onto the terrace. 'Bonjour mon ami, bienvenue!' I heard him say as I followed him out, relieved that we would not be alone with Lara. A sun tanned man with white hair and twinkly eyes walked onto the terrace, followed by a dark haired woman, just as Lara came up the steps with the bread. As the man stepped over to greet Lara, the woman came towards me and took hold of my hands warmly,

'You must be Alice,' she said. 'How lovely to meet you at last, my name is Valentina Chagall, my friends call me Vava and this is my husband, Marc.'

Marc stepped forward and kissed me on both cheeks,

'Enchanté my dear,' he said. Then, turning to Xavier he said, 'You dark horse, how could you have kept this beauty from us for so long?' I smiled, relieved, and said,

'Lovely to meet you both, shall we sit down?' Vava put her colourful bag down and we sat on the bench against the white wall of the house. Her dark hair was neatly pinned in waves around her face and her deep red lipstick offset olive skin and smiling eyes. Xavier came out with some beer for Marc and I handed Vava a glass of wine.

'Santé,' I said, and this time it was me who added, 'To new friends,' as I raised my glass to the Chagalls. 'I'm still marvelling at the view from up here! How clever of you to find this house for Xavier,' I said turning to Lara.

She had the grace to look awkward for a moment, then raised her glass to Xavier, 'To good neighbours!'

'And good friends,' added Marc.

'I'm going to bring some lunch out for us all soon, so in the meantime, relax and enjoy the view,' I said, walking back inside. Lara followed me with the bread,

'Do you want me to cut this up?' she offered.

'Thanks, there is a basket in the cupboard over there, but you probably know that already,' I said, opening the fridge to take out some thick slices of smoked salmon and lemon wedges. I cut up some avocados and squeezed them with lime juice, then arranged them over the top of the green salad.

'What else can I do?' asked Lara.

'You could take the plates out for me and there is another bottle of wine in the cooler.'

'Bien sûr,' she said, making her way outside again, her slim body showing in silhouette through the white muslin dress she had put on after her swim.

'This looks delicious,' said Vava as we sat down to eat. Xavier smiled at me,

'Alice picked the avocados from our tree this morning. Nothing tastes more delicious than home grown food, does it?'

'So true,' said Marc. 'We have never managed to grow avocados have we ma chérie?' said Marc turning to Vava.

'Indeed not, bravo Alice, et merci!' she said, and they raised their glasses to me.

When we had finished our salad, Xavier collected some ripe figs from the tree and I brought out some chèvre and honey to accompany them. Later, as I cleared the dishes, Vava came in to help me, she was a comforting presence. As we washed and dried and tidied, I could hear Marc and Xavier chatting contentedly outside. Lara had absented herself after the meal, taking the wire of tension that hovered in the air, away with her.

'Don't worry about Lara,' Vava said. 'She's just another one of his hangers on. It's you he loves, he mentions you often and tells us about the studio you share in Normandy. He calls you his muse.'

'Really?' I said, amazed. 'He never said.'

'Well, he wouldn't,' said Vava, 'he's afraid of breaking the spell. It is unspoken between Marc and me too, he paints us flying through the air together, with goats and horses.' Her voice went quiet. 'He's a genius, but I don't think he knows it, not really. Anyway, that is what you do for Xavier, you inspire him, you feed his creativity, just by being you.' She looked at me and smiled.

'Thank you Vava, that really helps. I have been feeling pretty low since Lara strode in this morning, as if she owned the place. I didn't know what to think.' She stepped forward and hugged me to her, then said,

'Now, why don't you and Xavier come to see us in Vence next week, I can show you the house and our garden.'

'I'd love to, thank you.'

When our guests finally left, I snuggled up on the sofa with Xavier, my head against his chest and he ran his hands through my hair. 'I had a great day,' I said, 'Vava was lovely, a bit like the mother I never had. You obviously get on well with Marc.'

'Mmm,' he said into my hair, 'he's a good friend, shares his considerable wisdom with me. The early part of his life was very hard. Perhaps through his work he's found God. That, I think, is what he means when he talks about working in a space between heaven and earth.'

'That probably explains why his figures are often floating,' I said. 'It's funny, but my father said something about religion relating to his art the year before he died.'

'What did he say?' asked Xavier.

'He created a huge sculpture of the Virgin Mary for a church in London. He said working on it was a religious experience for him.' I paused as we both reflected for a moment.

'By the way, Vava invited us for lunch next week, I forgot to say.'

'When?' asked Xavier.

'Wednesday, is that ok with you?'

'Fine,' he said, pulling me closer again. I smiled, my head against his chest, everything right in our world.

Lara dropped in every now and then, and I tried not to mind. Xavier spent most of his time in the studio and she was company for me. There was only so much relaxing by the pool I could do, and the studio wasn't big enough to share.

'Do you want to go exploring?' she asked one morning, arriving unannounced as I was finishing my coffee.'

'Yes, why not,' I said. 'What did you have in mind?'

'I don't know, a drive along the coast, lunch?'

'How about the parfumerie? Xavier mentioned it was nearby.'

'Why not,' she said. 'We could go to Fragonard in Grasse.'

Half an hour later we were on our way. Lara slid back the roof of her sports car, and as we bowled along the road towards Grasse, the wind in our hair, I was exhilarated!

'How far is it?' I shouted above the roar of the wind, my hair whipping across my face.

'Maybe 20 minutes,' she shouted. I leaned back in my seat and closed my eyes, the warm sun on my face, enjoying being on the road. Soon afterwards, we wound our way up into the medieval town of Grasse and Lara pulled up in front of the Fragonard Parfumerie. It was set high on a hill, painted in soft yellow, white louvred shutters framed the many windows, and the words 'Parfumerie Fragonard' were painted in neat grey letters across the front.

We walked around to the side of the building where a path led us to the entrance and a terrace with breath-taking views of the Alps. The parfumerie was nestled between the mountains and the Mediterranean Sea, the conditions perfect for the fields of roses that surrounded it.

'This is magnificent!' I breathed.

'Isn't it,' said Lara. 'Did you know that the roses and jasmine can only be harvested early in the morning, when the scent is at its strongest? They cultivate the plants all through the winter and when the flowers bloom in May, they are picked early each morning while it's still cool.'

'How do you know so much about it?' I asked, impressed.

'I've grown up with it,' she said, 'I helped with the harvest every summer to earn extra money. We were given hessian sacks to gather the flower heads, it was the most beautiful work. The scent was heavenly, like nothing I have ever experienced before or since.'

'Wow,' I said. 'Shall we go inside and take the tour?'

'You go,' she said, 'I've seen it before, you'll love it. I'll have a look in the shop.'

The tour began with an introduction to roses, orange blossom, jasmine and tuberose, the primary flowers used in Fragonard perfumes. The flowers were laid carefully in flat glass cases, their petals open onto paper to extract their fragrance. We saw the copper vats where the scent is distilled, then the process of filling, sealing and packing the crystal bottles.

When we finally emerged into the shop, Lara waved me over. 'What did you think?' she asked.

'I loved it, I had no idea the process was so complex, or that so many flowers were used to make each perfume.'

'Do you want to try some?' she asked, leading the way to the glass counter, laden with crystal bottles.

We sampled several fragrances, and finally, I chose an eau de toilette of tuberose, along with a small gift for Vava, before we headed home.

XAVIER

I don't think Xavier could have heard the car arriving home and I approached his studio quietly, to find him working on his recent portrait of me. I watched as, slick with oil paint, the tip of his finger slowly traced the outline of my face, pressing into the board with an intensity and gentleness that seemed to hold every grain of his love. The need to perfectly capture me was in every fibre of his being. He could barely contain the strength of his feelings about so many things and yet he couldn't seem to express them, except in paint. Only his grey eyes were windows to the truth of him and the myriad of emotions burning within.

He told me that meeting Marc had been a revelation for him; Marc understood the intense emotion of creativity, the way it pulled you into its flow, the way that hours could pass unnoticed, leaving you blinking and disorientated when you emerged. Marc had shown him a path to something much greater than himself and his human experience. Xavier had once wondered aloud, was it God he could feel around him when he was in his creative flow?

Xavier had never been religious, but lately he had been questioning everything he had ever known about himself. He told me it started when he met me. His protective layers began to fall away, as I opened his heart to love, for the first time. The feeling hit him like a thunder bolt, leaving him exposed, but at the same time, he said it released a joy in him he would not have believed possible. It bubbled up within him and poured into his work. He described it like a cork being taken out of a bottle, opening him up to a world he could see with fresh eyes. In meeting me, he said, he met himself; not the party self, not the brooding self he reflected to the world, but something much deeper.

He did his best to articulate this to Marc, late one night over cognac, trying to make sense of it. Marc immediately understood, 'It was like that for me when I truly fell in love for the first time,' he said. 'Love opens us up to the core of who we are, to our very souls and that is where we meet the divine. I have found that love for another person can wax and wane, but God has remained, ever present in my heart. He appears in my work and he appears in my mind. Ever since early childhood I have been captivated by the Bible. I think it's the greatest source of poetry of all time.'

Xavier leaned back in his chair, he had always had a weakness for women and he couldn't help the fact that he only had to look at them, it seemed, for them to fall into his bed, it was too easy. From the very beginning Lara had let him know she was available too, in the subtle and not so subtle ways she had.

It was only since meeting me, he could see how shallow these encounters had been. One afternoon, relaxing by the pool after a late lunch, we talked about the night we met. 'If I'm honest with you babe, I thought you'd be just another one. Then I experienced a moment of absolute clarity looking into the depths of your amber eyes.' He paused, 'Perhaps it was the pain of unspeakable loss I saw there; vulnerability and quiet strength. Suddenly as I kissed you, I felt an urgent need to paint you, the need to capture your essence overwhelmed me.'

I remember he spent hours that night, lost in the creation of the first of his 'bed as a river' series as I slept. When we made love afterwards our communion was deep and absolute.

'I tried to run from it, but I couldn't settle.' He went on, 'Even here; you changed everything Alice.' It was true that I instinctively understood him, his life as an artist, the intensity of the creative process. He spoke quietly as if musing to himself and I was half dozing as he spoke, afraid to do anything to interrupt this rare flow of truth from Xavier.

'For the first time I felt complete, I felt the symmetry of two souls aligned, but most of all, I felt your acceptance and enduring love. My life on the Côte d'Azur has always been separate and distinct from what I thought of as my 'real' life in Paris, and I've kept it closely guarded. Now I wonder if perhaps this is my real life after all, the place where all the pieces of the puzzle fall into place.'

I realised as I mused that Xavier had stopped painting and moved to the sink to clean his brushes. I put down my packages and walked towards him and he turned, surprised and delighted to see me. 'There you go again, smiling that calm, loving smile that renders me helpless,' he said, taking me into his arms.

'Shall we have a swim?' I said, stepping out of my clothes right there in the studio, before turning and walking naked down the stone steps towards the pool. I stopped and looked over my shoulder at him as I passed the bright bougainvillea, shielding my eyes from the sun.

THE CHAGALLS

Vava and Marc's home was of pale grey stone with tall windows, flanked by narrow white shutters. The house was surrounded by lemon trees, and at the boundary, a row of silver birch twinkled in the breeze, offering tantalising glimpses of the Alps against a clear, blue sky.

Vava came out to greet us, wrapping me in a warm embrace, as if I had known her for years. 'Come in, come in,' she said. 'I'm so glad you are here. Marc is in his studio, but he won't be long.' She led us into a large, neat salon with a woodblock floor. The walls were white, with well stocked bookcases on either side of the chimney breast. The fireplace was stacked with pale wood, and above it hung a large, colourful painting. It showed a bride and groom on their wedding day, floating on the back of a large rooster. The Eiffel Tower rose up behind them, as a goat playing a fiddle peered through the clouds.

We all paused for a moment, drawn to the vibrant colour of it. 'What do you think?' asked Xavier, turning to me.

'It's magnificent,' I said, recognising it as one of Marc's. 'Is this you and Marc on your wedding day?' I asked Vava.

'No,' said Vava, 'it is actually Marc with Bella, his first wife. He started it in Paris in 1939, and eventually finished it in New York a few years after her tragic death. It has always hung there, and I imagine it always will.' She sighed and smiled, 'Ah, the rich tapestry of life. Come on, let's go outside. Vava led us out onto the terrace, where abundant passion flowers snaked over the pergola. We sat down in comfortable, white wicker chairs, and I leaned back to take in breath-taking views of the sea.

'How lovely,' I said.

'Isn't it,' said Vava. 'I never tire of this view.' Then, remembering the gift, I pulled out a small, beautifully wrapped bottle of Fragonard perfume and handed it to Vava.

'I chose this for you in Grasse,' I said smiling.

'How thoughtful you are my dear, thank you,' said Vava as she pulled off the paper and sprayed a little onto her wrist. 'Mm, I love it,' she said, as Marc came out, a beer in his hand.

'Bonjour, bienvenue!' he said, raising the bottle in our direction. 'What do you think of our view Alice?'

'Marc, bonjour! I love it.'

'How is it going friend?' said Xavier.

We enjoyed drinks together and lingered over a long lunch. Vava talked delightedly of the day Marc proposed to her and when, soon afterwards they found this house, and lovingly made it their own. Marc spoke of the importance of his Jewish heritage. He told us about his time in Jerusalem, where he received a commission to create his first stained glass windows for the Abell Synagogue.

Interested in his religious perspective, in the light of my recent conversation with Xavier, I mentioned the sculpture my father made in London and the impact it had on him. I wondered whether Marc had experienced anything like it in his work.

'Oh absolutely, yes I have,' he replied, 'particularly with the windows. For me, glass is like a transparent wall reflecting my heart to the world and it back to me. When I am in the creative process, nothing else exists, it is pure beauty.' He was quiet for a moment, as if considering his next words. Then he said, 'Strange as this may sound, as I was working on the windows for the synagogue, I felt my mother and father looking over my shoulder. Behind them were Jews, millions of other vanished Jews – of yesterday and a thousand years ago.'

We were all silent as we took in his words, letting the realisation of his experience settle around us. After a moment, I asked,

'What were the windows like Marc?'

'There were 12 of them, each representing one of the tribes of Israel. The colours were glorious, every window a different colour; I worked on them here, in Vence.'

'Wow,' I said, 'when was that?'

'About 12 years ago,' he said. 'The project took me two years. When the windows were finished they were exhibited first at the Louvre and then in New York, before finally going home to Israel in 1962. I dedicated them to the Jewish people, to friendship and peace.

'Do you have any photographs?' asked Xavier.

'Better than that,' he said, 'I have the original designs in my studio. Shall we go and have a look?'

It was dusk by the time we got home. I could feel the air cooling and the threat of rain as we sat outside together. After a long, quiet time, Xavier pulled away and looked at me.

'I'm sorry mon petit chou, but I have to go to Paris.'

'You don't mean now do you?' I said, looking out at the rain beginning to spit against the windows and the darkening sky. It was already 9pm and he would have to ride all night to be there by morning.

'I have to, I must be there for my exhibition early tomorrow,' he replied. I wondered why he hadn't left sooner, and my heart clenched with worry.

'Please don't go,' I said, putting my arms around him. 'It's raining and it might get worse.'

'I must, but I'll be back soon, I promise,' he said, going inside to get a change of clothes. As I was putting some food and hot coffee together for him, he came up behind me and I turned into his arms. He held me close as I closed my eyes, wishing he wouldn't go, knowing it was futile to try to dissuade him. Then he whispered into my hair, 'I could not wish for more than I have with you Alice, right at this moment, you make my world complete.' I looked up into his face, filled with love, his pale grey eyes burned into my soul and for a moment, we were one again. I drowned in his enigmatic gaze and as our lips met for the last time, he said, 'When I come back from Paris, I'm going to marry you.' Then, he picked up his small canvas rucksack from the kitchen and walked out into the fading light. As his motorbike roared away, a shiver went down my spine and I closed the door against the rapidly cooling night.

When I eventually went to bed, the rain tapped against my windows and it was some time before I fell into a deep, dreamless sleep.

NEW DAWN

The shrill ringing of the telephone woke me as the first light of dawn began to seep through my bedroom curtains. I struggled to get my bearings, blinking in the half light as I reached for the receiver, my heart pounding at the intrusion.

'Bonjour Mademoiselle, est-ce que c'est bien Mlle Alice Gardener a l'appareil?' A deep sonorous voice spilled into my ear as I tried to sit up.

'Oui,' I confirmed, as the man went on to introduce himself as a Gendarme from a small town outside Lyon. He asked me to confirm that I was a close friend of Xavier de St Jacques.

'Oui,' I confirmed again and my blood ran cold as I waited for him to continue.

'I am so very sorry to inform you Mademoiselle that there has been an accident.' He paused, 'Monsieur de St Jacques' motorbike slipped on a wet road and slid beneath a truck.'

'Oh my God!' I said and felt the blood rush to my face as he continued,

'I'm afraid he was killed instantly.' Another pause, 'I'm so sorry Mademoiselle.'

There was a long silence before I heard the sound of screaming filling the space around me, ringing in my ears and deafening me as I slammed down the receiver. I threw myself onto the bed, as raw grief spilled out of me, the deep keening sounds of an animal shook my body as I cried and beat my fists against the mattress. Finally exhausted, my eyes red and swollen, I slept again, waking to bright sunshine filling my room.

The memory of the night before hit me like a hammer blow and I cried again, gasping for breath, thinking of our last moments together and the feeling of dread I couldn't explain as Xavier drove away. The next days passed in a blur of grief. Marc took care of all the arrangements and I was grateful, still too stunned and shocked to be of help to anyone. I was exhausted, empty of tears and devoid of feeling, longing to be home in Normandy.

Once there, it was many months before my recovery began and I resumed some semblance of my normal life. In the early days, Isobel came and went, making sure I ate and doing her best to keep my spirits up. Vava phoned me often and we reminisced about Xavier and cried together. Isobel often took me to Kiki's for short periods in Paris, but I was restless in the city, yearning for the countryside and my garden.

Alexandre called and tried to persuade me to go to London too, but as kindly as I could, I told him I needed to be alone.

'My poor darling,' he said. 'Of course I understand. Don't think that will get you off the hook though. You can expect regular phone calls from your Uncle Alex to supply you with gossip to cheer you up.' Alexandre was an interior designer and he always had funny stories about his clients and their idiosyncrasies; as well as the latest ideas and colours that were in Vogue. Mostly when he called, I just listened, soothed by his familiar voice, with no pressure to be anything other than myself.

The garden became my sanctuary, slowly helping me to rebuild a sense of purpose. I found I could immerse myself in the plants for hours at a time. Despite the hard work, it refreshed me and gave me a sense of being part of something bigger than myself and my grief. I would lie back sometimes, in the shade of a tree and just stare up at the sky, surprised to find tears running down my cheeks.

Rosa and Jack had been living with Juniper's family in London for some years, and I was alone on the estate. I welcomed the solitude, especially now, as I tried to come to terms with Xavier's death and the knowledge that he would never be back. I wandered through the woodland, and along the stream, stooping to look at wild flowers, the dew still on their petals. I stared into the water as it rushed along, separating out the colours, imagining how I might paint the mix of browns and greys reflected from the river bed. Mixed with reflections of the sky, they made the water look a deep, navy blue. I reached into the stream to pick out a pale grey stone with flecks of white, shining in the sunlight. Unexpectedly, it brought Xavier's grey eyes to mind. As the cool water rushed over my hands, the gentle caress of it made me squeeze my eyes shut as I tried to block out the pain. I remembered the last time we kissed, the feel of his lips on mine. The way he looked into my eyes, drinking in every part of me before he left. Neither of us could have known that it would be for the last time.

Was there more I could have done to stop him? I stood up and took some deep breaths, I needed to try to let it go and move on with my life.

Nature became my friend, I strolled along winding paths, listening to birdsong and the rustle of the breeze through the trees. Weeks slipped into months, the seasons changed and I began to paint again. At first it was small flowers that I picked on my walks. I would lose myself in the tiny details, the nuances of their colour and the little fibres on their fine stems. The smell of the paint soothed me, and I felt my mother by my side, comforting me.

As I painted, I remembered the way Marc talked of his heart communing with the world as he worked, and now I could feel it too as I reconnected with my love for Xavier. For the first time I could feel it without being overwhelmed with grief; I learned to let it flow through me into my work, so that he could be with me as I went on living. Hours would pass unnoticed as I painted, and slowly, over time, I began to heal.

ALICE, NORMANDY FIVE YEARS LATER 1975

One high summer's morning, the day dawned bright and clear and I decided to spend the day outside, clearing the stream of its weeds. It was a job I had been thinking of doing for some time. After a light breakfast, I pulled on some old clothes and my waders, doing up the stout clips as I stepped outside into the sunshine. The developing heat of the day warmed me as I made my way through the garden and down the slope towards the pond. It was fed by a stream from the lake further up and every couple of years I made my way along in the rushing water, clearing the plants and old sticks that slowed and sometimes blocked its progress. I loved the tranquility of working in the water, under the leafy shade of the trees. It was a sanctuary in the heat of the day.

The rush and flow of the water over the rocks rang in my ears and enveloped me in its world. The plants lifted easily out of the silt with a light tug, and I settled into a rhythm, feet planted firmly on the rocky bed of the stream. I reached out first to the left and then right, pulling clumps of green and throwing them onto the bank, forming a soaking pile of debris to be moved to the bonfire later. I scooped my hand along the crevasse between two rocks blocked with twigs, then heard the satisfying surge of water as it cleared, rushing over my hands and onwards down the stream. I worked slowly, stopping every so often to enjoy the progress of the blue and emerald damselflies, catching the light as they danced over the water. Ferns overhung the shady bank, their leaves sparkling with moisture as they arched into the water. I moved carefully along the rocky bed, which gave way to silt in places. A myriad of long leaves flowed in the current along the surface of the water, their roots held fast. They reminded me momentarily of my floating hair in the painting Xavier had made of me lying in the stream, and my heart clenched, then I tried to smile. I was slowly learning how to let him into my thoughts, enjoy the feeling he was with me and carry on.

I took my gloves off and threw them up onto the bank, putting my bare hands into the coursing water, allowing the soft silt to slip between my fingers as I reached in to pull out the plants. Suddenly, there was a loud snap of a twig, breaking my thoughts and my solitude. I stood up straight, feeling disorientated as my eyes adjusted to the light away from the water. For a moment I thought I saw Xavier standing silhouetted against the glare of the sun beyond the tulip tree. I rubbed my eyes, I had been struggling on and off with a nagging pain in my abdomen, painkillers helped a bit, but now I wondered whether the medication was playing tricks with my mind. The light made me dizzy, and I sat down heavily on a rock at the side of the stream and covered my face with my hands.

Then I heard a voice, 'Alice are you alright?' I looked up. It was Monty, he looked worried and I smiled with relief to see him. He visited Juniper's family house fairly regularly, partly to keep an eye on things for them, since Rosa and Jack had moved away and partly, I suspected, to see me. On those days we ate together and some evenings, when I needed to be held, I shared his bed. At first it felt strange, but I gradually got used to having him nearby. He arrived unannounced every now and again, and he was a comfort to me, filling the void of my loneliness.

I discovered there was a sensitivity to him, hiding beneath the brash bluster of the person I first believed him to be. He admitted that outside the army he struggled to find his place in the world, a bit like a fish out of water.

'I overcompensate sometimes, I suppose it's nerves. I know when we first met I must have come across as a bit of a wolf, I regret it now, that's not really who I am.'

One night, after drinking quite a lot of wine together, we were lying side by side in his large bed. He began to talk about his life in the army and his men. 'Despite and perhaps because of the dangers we have faced together, I miss them. I was like a father to them I suppose, and they were so much more to me.' He said it quietly, as if lost in his thoughts.

Monty leaned up on his elbow then, and as he looked down into my face he said, 'I have come to love you Alice, in my own way,' and he smiled, a gentle smile that laid his soul bare as he looked into my eyes. 'Would you do me the honour of marrying me? I would not ask too much of you, but I would have the joy of a beautiful woman on my arm in London and otherwise, we could live our lives as we pleased.'

'Monty, you are sweet and I am truly touched,' I put my hand to the side of his face, 'But I don't think I can marry you or anyone else.' I looked at him kindly and he sighed, already resigned to my refusal. 'Perhaps convention says that we should live our lives in a certain way,' I said, 'but I have never really been a part of that, I don't mind what people think of me. I suppose I will always dance to my own tune.'

'You are lucky, I only wish it was as easy for me. My parents will not be happy until I have found a wife and settled down. I have found such acceptance with you Alice, I can just be me, and I love you for it.' I had come to love him too in my way and we were friends.

Monty was a perfunctory lover, but the arrangement was comfortable and familiar. There was so much missing, and I tried my best not to think about Xavier and the raw, unapologetic sensuality of him. Monty withheld himself from me in moments of intimacy, unreachable. I too retreated into my own world, closing my eyes and imagining it was Xavier's hands on my body, his gaze burning into my soul, until I cried out with release, hot tears sliding down my cheeks.

LYDIA AND ROGER

Monty was away for weeks at a time either on army business, or visiting his sister in London. The last time we spoke of Juniper's children, he reminded me that they were almost adults now and hardly ever at home. I struggled to picture them leaving their childhoods behind. In my mind they were still as they were when they used to come to France, for the school holidays with Juniper. They would visit me often at Les Lavandes, while Juniper remained up at the house.

Roger was creative even then, he would find stones and small pieces of wood in the garden and create towns and villages in the conservatory, lining up daisy heads to represent all the people. Lydia, by contrast, was reserved and a bit shy, she seemed to be searching for acceptance in a world where I don't think she felt very loved. She would come and sit beside me while Roger played on the floor, asking me if I knew how to bake biscuits and whether I had a best friend. So I asked her about school and her life in London, trying to draw her out, remembering my own school days and sighing at the memory. I put my arm across her slight shoulders and pulled her to me, 'School isn't always quite as much fun as grown-ups say it's going to be, is it?' Lydia looked up at me, waiting for me to say more. 'You are not unhappy there are you?'

'No,' she said simply.

Juniper was as self-contained as she had always been on the rare occasions I saw her, and she kept her distance. I wondered whether she was as distant with her children, and it saddened me to think of it.

It really was time I saw them again I thought, as I worked in the garden at the back of the house. Rampant honeysuckle just coming into flower, had tangled itself around climbing roses, its pretty white buds waiting to bloom. Full-blown petals were falling and dead rose heads needed taking off, so that the blooms would continue through the coming weeks. I was working on the shady north side of the house, but even here, I could feel rivulets of moisture forming and running down my neck and chest. My stout gardening gloves were hot on my hands and every so often I threw them down onto the grass, only to find that a moment later, a vicious thorn would catch the delicate skin on the back of my hand. The long Virginia Creeper shoots had begun to climb the stone walls towards the roof, and I tugged them down one by one before they tangled themselves into the gutters.

At 38 I was still fit and strong. Piles of foliage were building behind me and I paused for a moment, surveying my efforts, before loading the wheelbarrow and heading out to the compost heap. When I had tidied away the weeds and my tools, I went inside for a cold glass of water, relaxing as I stepped into the coolness of the kitchen. Its stone walls were chilly in the winter, but I was glad of their refuge in the heat. I ran the tap for a while longer, ensuring it was nice and cold before I filled a large glass, and sank gratefully into a chair beside the french windows. I put my feet up and breathed a sigh of relief, taking a long swallow.

Perhaps I would bake a batch of scones for tea. I ran the tap until the water was steaming then soaped my hands, letting it run over my skin, scrubbing my nails with the little brush and finally drying them on the fluffy towel. I put a clean apron on and began to gather what I would need. I got out the weighing scales, switched the oven to high and pulled the ingredients from the cupboard; self-raising flour, sugar, milk. One at a time I lined them up on the worktop and finally lifted my much loved old mixing bowl from the cupboard. It brought back happy memories of cooking with Bella, and I treasured it. The powdery thud of the flour as it fell into the bowl pleased me, little white puffs flew out from the sides as I carefully added cubes of butter. Plunging my hands into the bowl, I deftly rubbed the butter through the flour with the tips of my fingers. There was a soothing rhythm to the task and I gazed out of the open window as I worked. The moist dough complete, I rolled it out and cut eight neat circles, placing them onto the hot baking tray in the oven.

The shrill ring of the telephone startled me and wiping my hands on my apron, I reached out for the receiver, 'Hello.'

'Alice, it's me, Juniper,'

It was very unusual for her to call me and I was surprised, 'Juniper, how are you, is everything alright?' there was a long sigh before Juniper came straight to the point. 'It's Lydia, Alice, I'm at the end of my tether. Étienne thinks she should come and stay with you for a while.'

'With me?' I said surprised, 'I thought Lydia was away at school.' I hadn't seen her for years, she must be 17 by now. 'Has something happened Juniper? '

'She was back at school and we thought she was doing well. She never talks about it of course, least of all to me, but I had no reason to think she was having problems. The last time she was here, I hardly saw her, you know how busy I am.'

I pictured Juniper, sitting erect, holding the phone in her immaculately manicured hand, much as Clémence would have done. 'Juniper you still haven't told me what happened.'

Juniper sighed again, 'The school telephoned me last week, apparently Lydia hardly eats and is very withdrawn. She's been at home for over a week now and frankly, I have no idea what to do with her.'

My heart went out to my angular and awkward niece. Juniper had never been affectionate with her and I imagined she organised her eldest child like another one of her committees. Lydia had been packed off to boarding school as soon as she was old enough, leaving Juniper free to attend beauty appointments, shop for hats and bring her fellow committee members into line.

'Oh Juniper, I am sorry to hear that, poor Lydia. When does she have to go back to school?'

'Well, this is the thing Alice, they don't want her back. She doesn't fit in apparently. They are afraid she may have,' there was a silence while Juniper searched for the right word, 'a negative influence on the other pupils. They say they don't have the resources to cope with her, but what do they think I can do?'

I kept my thoughts to myself, struggling to imagine Lydia being a problem to anyone and wondering why, after all these years and having made no effort at all, Juniper was turning to me.

Stalling for time I said, 'What does Étienne think?' Étienne had an easy going relationship with his daughter as far as I knew, but the trouble was, he was hardly ever at home.

'Oh you know what he's like Alice, he can't see the problem. He has no idea how busy I am.'

'Does Lydia actually want to come to France?'

'Of course she will want to. The only place she ever wanted to be when we were there was with you, at Les Lavandes. She loves you Alice, always has. I haven't said anything yet, I wanted to speak to you first. What do you think?'

I pictured Juniper leaning back a little in the antique chair, examining her nails and taking a quick look at her watch, wanting to bring this to a successful conclusion, but I imagine she knew better than to pressure me. Playing for time I said, 'Let me give it some thought, I'll call you back this evening if you don't mind.'

'Yes, of course,' she said, then added as an afterthought, 'I'm sorry Alice, in the upset of it all I completely forgot to ask about you.' Not wanting to prolong the conversation, I cut her short.

'I'm fine Juniper, but I must go, I have some scones in the oven. I'll call you later! Bye for now.'

I cut off the call and dashed into the kitchen just in time to pull the scones out. They were perfectly risen and brown and I eased them onto the cooling rack, allowing their sweet freshly baked scent to fill the kitchen.

Juniper and I were never close, but I had always made an effort with her for Étienne's sake. Nevertheless, the conversation helped me quite suddenly, to come to a decision. Monty had been suggesting for some time that I move back to London. He wanted me to move in with him, and since he would continue to be away on Army business for much of the time, I realised that it might work. I could remain independent most of the time, and Lydia could visit me closer to home.

I was not to know then that a few months after my return to London, on a beautiful spring morning, I would be told that I was dying.

ALICE, LONDON 1978

The more I came to know Monty in his home environment, the more I could see how ill-suited he was to life in Normandy. I was at my happiest in the countryside while Monty thrived in the city.

He lived in Ashley Gardens, not far from Westminster, in a gracious red brick Victorian building. The lift was old and slow with a brass grille that slid across to close it. A wide carpeted staircase with polished bannisters snaked around the open lift shaft, illuminated by stained glass windows on each landing. Monty lived on the first floor, his polished front door opened into a long, narrow hallway, with a faded red carpet.

The rooms were large and little used. Monty spent the rare occasions he was at home at the old pine table in the kitchen, listening to the radio and reading the papers. When I first arrived, I opened heavy drapes on rooms that had not seen the light of day for months, pulling open the sash windows to let in some air. Monty's bedroom was small, with a narrow single bed and iron bedstead, reminding me of boarding school. He seemed not to have considered the practicalities of where we would sleep, so I opened up the large, unused master bedroom suite at the far end of the hall. Apart from some dust and the need for an airing, it was a beautiful room. The double fronted windows were large and bright, and outside, leafy trees offered privacy and shade from the sunny aspect.

There was a serene and elegant drawing room halfway along the hall, and as I stepped inside, filtered sunlight dappled its leafy pattern onto the pale Aubusson rug in the centre of the room.

Soft, yellow armchairs stood on either side of it and long French doors led to a balcony from which I could almost touch the leafy, overhanging branches. I sighed contentedly, knowing I had found a place in the apartment where I could practise my yoga and make my own. From the hallway, a door opened onto an iron staircase to the garden, where an oak bench encircled a beautiful, old tree.

The spacious dining room was used as a store room, housing piles of things that appeared to have been there for years, so I left it that way. As far as I could tell, very little cooking had ever taken place in the old kitchen. When Monty was home, we would usually stroll out for drinks and dinner nearby and I was glad not to have to spend much time in it.

I was distracted and ill at ease in London, secretly hankering after my quiet life in France where I was free to roam the woodland and gardens and find inspiration to paint. Monty was away for long periods and I used those opportunities to catch up with London friends and get to know Lydia. At first I called in to see her in Richmond, but lately, she had been taking the 30 minute train ride to Victoria to visit me at Ashley Gardens.

Her angular awkwardness had given way to beauty; she was tall, with long dark hair and a haunted look in her eyes. They would dart about as we struggled to find common conversational ground, but once I accepted that she was happy just to be here, I relaxed and so did she. We found an old puzzle in one of the cupboards and with every piece that fitted together, I could feel her coming closer to telling me what was on her mind.

'Do you know why I had to leave my school?' she asked me suddenly one day, leaning back in her chair.

'No honey, I don't,' I said casually.

'They said I was making myself sick after meals, but I wasn't,' she said quickly.

'What made them think that,' I asked, 'and who is they?'

'Oh everyone, the whole school ganged up on me. Friends, teachers, everybody, they were all whispering behind my back.'

'Why would they do that?' I asked.

'Everyone hates me, especially Mummy,' she said, looking at me defiantly, her dark eyes burning like coals. 'Everyone tries to trick me, to make me eat too much food, and then they torment me. I can hear them whispering, telling me to be sick, to look at how fat I'm getting. You're the only person I know who doesn't go on and on about it,' she said.

I went to sit next to her, and looked at her kindly, I knew I was out of my depth with this, but recognised that Lydia was trusting me with something important and very real.

'Come on,' I said, 'why don't we leave the puzzle for a while and go out for a walk. We could go and see the ducks in St James's Park if you like.' As we walked, she began to speak more about school, but didn't directly refer to the food issues again. I knew that in time she would tell me more if she wanted to, but nevertheless, I was worried, and decided I would have another chat with Juniper.

After seeing Lydia onto her train home, I took the stairs back up to the apartment and unlocked the front door, to find the phone ringing.

'Hello,' I said breathlessly.

'Daahling, at last!' said Alexandre. 'How are you ma chérie?'

'All the better for hearing from you,' I said. 'How are things?' I hung my coat on one of the hooks inside the door, and sat down in the small armchair next to the phone.

'So, so,' he said, 'George has been uncharacteristically cantankerous lately. He's repairing a clock that has given him no end of trouble. I for one, will be glad to see the back of it. Anyway daahling, that brings me onto the reason for my call; he will be finished on Friday, so I'm hosting a little soirée. Can you come?'

'I'd love to,' I said. 'Shall I make my summer pudding?'

'Oh George, Ali is going to make her summer pudding,' I heard him say in a stage whisper, followed by exclamations of delight from George in the background, who must have come in from his workshop.

Alexandre and George shared a mews house in Chelsea, tucked away in a leafy courtyard near the river. The small garage served as a workshop for George to repair his clocks, while Alexandre used a corner of the large living space to work on his interior designs.

'Who else is coming?' I asked.

'Just a few friends,' he said, 'not sure yet, I'm just ringing round. Come at 8, see you on Friday.' In the end, when I arrived, there was just one other person there, John, making four of us, and

I was relieved. There were a few things I wanted to talk over with Alex, and so while George was in his element discussing clocks with John, who was himself a collector, I had my chance.

'So daahling,' said Alex, leaning in towards me, 'How are things?' he asked winking. 'You haven't been your old self lately and your Uncle Alex has been worried about you.'

'Haven't I?' I said looking at him, trying to force a casual smile.

'Come on,' he said, 'out with it, you know you can tell me anything.' I did know, Alex was an unofficial guardian from my old life and he had known me since long before my parents died.

'I don't know where to begin,' I said, running my hands through my short hair, leaving it dishevelled and spiky.

'So there is something,' he said, 'I knew it.'

'I'm not sure I've done the right thing moving to London,' I said, 'I miss France, especially my garden.'

'Then why did you?' he asked.

'It was prompted in part by Juniper; she wanted to send Lydia over to stay with me, she's been having some problems at school. As Monty has been asking me to move here for ages anyway, I thought it might be easier to do that. A chance for me to make a fresh start, leave painful memories behind me and so on, but it hasn't turned out that way.'

'Why not?' he asked 'and anyway what's up with Lydia? Why does the old witch think you should be the one to help her daughter?'

'No idea,' I said. 'I've always tried with Juniper as she's Etty's wife, but we've hardly spoken over the years, at least not in any meaningful way. I don't think Lydia feels she can talk to her either, she's always been quite remote.'

'Poor kid,' said Alex.

'Lydia deserves better from her family,' I said. 'She's never wanted for anything materially, but I suspect there has been a shortage of love and attention from her parents. She's been visiting me regularly, we've walked and talked quite a lot, in the park mostly. To be honest, I think she may need professional help to sort herself out.'

'Well in that case, you need to hand the problem back to her mother. You don't seem too good yourself,' he said looking at me carefully. 'You look pale and you've hardly touched your wine.'

'I'm not great at the moment,' I said. 'I've been having dizzy spells, probably just some tablets I'm taking.'

'Dizzy spells, tablets, what's all this about Ali?'

'Oh, I keep getting pains in my stomach, the doctor just thought it was indigestion. It's probably nothing, but sometimes the pain is so bad I have to lie down.'

'You need to go back and see him then,' he said. 'This isn't like you at all.'

'I know, I've been meaning to go back,' I said. 'It's just that I've had a lot on my mind.'

'I'll bet you have, trying to sort out Juniper's family for her, and what about Monty, where is he in all this?' Instead of waiting for an answer, he added, 'They all seem as bad as each other if you ask me.'

Just then, there was a lull in the conversation about clocks and John turned to me and smiled, 'Alice please forgive me! I have monopolised George and hardly spoken to you and Alex. I hear you are a painter,' he said, trying to draw me into a conversation I had no heart to pursue.

'Yes, I do paint,' I said, 'but I haven't for quite a while. My studio is in France, somehow the city hasn't brought it out in me. How about you?' I asked, wanting to change the subject. 'How long have you been collecting clocks?'

'Oh as long as I can remember,' he said,' but enough clock talk, I'll go on all night given half a chance.' I smiled at him and stood up to take the plates into the kitchen, where the summer pudding was waiting to be served. 'That sea bass was delicious Alex,' I heard him say.

'Actually George was our chef this evening, I just did as I was told,' said Alex. I saw him wink at George as he said it.

The juices of the pudding had soaked through to perfection and I served generous portions with cream and extra blackberries. 'My all-time favourite!' said John, putting the last creamy spoonful into his mouth. 'Alice, I think I need to get to know you better,' he turned to me and winked, letting his hand fall briefly over the back of mine. I smiled, but when he suggested we go out together one evening, I thanked him and declined. I felt the need to wind up my responsibilities to others and draw into myself for a while.

DOCTORS

The next morning I picked up the phone and called Juniper, 'Hello Juniper, it's me, Alice.'

'Alice, is everything alright?'

'Not really no,' I said, taking a leaf out of Juniper's book and getting straight to the point. 'I wanted to update you on how things have been going with Lydia. Did you know she has been coming to see me a couple of times a week?'

'No I didn't,' she said, sounding surprised. 'Has she been bothering you?'

'Not at all, 'I said, 'but I am concerned about her.'

'Concerned about her? In what way?' she asked.

'It has taken her a long time to open up to me, and I feel I am breaking her trust by speaking to you, but unfortunately, I don't think I have any alternative. This is not something I can deal with at the moment, Juniper.'

'Alice you are frightening me, what on earth has happened. Is Lydia alright?' I marvelled at the fact that Lydia was living at home with Juniper, and yet she might as well have been on Mars for all Juniper seemed to know about her. I plunged in again,

'I think she may have some kind of eating disorder.'

'Eating disorder?' said Juniper, sounding incredulous.

'Do you think you would be able to talk to her about it? I said.

'Talk to her? What on earth would I say Alice? I have no experience of dealing with something like this.'

'Perhaps start by taking her to your doctor,' I said. 'See what he suggests. Perhaps you can get her to talk to someone, I think she may need professional help.'

Two weeks later, Juniper phoned me to say that Lydia had been admitted to The Priory clinic. 'You were right,' she said, 'Lydia has been suffering from bulimia.'

I was thankful not to have to worry about her after that, I had enough problems of my own. The aches and pains in my abdomen persisted and I knew I needed to take my own advice, and arrange to see my doctor. Monty was away so much that he hadn't seen the occasions when I was suddenly dizzy and needed to lie down. Could it be the pain killers I was relying on, maybe they no longer agreed with me.

A few days before my appointment, six months after moving to London, things came to a head. I was making my way up the stairs to Monty's front door after a stroll in the park, when I was gripped by a pain so intense that it took my breath away. I doubled over in agony and must have fainted, because when I came round I was in hospital. Monty was away as usual and it was Mrs Peacock, a widow living in the apartment below, who heard the thud as I fell, and raised the alarm.

'Ah, Miss Gardener, you are awake.' A pleasant, older man in a white coat made his way to my bedside. 'I am Dr Spencer, how are you feeling now?

'A little better, I think,' I said. 'What happened and where am I?'

'You fainted my dear, your neighbour called an ambulance and we brought you straight here. You are in St. Stephen's Hospital.'

'I see,' I said, trying to remember. 'What exactly is wrong with me?'

'We're not sure yet, I'm running some tests, but in the meantime have you had any health problems you want to tell us about, any dizziness or pain anywhere?'

'Well yes, I have had quite a lot of pain in my lower abdomen,' I said, 'and recently I have been dizzy too.'

'Since when?' he asked.

'It has been quite a few months since the pain started,' I said, 'and lately, it has got worse.' Part of me was relieved to be here, I had been more worried than I cared to admit.

'Have you seen your doctor?' he asked.

'Not yet, but I do have an appointment booked for next week.'

'Alright,' he said. 'Well, now you are here, the nurse is going to get some details from you for your admission documents and then, I'll arrange a CT scan. We should have the results later tomorrow.'

'Thank you Doctor,' I said, lying back against my pillows, hoping it would be nothing serious.

'Is there anyone we can call for you?'

'Not for now,' I said, 'but thank you.' I struggled to sleep that night and the next morning, I waited anxiously for the doctor and the results of the scan. When he eventually came and sat by my bed, his face was grave.

'Miss Gardener, I have some very difficult news for you; I'm afraid you are seriously ill. We have found a tumour that is putting pressure on your intestine. It has been growing for some time, and it is this that has been causing you pain.' There was a long pause as I waited for him to talk me through the treatment plan, and as the pause lengthened I said,

'So what needs to happen now?' I looked at the doctor and the nurse stepped forward and took my hand in hers, smiling reassuringly.

'Miss Gardener,' he said, 'there is no easy way to tell you, I'm afraid you have cancer, rather too advanced to treat. If we try it will be futile and make you feel much worse. I am so sorry my dear, there is nothing more we can do for you.'

'What do you mean nothing can be done?' I said shocked. 'Do you mean that I'm going to die?'

'The tumour is inoperable and it has spread,' said the doctor. 'If we leave it alone, you will have some quality of life left to you and we can give you medication to control the discomfort.'

'How long have I got?' I asked, as if I was speaking in the abstract and not about myself.

'Maybe a year,' he replied, ' maybe a little more. I'm so sorry Miss Gardener.' Tears began to run down my cheeks as my worst fear was confirmed.

The kindly nurse came and sat beside my bed, 'Are you sure there is nobody we can call for you?' she asked.

'No there isn't,' I said, 'I prefer to keep this to myself for now, but thank you.' The nurse patted my hand and got up.

'I'll leave you to get some rest,' she said. 'Take these tablets they will help with the pain and make it easier for you to sleep.' I swallowed them down, then the nurse gave me a smile and another pat on my hand, before walking away.

I was numb with shock and glad of the tablets to help me sleep. When I finally awoke several hours later, the reality of my illness hit me and I knew I would need time and space to come to terms with it. I also needed to consider how I wanted to spend the last year of my life and knew with sudden clarity, that I did not want to spend the precious time I had left, living in London.

I wasn't sure how I had allowed myself to drift into the current living arrangements, allowing the essence of myself to be slowly eroded by city living. In the light of my failing health, I felt a powerful urge to find my own rhythm again.

I would write a letter to Monty telling him I was going back to Les Lavandes. He was not due back for another fortnight so there was no reason to delay my trip. Once I was back at Ashley Gardens, with a raft of medication and instructions, I phoned Alex.

'Daahling,' he exclaimed, 'how are you now? Have you seen the doctor?'

'Yes,' I said breezily, 'Nothing to worry about. He said I need to drink more water and get plenty of fresh air. Actually that's why I'm calling, I've decided to go back to France for a while. I'm going to leave Monty a note.'

'Good girl,' he said. 'Best thing for you, let everybody sort out their own problems.'

'Thanks for the other night Alex. Give George a hug for me won't you.'

'I will,' he said 'have a safe trip. Au revoir chérie, see you soon.'

NORMANDY, A FEW MONTHS LATER

It didn't take me long to settle in, I felt such profound relief to be home again. There was plenty to keep me busy, the barn was still full of paintings Xavier had made. I hadn't been able to look at them since his death, but I would do so in the coming weeks. I needed to set my affairs in order because before long, I would find myself running out of time.

My medication kept me comfortable, if sometimes a little detached from the world. It wasn't an unpleasant feeling, but my progress with sorting things was slow and I didn't have much of an appetite. I found I could write though, very easily, the words flowed out of me as if I could see my life passing once again, before my eyes. Words were something I could leave behind, something that would make sense of my life.

A few months later, during which I had eaten little and seen nobody, I was out walking in the woods. I was thinking about nothing in particular as I ambled along, making a path through the leaves as I walked, when I stopped, frozen in my tracks. There, some distance ahead, leaning against the old oak tree was - but it couldn't be - I rubbed my eyes, it was Xavier as I had first seen him in Paris! I couldn't move or take my eyes off the ghostly apparition.

Tears began to run down my cheeks and I tried to shout out to him, but no sound would come. I ran towards him, tears blurring my vision as my feet kicked up the dry leaves and snapped twigs underfoot. Suddenly, my boot caught on a branch and I fell in a flurry of leaves, frightening the birds who took off into the afternoon sky, their calls echoing around me. When I recovered myself and got up from the ground, he was gone. I rubbed my eyes again, strangely comforted by what I had seen, but realising I must be losing my mind.

I walked quickly towards the tree and could see that the leaves at its base had been flattened. The remains of a cigarette had been hastily stubbed out on the root. Was I going mad, had my mind played a trick on me, showing me what I so desperately wanted to see? Of course not, I reasoned, raking my fingers through my short hair to dislodge leaves and twigs. It was probably someone who shouldn't have been in the woods at all, why else would he have run away without acknowledging me.

The following week there was a knock at my door, I was alone on the estate and confused, who could it be? The idea of seeing another person suddenly made me desperate and I ran to open the door, delirious with the idea that I might find Xavier standing there after all, as he had been so many times in the past.

When I swung it open I don't know whether it was Juniper or myself who was the most surprised. 'Juniper! I said, 'what are you doing in France?' as she said, simultaneously,

'Oh Alice, what has happened to you, you are wasting away!' I flung my arms around her.

'Juniper, I'm so pleased to see you,' I realised I was crying and it surprised me. The two of us had never had all that much time for one another.

'Alice what on earth is wrong, have you been eating properly? You are as thin as a rake,' she said, her hands still on my shoulders.

'Just another faddy diet, you know how it is,' I said, quickly wiping away my tears. 'Why are you here?' I said, 'I thought you were all in London.'

'We were,' she said, 'but Lydia came home from the clinic last week and she particularly asked if we could come here for a few days. She's hoping to see you, Alice. I told her we mustn't intrude, Monty said you wanted time alone.' I looked at her, jolted into the recollection of what seemed like another lifetime, in London. Juniper continued, 'I won't stop now, why not get yourself ready and come up to the house for dinner this evening. Étienne is in Paris as usual, so it'll be just the two of us and the children. Well not children exactly, they are quite grown up now, but you know what I mean.'

'Thank you Juniper, it's so long since I've seen Roger; and how is Lydia now?'

'Much better, you'll see,' said Juniper.

Once Juniper left, I ran myself a bath and changed into a floor length floral pinafore dress and a lacy white blouse. Standing in front of the mirror, I saw myself as they would see me; for the first time acknowledging the change in myself. My cheeks were hollow, my face pale and I had dark circles under my eyes. The dress and blouse hid my bony shoulders and thin arms, but I looked more like a diminutive child than a woman approaching 40.

I decided to take the car along the lane to the house, to avoid returning on foot in the dark. I put a bottle of red wine into my basket and picked a small bunch of flowers for Juniper. A few minutes later I was pulling the bell outside the kitchen door, and Juniper ushered me in. The delicious smell of boeuf bourguignon wafted towards me as I stepped inside, and I realised how hungry I was.

'Come on through Alice, what would you like to drink?' Juniper asked over her shoulder, as she led me into the salon where a huge fire was burning in the grate.

'Whatever you are having would be lovely,' I said 'thank you.'

'Red wine it is then,' said Juniper.

'Hello Auntie Alice' said Lydia, and in the firelight I saw a tall young woman with long dark hair and beautiful eyes.

'Lydia, you look beautiful darling, come and give me a hug!' Lydia got up from the sofa, dwarfing me with her height as she wrapped my thin frame in her warm embrace. It reminded me of a time not so long ago, when it was she who was thin and in need of me.

'How have you been,' I asked her.

'Pretty good,' she said, 'I've got my confidence back. Thanks for paving the way for me with Mummy, things are much better now.'

'Here we are!' said Juniper, coming in with two glasses of wine and handing one to me. 'Santé!' she said, as we clinked glasses. I felt the smooth wine in my mouth and then as I turned to find my way to the sofa, there he was.

'Oh my God!' I said, as my vision blurred for a moment and I rubbed my eyes, taking in the sight before me. It was Xavier in his prime, and then I knew I was losing my mind. My glass slid out of my hand, landing softly on the rug, my red wine silently soaking into the pale, yellow wool.

'Alice,' said Juniper, 'are you alright? This is Roger, you remember.'

'Hello Auntie Alice,' he said, ignoring the glass and stepping forward to hug me, as my eyes tried to make sense of what I saw.

As he held me, I felt myself melting into his arms, Xavier had come back for me. His strong arms around me, the width of his shoulders, even the smell of him transported me. Had I already died and gone to heaven?

Juniper told me later that I had what she called a funny turn, falling into a semi faint and speaking deliriously. She immediately called the doctor to the house, who examined me thoroughly. It didn't take him long to establish that I was in the terminal stages of illness, and my secret was out.

Juniper was shocked by the news, and insisted that I stay with her for a few days. The children had to return to London the next day, she said, so it was to be just the two of us. I had my doubts about spending time with Juniper alone, still confused and longing for the feeling of Xavier's arms around me again. Although I felt foolish, I truly believed he had come back for me. The thought of him leaving, even though Juniper kept repeating that it was Roger, left me desperate. When he came to say goodbye the next day, I clung to him as if my life depended on it, embarrassing everyone, but I no longer cared. I lay back on my pillows, spent and exhausted, fearing that on top of everything else, the burden of me and my illness would be the last thing Juniper wanted, but she surprised me.

I was coming out of a long sleep as she came awkwardly into my bedroom carrying a tray, she put it down on the table and sat in the armchair near my bed.

'I've brought you some tea,' she said hesitantly. 'How are you feeling now?'

'Oh, you know, not too bad,' I said. 'Better for sleeping, thank you. Did the children get away alright?'

'Yes, they did, thank you.' There was a silence as she poured our tea, the smoky fragrance of the Lapsang rising into the air. To my surprise, the conversation took an unexpected turn.

'Alice, I'm ashamed of the way I have treated you over the years; you haven't deserved it. I wanted to say that to you, I'm so sorry.'

'You have nothing to be sorry for Juniper,' I said.

There was so much more we would say to each other over the coming days; but that day, I could never have imagined that Juniper would become one of my closest friends. I know now that there is clarity in death; life's clutter is swept away and a bright flame illuminates the path to hope and friendship.

ALICE AND JUNIPER

We fell into a routine over the next few days, talking over cups of tea, and slowly Juniper opened up to me.

'There is so much you don't know about me Alice. I have always envied your ability to be so carefree, to draw people to you without even trying. Even Lydia prefers your company to mine. It all came out during family counselling sessions at the Priory, I was forced to see myself as others see me and I can tell you, it was not a pretty sight.'

This was unexpected. I was lost for words as she continued, 'Now I find you are terminally ill.' She hesitated and looked up at me, twisting her lace handkerchief in her lap. 'It changes everything.' I had never seen Juniper like this, she lifted the handkerchief and dabbed her eyes.

'Juniper, what has brought this on, please, don't be so hard on yourself.' I said. She took a deep breath,

'Thank you,' she said and smiled weakly. 'Anyway, enough about me, let me top your tea up.' I held my cup out to her.

'What a nuisance I'm being,' I said, 'thank you for being so kind. I can't think what came over me the other night, I'm just sorry to put you to all this trouble.'

'It's no trouble,' she said.

'I thought I was dreaming you see, my medication plays tricks with my mind and I've been having hallucinations, quite often actually. When I saw Roger, I thought it was Xavier, it's not the first time it's happened.' The colour drained from Juniper's face, I was obviously upsetting her. 'Sorry Juniper, I didn't mean to go on.'

156

'No, it's fine,' she said, getting up to clear the cups. 'I'll leave you to rest now,' and she left the room, closing the door quietly behind her.

Some afternoons Juniper read to me from 'The Secret Garden', it was one of her favourite childhood books; I wondered whether she had noticed the parallels to my own story. I was comforted by the sound of her voice, and I think we were both soothed by the idea of the little garden the orphan Mary discovered.

'I wish I'd taken the time to read to my own children,' Juniper said one day, looking up from the book, 'I had no idea how relaxing it could be. They asked me so many times, but I was always too busy, and now it's too late.'

'It's never too late,' I said. 'Just do the best you can for them going forward. You only have to take the time to listen to them, and things will improve.'

A few days later I awoke feeling stronger and wanted to return to my own home. I was a little light headed, but made my way downstairs. Juniper was already in the kitchen. 'How are you feeling?' she asked.

'Oh I'm fine, don't worry about me Juniper, I'm coming to terms with my illness as best I can. I'm just sorry to burden you like this.'

'You are certainly not a burden, in fact, I'm glad of the company, things have been so difficult lately with Lydia. I've had nobody to talk to you see Alice.' Juniper turned to pour some coffee for me and I gripped the edge of the table to steady myself, as a moment of dizziness washed over me. 'There is some fresh bread and jam if you can eat it,' she said.

'Thank you,' I said, sliding myself onto one of the kitchen chairs. After a moment I said, 'Juniper I'd like to go back home today, you've been so kind, but I need to have my own things around me again.'

I knew once I was home I would feel stronger and better able to offer Juniper the support she seemed to need. Over breakfast, wanting to lighten the atmosphere and tether my mind to something calming I asked, 'Have you ever thought of taking up yoga Juniper?' she looked surprised,

'Yoga?' she said. 'No, why?'

'Oh it's the most calming thing, I'm not sure where I would have been without it.'

'Isn't it just a form of exercise?' she said.

'It's so much more than that, for me it's a mind and body experience, a kind of meditation.'

'Meditation?' said Juniper. 'What is that exactly?'

'It is a form of relaxation, I think it will help you. Close your eyes and relax for a moment, focus on your breath.' Juniper rested her hands in her lap and closed her eyes. 'Take a few deep breaths, feel the cool air coming in through your nostrils and the warmer air leaving through your mouth. Breathe gently and if your thoughts wander, bring your attention back to your breath.' I paused a moment before slowly continuing, 'Now, I want you to visualise stretching out on the lawn, blue sky over your head,' I said. 'The blades of grass are tickling your heels and the backs of your hands.' I had already lost myself in this visualisation when the harsh sound of Juniper's chair scraping against the floor as she stood, jolted me back. To my amazement, she looked distraught and said,

'Alice there are things I need to tell you. I can't bottle it up any longer. For the first time in my life I need to speak freely and honestly. No more secrets, I can't do it any more, it's killing me.' She wiped a tear from her eye, 'I've been holding so much inside me for so long that it is beginning to destroy me, but I haven't known how to change, how to let it out.' I looked at her, shocked at her outburst and then with concern, as she continued, 'The counselling has helped me as much as it has helped Lydia. It has been a shock to find that I haven't been everything I could have been to her. I see the way she looks up to you Alice, it has opened my eyes, made me realise what matters. I want to change, I really do.'

I got up from the table and held Juniper as she cried, and the tightly controlled detritus of her life poured out.

'Juniper, I'm so sorry you feel this way, I wish I had the strength to do more for you,' I said, as I held her to me. 'Do you think you could help me to get home today? Once I am settled in, I want us to sit down together and talk, you can tell me everything.'

As my illness progressed, I began to rest in bed every afternoon for several hours, and soon, these afternoons became whole days. Juniper wouldn't leave me, she arranged for a girl from the village to come in each day to prepare meals and take care of my needs. She talked and talked to me, laying herself bare; she told me about the childhood abuse she had suffered, her misery at loving the absent Étienne, whom she felt certain was having an affair. She talked of her jealousy and envy of me; my freedom and apparently effortless life. 'Everything has always been so easy for you Alice, you have free wheeled through your life and yet everybody loves you. I try so very hard and yet I seem to drive people away.' This was not the moment to contradict her so I let her speak, seeing the relief this unburdening of her personal truth was bringing.

'Juniper, I hate to see you so unhappy.' I reached for her hand, 'You must learn to value yourself, trust yourself. Waiting for other people to bring you happiness will always leave you disappointed.' Juniper wiped away a tear as I continued, 'If you take control of your own life, live it in a way that is true to who you are, I promise you will find contentment. You will never find that while you are trying to be what other people want you to be. Can you see that?'

'I think so,' she said, 'but I don't think I've ever thought about who I really am, underneath the person I've pretended to be all my life I mean. Perhaps I have, but in a superficial way, to gain approval; what I would wear, the impression I would make and so on. Beyond that, I honestly don't know.' There was a pause as we both reflected on her words. Then I said,

'Juniper, I know I've mentioned yoga and meditation before, but it might be a good place for you to start. I can't promise it will be easy but it may help you find a sense of equilibrium and calm.'

'If you really knew me Alice, you would feel differently about me. I am not a nice person. The more time I spend with you, the more I know that to be true.'

'We all have good in us Juniper, we just have to look for that part of ourselves and connect with it, make it a way of living. I have been through the most unspeakable pain, pain that broke me from within. It was only when I felt there was nothing left of me, that I began to find meaning. I know that sounds strange, but hidden in the depths of my pain, I found the light of love, spiritual love like a burning flame in my heart and it saved me.'

I still wasn't sure that Juniper understood what I meant, but I really wanted things to be different for her. As I allowed her time to take this in, she surprised me by saying quietly, 'Alice, there is something more I haven't told you,' she paused and looked at me, a serious expression on her face and sadness in her eyes. 'Do you remember your house warming party all those years ago?'

'Of course I do,' I said, 'why?'

'I did something dreadful that night, something I've carried with me ever since, and there are times when it feels too much to bear.'

'What do you mean?' I asked her, 'I don't remember anything, are you sure?'

'Oh yes,' she said, 'beyond a shadow of a doubt. I'd had so much to drink that night, I hardly knew what I was doing.'

'Juniper, you were no worse than the rest of us as far as I remember,' but she continued as if I hadn't spoken,

'I disgraced myself that night.'

'Juniper you are so hard on yourself, I'm sure you don't deserve that.'

When Juniper finally told me what she had done, it was so unexpected, so profound that I broke down and cried. Juniper came over to me, her voice shaking, and said,

'I'm so sorry Alice, how can you ever forgive me?' She put her arms around me and we clung to each other once again.

'You have needed a friend so badly, I just wish I had known,' I said. 'Of course I forgive you, as you must forgive yourself. It was all so long ago, it's been a shock, that's all.' We both went for the box of tissues at the same moment, and as we dabbed our eyes, we smiled at our unlikely friendship.

I won't say more about what Juniper told me that day, for it has the power to change lives. I can only leave it in Juniper's gift to share it if and when the time is right, that will be up to her. For me, I cannot overstate the meaning her words brought to the final months of my life.

My bedroom has a large, low window with a wide sill. As I lie back on my pillows, my strength ebbing away, I look out at the beautiful magnolia tree, in glorious bloom, filling my window. A little pine birdhouse with a green roof is attached to its mossy trunk and below it, a post holds three tubes of bird seed. Goldfinches visit the tree to feed every afternoon. I watch their red and gold feathers illuminated in the late sunshine, as they flit from branch to feeder. Occasional gusts of wind bring the pink magnolia petals fluttering from the tree in the sunlight, like confetti onto the spring garden outside. The seasons change so quickly, the cycle of life renews and repeats, each generation learns from the last, like the trees, and so we go on.

ROGER 1979

The holiday in Cornwall with the Ashcrofts all those years ago was the beginning of Roger's life-long love of art. From the first moment he put paint to paper on the beach with Caro, he discovered a part of himself that was soaring and free. It made him want to laugh a deep belly laugh of joy. His brush strokes were tentative at first, but with Caro's guidance and encouragement he began to show real flair, not just for painting but for design too.

He would spend hours drawing an intricate shell, losing himself in the lines and flow of it, carefully adding the blush of colours that tinted its undulating shape. Roger was often invited on their family trips to Cornwall. The year he was preparing pieces for his portfolio to submit to Kingston School of Art, Caro had been only too happy to help and advise him. He collected pieces of wood and rope from the beach, and made necklaces out of shark's teeth. He bought white calico fabric and created a richly coloured, hand painted dress for Caro, embellishing it with small shells which he pierced and stitched around the scooped neckline.

When Roger was accepted for the course, it was Rosa and Jack who helped him pack up and move to the college campus. He had a small room of his own and a shared bathroom and kitchen, as well as a communal canteen. On the first day, he along with the other newbies, gathered for a welcome talk by the head of the art faculty, Jennifer Meacham.

'First I want to welcome you all to Kingston School of Art, congratulations on being selected.' She paused for a moment, looking out across the hall. 'It may be that some of you thought that by choosing Art you were taking the easy option, a comfortable ride.' There was a ripple of laughter before she added emphatically, 'Not so! We want to bring out the best in all of you, draw out your creative ideas. You will need to research to inform your work and never give up the quest for new ideas, new forms, new boundaries. As artists, that is our job and the pledge we make in the name of free expression.' She paused, 'I am here for questions if you wish, and as you leave the hall, please pick up a copy of your timetable and a map of the campus. Familiarise yourselves with the layout today and allow plenty of time to get to your studios and lecture rooms. I hope that among you there is an artist waiting to be discovered, it is there for the taking. Don't waste this opportunity!'

Relieved that it was over, Roger turned to the girl next to him and introduced himself, 'Hi I'm Roger.'

'Julie,' she said, smiling quickly.

'Well if we're doing intros, I'm Mark,' said a lanky youth with curly shoulder length hair.

'Hi Mark,' said Julie. 'Mark, Roger' she said, gesturing between them.

'That was a right load of tosh wasn't it,' said Mark before turning and sauntering towards the door. Roger caught Julie's eye and she grinned. As they exited the hall, pamphlets in hand, a girl with short dark hair waved at Julie.

'That's my new neighbour, Sal' she said, heading over to talk to her. 'See you around Bones,' said Julie as she walked away. Roger looked behind him to check that Julie had been speaking to him and he flushed slightly when he realised she had, then grinned. Why Bones? he wondered.

'Our first project is going to be about pop art. What is it, who started it, who bucked the trend and what did all this mean for the evolution of Art. Please write down these questions and do some research, there is no right or wrong answer. If you have an opinion, tell me, but you must underpin your statements with facts and research. You have the library at your disposal. London is full of galleries, go to them, be inspired! Produce some work in the pop art style to support your project and most of all, enjoy it!' As the lecture came to a close, Roger heard a voice behind him,

'Hey Bones,' it was Sal. Julie must either have mentioned him or she'd heard his new nickname yesterday.

'Hey, Sal isn't it?'

'Yeh right, you going to get some lunch?'

'Yes, I'm starving.'

The students shuffled slowly out of the lecture room, picking up the handout sheet as they left, then headed collectively along the corridor, towards the canteen and food. Roger chose sausages, mash and beans, Sal had fish and chips and Julie a salad. They chatted as they moved towards a table by the window with their trays, keen to sit down and enjoy their first proper meal.

'Thank God for some food,' sighed Julie between munches, a trickle of French dressing running out of her mouth.

'Any thoughts on our first project?' said Roger.

'Are you kidding?' said Sal, 'I have no idea where to start, you?'

'Well I suppose my first thought is to go to see some pop art at a gallery, to get a feel for it.'

'Christ,' said Julie, 'you're keen.' Bones said nothing as he continued to spear and cut his sausages, spreading mash over the top of each mouthful before layering on some beans and forking it into his mouth.

'What are you planning, Ju?' said Sal.

'I don't know yet, but I can feel my inner cogs beginning to turn and they can only get better after some chocolate pudding,' she said. 'My best ideas come to me in my sleep by the way, so watch this space!'

They all scattered after lunch and Roger headed over to the library to find out if there were any pop art exhibitions on, and he was in luck. The Hayward Gallery was showing works of Andy Warhol, Richard Hamilton and others. He grabbed his rucksack and a sketch pad and pencil and headed to the station.

When he arrived, the gallery was quiet. He walked slowly into the exhibition space which was a huge, white, rectangular room. The brightly coloured works had been arranged chronologically starting with a 1956 piece by Richard Hamilton, 'Just What is it That Makes Today's Homes So Different, So Appealing?' Reading the information beside it, he learned that Hamilton was considered by many to be the father of Pop Art. The piece was quite small, only 10 inches square and created in the mid-sixties, not so long after the end of the post war period. The work, he read, was filled with 'aspirational images'. Roger leaned in to study the picture, practically choking when he saw the central figure of a muscular, almost naked man, literally popping out of his pants and a seated, topless woman. He flushed as he leaned in for a closer look, only later registering the tin of ham and a television set. He struggled to imagine these items being aspirational.

Moving along, there were Andy Warhol paintings of Marilyn Monroe, colourful and spare, like sets of stamps. Rows and rows of red and white Campbell's soup tins were next, printed onto a larger canvas. The information said that these had been painted in 1962, and were chosen to represent images of people in the public eye, as well as the everyday things most people might have in their kitchen cupboards. Roger took out his camera and stood back to take a shot, and just as he was fine tuning the focus he heard the guard shout, 'No photos!' He put the camera away, disappointed and mouthed 'sorry' to the guard.

The next painting was larger, it showed a woman floating in a stream, on her back. Her skin was pale, almost translucent and her eyes were closed. Flowing around her among the reeds were unexpected images of soup tins and Coca-Cola bottles, bobbing under and on the surface of the water. Roger looked at the information beside it. It had been completed in the early sixties by someone called St Jacques, described as a rebellious genius. The subject is unknown, it said, and the style of the work pays homage to both the Victorian painter, John Everett Millais and the contemporary Andy Warhol. The painting was apparently unique in this regard.

Next was the artwork for the sleeve of the album everyone still talked about, 'The Beatles, Sgt Pepper's Lonely Hearts Club Band' by Jann Haworth and Peter Blake. After examining the sketches that would lead to the final piece and reading the notes beside it, Roger sat down on a wooden bench in the centre of the exhibition space and got out his notebook. He made a couple of quick sketches and added some notes, then he stood up, smiling to himself.

Their first two terms passed quickly and by the end of April, they were enjoying warmer weather. They would take bottles of beer and canteen sandwiches down to the river, rolling up their sleeves, kicking off shoes and lying back in the grass after lunch. Roger, lost in a warm haze of sleep, suddenly felt something tickling the side of his face. He was about to flick it away, when a voice whispered into his ear, 'Hey Bones, do you want to get together sometime?'

As he opened his eyes, Julie moved her face away and lay back down on the grass next to him with her eyes closed, as if it hadn't happened. Roger, deciding he must have imagined it, carried on sleeping, but he began to look at Julie in a new light. He noticed that her legs were long and slim, that she wore pink fitted jeans that flared voluminously from the knee. Her profile was shapely with long lashes and a turned up nose. Every now and again, she would catch him watching her and give him a flirty little smile, but instead of smiling back, he looked awkwardly away. A couple of months later, he saw that the new James Bond film was on at the local cinema, and found the courage to ask her out.

'Moonraker?' she said slowly. 'I don't know whether I'm free tonight.'

'Oh, don't worry,' Roger said quickly.

'You ninny, of course I'll come out with you, I thought you'd never ask.'

'Really?'

'Yes, really,' she said smiling. 'What time?' Encouraged now, Roger said,

'If you like we could go out for a pizza first.'

'Why not, that would be great.'

'Ok,' he said, amazed, 'I'll meet you outside the Art Department at 5.'

Over dinner, Roger found himself telling her about his trips to Cornwall and the beginning of his love of art. 'I've always been quite shy,' he explained, 'and I found that through art, I could express myself without feeling awkward.' Julie listened closely, giving him her full attention.

'So if it hadn't been for Caro, you may never have found your vocation?'

'Yeah, maybe that's true,' he said. ' How about you, did you always know you would study art?'

'I come from an arty household, my mum used to model for an artist, and occasionally dabbled with paint herself, so it seemed natural for me to follow in her footsteps.'

As they left the restaurant to stroll to the cinema, Roger felt a sense of contentment he couldn't remember feeling outside of painting. 'Thanks for the pizza,' said Julie, taking his large hand in hers as they walked. When the film was over, they walked slowly back to their halls. Julie stopped to point out the moon reflected on the river and the hundreds of stars over their heads.

'Wow isn't the sky incredible,' she said. Roger, who gazed up at it often, always in awe of its vast beauty, put his arm around her.

'Look' he said pointing, 'Do you see that upside down W in the sky? That is Queen Cassiopeia on her throne. Legend has it that she was so vain, she declared herself more beautiful than the sea nymphs and it angered the gods. They punish her each night by plunging her into the sea, as she circles the celestial pole.'

'What a story,' said Julie as they strolled along, his arm still around her.

'I had a great time tonight,' he said.

'So did I, thank you.' She looked up at him and stood on tiptoe to kiss his cheek. Roger felt his heart lift in his chest and smiled as she walked back inside. It was the first of many evenings together and Roger began to feel his life settling into a satisfying rhythm.

He was well into his second year when, returning to his room one evening, he met Mark coming down the stairs.

'Hey mate, there was a phone call for you, urgent apparently.'

'Who was it?' said Roger, surprised.

'Your dad I think, whoever took the call wrote a note and slid it under your door.'

'Thanks,' he said, taking the remaining stairs two at a time and hurrying to unlock his door. A folded piece of paper lay on the carpet and he picked it up, scanning the text quickly. 'Call your dad as soon as possible,' it said.

'Why is Pa phoning me here?' thought Roger, 'He never calls me. I hope Mother is ok.' These thoughts rushed through his mind as he searched for some change for the payphone, before heading along the corridor to dial his father's number. When the call was answered after two rings he said,

'Father, it's me, Roger. I received an urgent message to call you, sorry it's late, I've been out.'

'No matter Rojay, it is good to hear your voice. I'm sorry to call you with bad news mon cher, I know I don't call as often as I should.' Roger waited, transported back to his life at home by the mention of his proper name, and in particular the way his father had always pronounced it the French way.

'Has something happened Father?'

'Yes, it has,' he replied, 'I have received some very sad and unexpected news. My cousin Alice has died, she was the closest thing I had to a sister.'

'I only saw her a few months ago, what happened to her?' said Roger.

'Apparently she had a long illness, nobody knew, apart from your mother. Even she was only told,' he hesitated, 'I believe it was soon after you last saw Alice in France. How was she then?'

'Well, to be honest, she was a little strange. She thought I was someone else and then fell into a kind of faint and started rambling. We couldn't quite make it out, Mother had to call the doctor.'

'Juniper never mentioned that to me,' said Étienne. 'Are you sure?'

'Yes' he said, 'Lydia and I were both there when it happened. We flew back to London together the following day, and Aunt Alice stayed on at the house with Ma.'

'Well she died here in London,' said Étienne. 'She will be buried next to her parents.' The conversation was punctuated by the tone of rapid little beeps, indicating that more coins were needed, and Roger fumbled in his pocket for another ten pence.

'I mustn't keep you,' said his father. 'I called to let you know that the funeral will be on Friday of next week. I have ordered a dark suit for you, please ensure that you are home in Richmond by Thursday evening.'

'Yes sir, I will,' he said, then added, 'Father, I am sorry for your loss.'

'Thank you,' he said. 'Goodbye Rojay, see you next week.'

Julie had a wide circle of friends and Roger struggled to keep up with her social life, but she often sought him out, and it made him feel hopeful for the future. Just the other evening she confided in him over some family concerns, but his hopeful frame of mind at their growing closeness was quickly extinguished by the conversation with his father.

Roger hardly knew Alice, the last time he saw her was one of the only times he remembered meeting her. He laughed with Lydia afterwards about the mad woman running towards him in the woods, and their realisation that it had been Alice. On top of that, his father's call this evening was an unwelcome reminder of the person he was at home.

Here at Kingston, he had taken on a new identity. He likened it to a suit of formal clothes he could leave at the door, changing into something that fitted him more comfortably. It started with the nickname Julie gave him on the first day. When he'd asked her, 'Why Bones?' She'd simply replied,

'Jolly Roger of course, skull and crossbones, get it?' He had, and grinned, it made him feel as if he could be a new person; cool, casual and full of possibility. This was the feeling he wanted to hold onto when he returned to his family for the funeral.

THE FUNERAL

Monty looked about him uncomprehendingly across a shifting sea of black, and began to feel unsteady on his feet. The church was packed for Alice's funeral and now the tide of mourners were here in his living room. He was overwhelmed by the noise and desperately looked around him for help. He found his anchor in the form of his sister moving through the crowd towards him. Beside Juniper was a woman he didn't recognise, her long legs approaching under a flowing cotton skirt, her feet unadorned but for the leather hoop of her sandal around her big toe. Monty felt himself become calm as he watched the gentleness in her walk, her flow of womanliness. He imagined her reaching out her arms to offer him a place of safety in his confusion.

Her hair hung neatly cut about her shoulders, reflecting shades of gold. She drew him in with her hesitant smile, blue eyes full of concern as she saw his distress,

'Monty, this is Isobel,' said Juniper, jolting him out of his reverie. 'She was a close friend of Alice's.' Isobel's hand reached out and touched him lightly on the shoulder, 'Monty, I am so sorry, if there is anything I can do,' her voice trailed off. Her simple compassion felled his defences and emotion overwhelmed him. He wanted to swim in her blue eyes and forget, pretending that everything was as it had been before. Instead he heard himself say,

'I'm bearing up, thank you for coming today, Alice would have appreciated it.'

'Are you alright Monty?' said Juniper, as Isobel moved away, 'You are not yourself. I have made up a bed for you at home in case you prefer not to be alone tonight.' She put her hand gently on his arm and he looked at her, exhausted, his eyes hollow and empty. She added, 'Don't forget there will be the reading of the will in Richmond later too, I think you should be there.'

'Thanks Juno, I think I will stay at yours tonight if you don't mind. Pretty dismal business all this, don't think I want to be alone.'

He shook hand after hand and received condolences from people he hardly knew, all with tears in their eyes. So many well-meaning friends and relatives had talked to him about how much Alice had been loved. It was as if they were speaking to him in a language he didn't understand, how could Alice have known so many people?

Walking away from Monty, having spotted Kiki on the far side of the room, Isobel felt a ball of grief roll up and stick in her throat. It was bad enough that dear Alice was dead, but to be faced with her past like this as well, so unexpectedly, it was too much. Overwhelmed, she pulled the garden door open and hurried down the steps, pausing at the bottom to take in great gulps of the chilly air. The gravel crunched under her feet as she followed the path to the old tree, where a bench overlooked a garden of hydrangeas, still bare but for a few new leaves, budding onto bare stalks.

She sat down and dabbed at her cheeks, trying to calm her breathing as she rummaged in her bag for a mirror and some lipstick. Closing her eyes, she took a deep breath and slowly let it out. This will be ok, she thought, taking another deep breath to steady her nerves. Seeing Kiki again so unexpectedly after more than 15 years, had thrown her. She had wanted to run into her arms and sob her heart out for the times they had shared in Paris, and for the loss of Alice.

At the sound of footsteps, she opened her eyes and saw David approaching across the damp lawn. 'Come on darling, let me take you inside, it's cold out here'. He smelt of tobacco and she knew he had been smoking in the garden, to relieve the awful stress of the day. It was soothing somehow to smell it on him, familiar. They walked back to the house together and Isobel made her way into the crowded room, seeing Monty on the far side, awkwardly holding a cup of tea. Then she caught Kiki's eye and turning to

David she said,

'I won't be a minute, I'm just going to speak to an old friend.' As she walked towards Kiki, Jack appeared beside her, his hair now peppered with grey; but Kiki saw Isobel approaching and moved towards her, arms outstretched,

'Darling Izzy, how are you?' she hugged her and then stepped back to look into Izzy's eyes, before planting a kiss on her cheek. 'How long has it been?'

Izzy looked into Kiki's face, still the same, a little thinner perhaps with lines around her eyes, but still they twinkled with mischief.

'Far too long,' said Izzy, 'and what awful circumstances.'

'I know, it's a tragedy. I thought Alice would always be here for us all, didn't you?' Kiki put her strong arms around Izzy and pulled her close as she spoke. Isobel wanted to relax into her embrace so very much, but she knew that if she did, she would be lost. She couldn't stop her tears though, and even as she pulled back and looked up into Kiki's eyes, they rolled down her cheeks. Kiki rummaged in the pocket of her black trousers and pulled out a colourful handkerchief for her. 'I know my darling, I know,' she said, as Izzy cried for so much more than the loss of Alice. Then David was at her side,

'Are you alright Isobel?'

'Yes, yes I am, just upset that's all.' Then, remembering her manners she said,

'David, this is Kiki, a mutual friend of Alice and I from our days in Paris. Kiki, this is my partner David.'

'Hey,' said Kiki, 'good to meet you David.' They shook hands and then Kiki began to move away. 'Actually, we ought to leave in a minute, we're taking the overnight train back to Paris tonight. Don't be a stranger Izzy,' she said, smiling, 'Paris is not so far away, you are always welcome, you know that.'

'Thank you,' said Isobel weakly. 'Have a safe journey.' Others began to drift away too, saying their goodbyes, glad to be making their way home.

'Take care old chap,' said Étienne, stepping forward to shake Monty's hand, his mother on his arm. Clémence was elegantly dressed in a black Chanel suit, she looked relaxed and tanned.

'I'm so sorry for your loss Montgomery, I know Alice meant a great deal to you, as she did to us all.'

'Likewise,' replied Monty sadly. 'Thank you Clémence, I appreciate you making the trip for her funeral.'

'It was the very least I could do,' she replied quietly, her face full of pain.

'I'll join you all later at the house for the reading of the will, Juno has invited me to stay over, I hope you don't mind.'

'Of course not, see you later,' said Étienne. Monty watched the mourners gradually begin to take their leave, relieved that it was over.

Finally, the house was empty, it had been a long day. Monty dropped his face into his hands as self-pity overwhelmed him, what a fool he had been. He had loved Alice in his way, naively assuming she would always be here for him. He had understood her need to be alone in France, but counted on her coming back. She had been his rock, but now it was too late, she was gone.

THE WILL

Back in Richmond and tired after the funeral, the family were called to the dining room for the reading of Alice's will. Lydia was abroad and had been excused, Monty had just arrived. Roger took his father aside and said quietly, 'I don't need to be here for this do I? I promised I would get back to Kingston early this evening to go over some work.'

'On the contrary Roger, you have been asked very specifically to attend, as have we all,' Étienne replied quietly.

'Oh I see, very well,' Roger sat down at the table.

Étienne had asked for some tea and sandwiches to be brought into the dining room, where they all sat around a large mahogany table with the de Montfort family solicitor. Mr Brightwood opened his briefcase, and taking a final bite from his cucumber sandwich, removed some papers and put them onto the table in front of him. He waited expectantly for the attention of the group, before he spoke,

'I was invited to this house a number of months ago by Mrs Juniper d'Apidae, née de Montfort,' he clarified, 'to enable Miss Alice Gardener to make a last will and testament. You may know Mr d'Apidae that we have been representing the de Montfort family for many years.' Étienne nodded, but said nothing, unaware until this moment that Juniper had been any more than slightly acquainted with Alice. Mr Brightwood continued to speak in a slow, sonorous voice, the kind of voice, thought Roger, which might lull him to sleep at any moment.

'Miss Gardener was relatively young when she died and

unmarried.' At this, Clémence's face contorted with pain, as he continued. 'She was without siblings or children and chose to live very simply, splitting her time between her home in France and those of various friends in London. However, she was a wealthy woman and leaves behind a large property in London, a home on the Côte d'Azur as well as her home on the d'Apidae estate, 'Les Lavandes.'

The solicitor paused as he concluded his introduction, leaning back in his chair to look at each of them in turn.

'Unless specifically requested, I will not read you the will in its entirety today, I know you are all tired. My intention is to give you the key details of Miss Gardener's wishes. May I suggest that for those of you who would like further information, I would be glad to receive you at my office at a later date.'

'Thank you Mr Brightwood, perhaps if we could now come to the point of our business today.' Said Étienne, wanting the whole thing to be over and done with, so that he could kick off his shoes and relax.

'Yes, yes indeed. Well it is really very straight forward,' said Mr Brightwood, getting straight to the point now. 'Miss Gardener has left her property on the Côte d'Azur to her friend and partner Mr Montgomery de Montfort. Otherwise, she has left her entire estate to Mr Roger d'Apidae.' Roger, who had been on the verge of dozing off, now jerked his eyes open and sat up straight.

'To me?' he said, 'why would she do that? She barely knew me. I think I only met her once or twice.'

'How extraordinary,' said Étienne, who had expected, as her next of kin, to find it had all been left to him. Only Juniper sat quietly, fiddling with her rings.

'There is one other thing,' said Mr Brightwood. 'Miss Gardener inherited quite a lot of jewellery from her late mother. She has left pieces of particular significance to Mrs Clémence d'Apidae. There is also a list of close friends, each of whom are to choose a favourite piece for themselves as a keepsake. There are also some cash legacies to some individuals.'

'Miss Gardener asks that the moonstone ring, which was precious to her mother, be given to you Roger. If it pleases you, she would like you to offer it as an engagement ring to your future wife.' This was becoming surreal. Roger wondered if he had in fact dozed off and woken in the middle of a dream.

'I really am confused, Mr Brightwood, why would Alice do this for me?'

'I cannot answer that young man; I can only offer any advice you may need in managing your inheritance. I have here a summary of Miss Gardener's properties and bank accounts for you to peruse, and I suggest we meet next week to discuss it further.' He handed Roger a large brown envelope with his name written on the front in a neat script. Mr Brightwood continued, 'Mr de Montfort, I have separate papers for you regarding the villa in France, but as yet have not received them in their entirety. They should be with you early next week.'

Mr Brightwood turned to Juniper next and said, 'There is one final thing. Miss Gardener left a letter for you Mrs d'Apidae.' He pulled a large A4 envelope out of his briefcase and handed it to her.

'Good heavens! This feels more like a book than a letter,' she said, holding the weighty envelope in both hands before setting it down in front of her. 'Thank you Mr Brightwood.'

'That concludes our business for today,' said Mr Brightwood. 'Do you have any questions before I take my leave?'

'No, not at the moment,' said Étienne standing up. 'Thank you for coming to see us today.' He showed Mr Brightwood out and then returned to the dining room where Roger, Monty and Juniper were sitting in silence. 'How extraordinary!' said Étienne. 'Did you know anything about this Juniper?'

'No, of course not,' she said, 'I only tried to help Alice when I realised she was dying, she had nobody else.'

'You knew she was dying?' said Monty, incredulous.

'Yes, I did, but she wanted to keep the illness from you Monty. She didn't think you would cope with your job as well the burden of it. She told me she didn't have the strength to shoulder your grief, as well as her own. I brought her back to London to help her get her affairs in order. As for you Étienne, you were away, no wonder you didn't know.'

'I see, ' he said, 'but it still doesn't explain why she has left nearly all her property to Roger. What about Lydia? I think it is all very odd.'

'I'm sure she had her reasons Etty, even if we don't understand what they were.'

'Well she always was a maverick, right from the outset, danced to her own tune. Maman used to say she was just like Amélie.'

'Amélie?' said Juniper.

'Yes, my aunt, Alice's mother.'

'Oh, yes,' she said remembering.

'Anyway, Mother, Father,' interjected Roger, 'I'm sorry to interrupt but I'm afraid I need to get back to Kingston now,' he said standing up. 'I don't suppose you could drive me could you Father?'

'Oh please don't go back tonight Roger,' said Juniper.

'Sorry, I must,' he said, ' Father?'

'Alright, yes,' said Étienne. 'Go and change as quickly as you can, I'll drive you now before I pour myself a whisky.' Turning to Monty he said, 'Go and help yourself old chap. You'll find whisky and a nice fire in the drawing room, I won't be long.'

'Come on Clémence, you must be exhausted. Let me show you to your room,' said Juniper. 'Can I ask Rosa to bring you anything?'

'No thank you,' said Clémence, 'but I must admit, I am tired. I'm looking forward to being back in Paris for a few weeks, before returning to America, it has been far too long.'

As Étienne's car moved out of the driveway, Monty poured himself a drink and sank into the sofa in the drawing room. With Clémence settled upstairs, Juniper, now alone in the dining room, poured herself a glass of wine, then sat down to open the brown envelope. Inside was a small, pink envelope with her name on it and another much larger one addressed to Roger. Juniper slit open the pink one and began to read Alice's flowing handwriting,

Dear Juniper

I can never thank you enough for the support you have given me over these last few months. I am only sorry we did not become friends sooner. I wonder why we let life get in the way? I thank you especially for sharing your closest confidences with

me, this cannot have been easy and I applaud you for your courage.

My life has been full of wonderful friends, but only one person among them has made my life complete. After the death of my own parents when I was a child, I felt that happiness would never be mine. It was almost as if I didn't deserve to be happy and then one night in Paris, I met Xavier. I learned through him what it is to love in a deep and visceral way, to love with all my heart and yet still be free. It was as if the very air I breathed was the universal love I felt for him. It was never a possessive love, Xavier needed to be free and he was, but we were free together, if that makes sense. It was my tragedy that the happiness I found was so brutally snatched away when he was killed, but I am thankful he has not been here to witness my decline.

I have enclosed with this letter some journals I have written, there is also a letter for Roger. I want him to have these. It will help him to understand his inheritance, which no doubt he is questioning, even as you are reading this. Juniper, they contain a full and detailed account of many of the conversations you and I had when you discovered my illness. I want him to know everything. However, I leave some parts of the story in your gift, it is yours not mine to tell. You may never want to tell it, but I thank you with all my heart for sharing it with me. It is this that made the last months of my life bearable, the feeling that none of it was, in the end, for nothing.

I wish you happiness in your life Juniper, and I embrace you with love and affection.

Alice x

ROGER 1981

It took Roger some time to get used to the idea that he was at last a man of independent means, and as a result, his confidence grew. He had lived in the shadow of his parents all his life, but gradually their power over him diminished. He put this down to his growing relationship with Julie, and he began to wonder what it would be like to see her away from Kingston. The Easter holiday was approaching and one day, over fish and chips in the canteen, Roger voiced the thought he had carried in his head for over a week.

'Julie, I don't suppose you fancy a few days away?' he said, uncertainly.

'Away, where?' she replied, not looking up from her fish and chips.

'Paris,' he said.

'Paris!' she shrieked, her food forgotten. 'Bones are you serious?'

'Yes, yes I am,' he said quietly, a slow smile spreading across his face. She leapt up from the table, did a little dance of excitement and rushed out of the canteen, leaving her rucksack on the table. She returned to grab it a few minutes later, saying, 'Lovely idea Bones, but I can't afford it, sorry. I've got to go, I'm late.' She bent down to plant a kiss on his cheek, 'Talk later,' then she was gone.

Had she turned down his invitation? Roger wasn't sure, but he hoped she would mention it again later. There was a church he wanted to see in the Latin quarter, as well as an art exhibition that would help his project. He had visited Paris many times before, but never without his family. The thought of strolling arm in arm with Julie, along the banks of the River Seine, made his heart soar.

Roger finally broached the subject again as they sat by the river swigging cokes from the bottle.

'You are such a sweetie Bones, but I can't come. I'd love to, but no funds,' she said, pulling out her empty pockets for dramatic effect. 'C'est la vie!' She put her bottle down and lay back on the grass, enjoying the sunshine.

This time it was his turn to surprise her as she basked in the sun. He leaned towards her and whispered in her ear, 'Hey Julie, do you want to get together sometime?'

She opened her eyes and giggled, as he leaned in to kiss her gently on the mouth. When she closed her eyes and sighed with pleasure, he kissed her more deeply before pulling away. 'So, will you come?' he said quietly. 'It's on me, so no worries about funds.'

'Are you rich or something Bones, you dark horse?' she asked him.

'No,' he said, 'but right now I'm flush! My father's cousin has died and for some inexplicable reason, she left me some money.' He decided not to mention the property for the moment, that part still felt unreal.

'You lucky sod' she said. 'Ok, I'll come, why the hell not.'

PARIS, A FEW WEEKS LATER

The spring sunshine warmed them as they strolled along the left bank of the Seine, holding hands, stopping to admire Notre Dame standing majestically on the Île de la Cité. 'That is incredible!' Julie sighed, pulling out her camera to take a few shots. They stopped to admire stalls along the river bank selling posters, books and trinkets. A little further along, they crossed the road into a cobbled street where cafés and boutiques thronged with people. As they rounded the corner into the Place St Severin, Roger indicated the curved outline of a beautiful church.

'This is what I wanted you to see,' he said, turning to Julie. 'It is one of the oldest churches on this side of the river. The architecture is really unusual and I think you'll love the windows.' They linked arms and strolled quietly into the dimly lit interior, marvelling at the luminescence of the great arched windows. They were a myriad of blues and then of pinks and reds, dancing in the light. The soaring stone pillars around the central part of the church were shaped like palm trees, their branches reaching towards one another to create elaborate stone arches. Julie smiled up at Bones.

'I love it,' she said quietly, 'I want to try to capture the shapes and colours.' She sat down in one of the pews and pulled out a sketch pad and the small set of watercolours she kept in her bag. Roger left her to it, strolling into an oval side room. The sun poured in through thick, yellow glass onto the arc of wooden chairs arranged to fit the curve of the room.

At the front was a small altar with a single painting hanging on its pale stone wall, and high up in the centre of the ceiling was a curved hollow in the shape of a shell. This, he read, represented the shell of St Jacques, the guiding symbol along the holy route of the pilgrims. He stood quietly, slowly taking in the tranquil space. Some candles were burning to one side of the altar and Roger walked over to say a brief prayer and light one, sending up a silent blessing to Alice for making this trip with Julie possible. As he looked up to the windows again, he was momentarily dazzled by the sun, and warmth flooded through him.

He felt a tap on his shoulder, and looked round to see Julie smiling up at him. 'Are you ready to go?' she said quietly. They made their way to a brown wooden door to exit the church and blinked in the bright sunlight, as they stepped onto the square. The pavement restaurants and cafés were thronging with people chatting over salad and glasses of wine. Little baskets of crusty bread and bottles of rich olive oil stood on the tables and impulsively Roger said, 'Shall we sit down and have some lunch?'

'Ooh yes please,' said Julie. A waiter waved them to a small table with a red and white checked cloth, and they sat down in the sun. Roger ordered the set menu of green salad tossed in lemon dressing, followed by pan fried fish in butter and herbs, in flawless French. When the waiter had gone, Julie smiled at him, 'Bones, you make me proud,' she said shyly, and he basked in the pleasure of it.

Later, relaxed after their food and wine, Roger paid the bill and they set off to stroll along the low, wide path beside the river. He pointed out the famous Shakespeare & Company bookshop as they passed, moving carefully through the little throng outside. 'That place is so well known,' said Roger. 'Famous authors come and read their work out loud. It still provides accommodation for writers in return for help in the bookshop. It dates back to Hemingway's day, even James Joyce frequented it apparently.'

'Wow!' said Julie, 'What a great location. Look at the view across to Notre Dame from here.'

He reached out to take her hand, leading her across the square. 'Let's head over this way, there's a slope we can walk down just beyond those stalls.' They crossed the road, weaving their way through tourists and locals alike, all enjoying the Quartier Latin. As they reached the cobblestone slope and began to descend towards the riverbank, they left the noise behind and the atmosphere changed. Only a few others strolled by the river, a young couple hand in hand, an old man with a stick, pausing every now and again to catch his breath. A lady walked briskly along with her dog, heels clacking on the stones. Roger put his arm around Julie's shoulders and pulled her close as they walked.

'Thank you for a lovely day,' she said, stopping suddenly and turning her face towards him. Julie stood on tiptoes to reach his lips and kissed him slowly, her lips soft and warm against his. 'You're not trying to make me fall in love with you, are you, Bones?' she whispered, wrapping her arms around his waist and putting her head against his chest. Roger's heart soared as he ran his fingers over her curly hair.

'Oh look!' she said as they strolled on, 'there is an actual house boat! I've always wanted to live on one, let's go and have a look.'

Just ahead of them, a blue barge swayed gently on its moorings. The occupants were seated at a small table, partially screened by trees and shrubs growing in pots on the deck. Laughter emanated from the group and Julie saw a woman with long auburn curls throwing her head back with mirth at whatever the joke had been. There was a half empty bottle of wine on the table and a scruffy dog lounged at their feet in the sunshine. 'Just imagine, living on a boat!' said Julie enthusiastically. 'We could just untie the ropes and sail to wherever we felt like living!' Roger loved her enthusiasm and smiled, pulling her closer. They continued to walk along the river bank, occasionally stopping to watch the Bateau Mouche carrying tourists along the river, the white foam behind the boat slowly fanning out towards them.

Up ahead they could see another barge painted pale green, little coloured flags lined the ropes from bow to stern, fluttering in the sun. The deck was obscured by potted hydrangeas and bundles of fresh herbs, and an old woman was dozing in her chair among the plants. When suddenly a dog barked, her eyes flew open in surprise and she looked momentarily confused before calling out to the young couple,

'Monsieur, Mademoiselle would you like to buy some lovely flowers or some fresh herbs? I have beautiful hydrangeas, rosemary, basil and lavender, they smell so good, come and look!' Roger, not wanting to walk on without acknowledging the woman, began to step towards the barge, but Julie had already leaped across the small gap and was on the deck laughing.

'How incredible!' she said, turning to the woman 'Bonjour Madame, votre bateau très joli.' The woman's suntanned face crinkled as she smiled and nodded at Julie. 'Come on Bones,' she called, 'what are you waiting for?' The woman gestured towards a wooden bench near her chair and Julie sat down. Roger had stepped aboard by now and in perfect French complimented her on the marvellous hydrangeas and the sweet smelling herbs.

'Asseyez-vous' she said, smiling and Roger sat down beside Julie. 'You are from England?' the woman asked.

'Yes we are,' said Julie, 'we are art students from London. I absolutely love your boat, it is my dream to live the way you live!'

'Oh I 'ave lived on the water for many years, it is my way of life. You want to see inside?' she asked.

'Oh yes please!' said Julie.

'We don't want to intrude,' added Roger hastily.

'Of course you don't intrude, please,' she said, indicating the entrance to the cabin down three pink wooden steps. They ducked below the strings of flags into a colourful galley. The small kitchen had mugs and saucepans on hooks against a pale turquoise wall. Pink and red painted flowers decorated shelves holding plates and glasses, and a table with a blue and white cloth had a bench seat covered in bright cushions.

'Oh look, a ginger cat!' said Julie, stepping towards the sleeping fur bundle, curled up between the cushions. 'What is your name?' she crooned quietly, gently running her hand over the cat's soft fur.

'Il s'appelle Cedric,' smiled the woman, revealing gaps in her lower teeth. 'Et moi, je m'appelle Astrid.'

'I am very happy to meet you both,' said Julie, standing up and giving an elaborate bow, 'enchantée!' Roger struggled to keep up with the situation, one minute they were walking along the river minding their own business and now they were aboard this strange woman's boat, with Julie behaving as if she had known her all her life.

'What a beautiful home you have, Astrid!' said Julie, 'I love it!' The woman's nut brown features crinkled again as she smiled back at her.

Then Astrid looked at Roger, becoming serious and said, 'Your girl is very special, take good care of her,' Julie looked at him and winked.

'Yes Bones, you need to take good care of me,' she said grinning.

'I will,' he said, looking at the woman and blushing awkwardly. He turned back towards the entrance and made his way out onto the deck. He would choose some flowers for Julie and then make their escape. He looked at the brightly coloured pots and selected a blue one containing a hydrangea covered in purple and lilac flowers. He turned to indicate his selection and only then realised that the two women were still inside. He dipped his head below and saw that they were deep in conversation. 'Julie, I think we ought to be going,' he called.

'Coming!' she said. He watched her take the woman's hands in hers, before coming towards him and back up onto the deck. Roger pulled a 10 franc note from his pocket,

'I would like to buy these flowers please Madame,' he said, his face half hidden by the huge blooms.

'Bones, have you any idea how funny you look peering through the flowers?' said Julie laughing as the woman took the note.

'Merci Monsieur, au revoir.' They stepped back onto the quayside, Roger peering round the plant so as not to miss his footing, as Julie leaped across the gap from the boat to the bank.

'Au revoir Astrid,' said Julie, 'See you soon!' she called, raising her hand in a wave. The woman raised her own as she watched them stroll away.

'That was amazing,' said Julie. 'Astrid said that I have a special light, an aura. She wants me to go back tomorrow afternoon for a Tarot reading. There is something she wants to speak to me about.'

'Are you going to go?' asked Roger from among the flowers.

'May as well,' she said 'I liked her and I'm curious.'

The next day as Roger made his way to a gallery to do some research, Julie walked back along the river to meet Astrid. It was an overcast morning with occasional drizzle and when she arrived at the barge, there was no sign of the old woman on deck. Julie jumped aboard and knocked lightly on the doors, before pushing them open and stepping down into the galley. 'Bonjour Astrid,' she called, pushing the doors closed behind her.

At first there was no sound or sign of life except the cat, who raised his head languidly before closing his eyes again. Suddenly the turquoise curtain was pulled aside and Astrid appeared in a faded patchwork dressing gown and an old pair of slippers, her grey hair hanging around her shoulders. 'Julie, bonjour,' she said smiling as she filled the small kettle and put it on to boil. 'Would you like some coffee?'

'Great, thanks,' said Julie. 'I hope I'm not too early for you.'

'Pas du tout' said Astrid, 'I sleep late these days, I like to rest my old bones.' Julie rummaged in her bag, pulling out a paper parcel, 'I bought some fresh croissants, shall we have them with our coffee?'

'Why not,' said Astrid, placing two steaming cups on the table and taking a seat at the far end of the table. They munched on croissants and sipped their coffee in companionable silence, as the cat licked his paws one by one. 'I knew you were coming to find me, I just wasn't sure when,' said Astrid. Julie stopped eating and looked up at her,

'What do you mean?' she said.

'I am a teller of fortunes and a seer, it is a gift I was born with. It allows me to know things before they happen, without always understanding the significance at the time.' There was a pause as Julie took this in, while Astrid continued to sip her coffee, in no hurry to continue.

'When we met yesterday, you said you wanted to read the Tarot cards for me,' said Julie.

'I knew it was your destiny to come here, there is something I need to ask you.'

'Of course, fire away,' said Julie, curious now.

Astrid continued, 'I am getting old and weary and I have not seen my only daughter for many years. She lives in Canada you see.'

'So how do you think I can help?' asked Julie.

'I would like to go and see her before my time comes but I cannot leave my boat, or my dear Cedric.'

Julie was beginning to see where this was leading. 'Astrid, you know I would love to help but I have to go back to London in a couple of days, with my friend.'

'Do you love him yet Julie?'

'What a question,' said Julie, realising she was blushing. 'Maybe, and what do you mean, yet?' Astrid smiled her toothless smile,

'Perhaps you are already feeling it.' She paused, 'For now, my question is would you be willing to come and live on my boat in the summer, while I go to Canada?'

'Astrid, are you serious? Of course I would, I would absolutely love to!' Then more quietly she added, 'The only problem is, I'm supposed to be working in July and August to earn some money, I'm not sure how I would manage if I didn't do that.'

'Well that is easy,' said Astrid. 'One of my neighbours has a restaurant barge further along the river, they always need extra help in the summer, I will see what I can do. Now relax and familiarise yourself with the boat, while I get dressed and run a brush through my hair, then I will get out my Tarot cards.'

JUNIPER

Back in Richmond, the responsibility of the envelope Alice had left for Roger weighed heavily on Juniper's mind. She hadn't discussed it with Étienne since the evening of the funeral, when he casually asked her what it was. She had made light of it, 'Just some journals, nothing of interest, Etty. Alice was so young, it's all so sad.'

'She lived in a world of her own half the time, Juno. I expect she's written about elves and fairies,' he said, pouring himself a large whisky.

Juniper knew that the story her son would find in the envelope would shake his world, and very likely her own as well. She couldn't hand it over to him without assuming that it would, thereafter, be in the public domain. It was a risk she was not ready to take. She went to bed, hoping to find clarity in sleep, but the cogs of her mind turned and sleep eluded her. It had been weeks now, why was this playing so much on her mind when she had lived with it untroubled for so many years?

When Juniper awoke, she resolved to put the whole thing out of her mind. After all, she hardly saw Roger these days and it was unlikely he would approach her to discuss the will. If he did, she could give further thought to the envelope. The matter settled, she opened the drawer of her desk and with some difficulty pushed the envelope into the drawer and locked it, breathing a sigh of relief.

Alice's death hit Juniper hard and she struggled. Although the two of them had never been close, those last months with her changed everything. By making herself vulnerable, trusting Alice with her deepest secrets and fears, Juniper learned compassion and love. Where previously she might have been critical, she found herself seeing the humanity in others and it felt good.

As her defences slowly eroded, and the deep truths of her life rose inexorably to the surface, Juniper knew she needed some help. What she was discovering within herself, had no place in the rigid world she had inhabited thus far. Alice had tried more than once to encourage her to take up yoga, saying it would be calming and help her cope. At the time, she had seen it as one of Alice's bohemian ways and didn't take it seriously. Perhaps now she really should consider it, she had nothing to lose.

The following week, Juniper noted down the number from a poster in her local church. It invited her to find inner peace and make new friends through yoga. When she picked up the phone and dialled the number, Hermione was enthusiastic and forthcoming. She told Juniper there was a regular class and suggested they meet for coffee to discuss it. Juniper found herself agreeing, and made a note of the address.

Hermione lived in a small red brick house on the other side of Richmond Park. Dressed in a batik kaftan, she greeted her warmly and ushered her into a colourful room with two oversized armchairs facing a large window. The bright space looked out onto a small garden with ornamental grasses and a pond. A stone statue sat peacefully surveying the water, which tinkled as a tiny fountain splashed into it.

Juniper found herself relaxing in Hermione's company. Her eyes twinkled as she spoke and her voice was calm and kind. That day was the beginning of a new friendship and Juniper was thankful. Hermione's large comforting presence made Juniper feel she could tell her anything, and very slowly she opened up about her life. She told her about Alice and then about Roger, finding comfort in the way Hermione listened with quiet attention. That had been a turning point, she reflected now, as she gazed out at the garden.

Just then the telephone rang. Juniper was about to pick it up when she heard Étienne answer it in his study. She heard him laugh and then gently close the door. She couldn't remember the last time he had laughed with her, or had any form of meaningful conversation. A pang of jealousy shot through her as she walked purposefully along the marble tiled corridor towards the garden.

Juniper took her gardening jacket from the hook and stepped outside, pulling her secateurs and gloves out of the pockets as she walked over to the rose bed. She would do some dead-heading, the charity dinner would have to wait. To her surprise, as she began to cut the rose heads, she realised a tear was sliding down her cheek. She quickly wiped it away with the back of her glove. What on earth was wrong with her?

She was not prone to sentimentality, but lately, it was as if a door had opened in her heart and mind, allowing things she had buried for years to seep out. She only had a short time with Alice before she died and in those last months, Juniper discovered what it was to put herself aside and think only of the wellbeing of another person. It was a feeling that had come from her heart. She was in awe of Alice, a person who had lost her parents when she was only a child, lost the man she loved and faced an early death. Yet, she listened with kindness and empathy to Juniper, as she finally found the courage to talk of things she never thought she would.

Juniper had come to see herself in a hitherto unseen light. She realised she had withheld her true heart and even her love, from her husband and children. She had been prickly and defensive with them, never wanting to let down the barriers she had built around herself as a child. No wonder Etty looked elsewhere for his companionship, he had certainly not found it in her, she wiped away another tear.

'You alright Mrs d'Apidae?' came a voice from behind her.

'Yes Jack I am, just a bit of hay fever, that's all.'

'Shall I get Rosa to bring you a nice cuppa tea?' he asked kindly. 'You could sit over there in the sunshine.'

'Thank you Jack, I will, a cup of tea would be lovely.' Another kind soul she thought, as she made her way over to the bench near the lilac tree. Why hadn't she noticed that before? Her defences were slowly falling away and she was seeing a new world, but she felt so vulnerable in it. Another tear slid down her cheek as she rummaged for a handkerchief. She blew her nose, wiped her eyes and sat up straight, taking a deep breath of the late spring air, slowly exhaling and relaxing her arms and back against the bench.

As she opened her eyes she saw Rosa making her way across the lawn with a small tray and managed a smile.

'Here you are Mrs d'Apidae, I've cut you a nice piece of my cherry cake too, in case you were feeling hungry.'

'Thank you Rosa, how thoughtful.'

'Shall I pour for you?' she said, setting down the tray on the little garden table.

'No, thank you, I can manage,' said Juniper, reaching for the teapot and pouring a steady stream of fragrant lapsang into her cup.

'Will there be anything else Mrs d'Apidae?'

'No, thank you for the tea Rosa and your thoughtfulness.' Rosa turned and walked away, and as Juniper looked towards the camelia in front of her, she noticed a robin hopping in the undergrowth. She gazed at it for a while before lifting the cup to her lips, closing her eyes as she sipped the tea, enjoying the smoky flavour. When she opened them again, she saw Étienne walking towards her.

'There you are Juno, it's not like you to be out in the garden. Is everything alright?'

'Of course it is Etty,' she said, taking another sip of her tea. Then she added uncharacteristically, 'And how are you?' Étienne looked momentarily surprised before replying,

'Actually, I'm just on my way to the airport, something has cropped up at the Paris office. I'll be back at the end of the week.' Juniper sighed. 'By the way,' he added, 'Roger called, he's coming home at the weekend. He's left a couple of books behind.'

'Oh what a pity, I won't be here much. I've promised to spend Saturday and Sunday with Lydia, helping with her move,' said Juniper, her heart jumping at the thought of Roger. This time Étienne sighed,

'Never the twain shall meet,' he said, leaning down to kiss her lightly on the cheek. 'I have a weekend of golf lined up, so he'll just have to fend for himself. Give Lydia my love when you see her.'

'I will, have a safe trip.' She watched Étienne striding back towards the house. It was fortuitous she would be out this weekend, she was not ready to see Roger yet. Perhaps she never would be able to face him with the honesty he deserved.

ROGER

Roger returned to Richmond for the weekend as planned, and when he emerged for breakfast on Saturday morning, his mother had already gone out for the day. Étienne too, was about to leave the house.

'Morning old chap, sleep well?'

'Yes, thank you Pa, I did, where's Mother?'

'She's gone to help Lydia get her new flat in order. I'm going out to play golf in a minute, do you want to join me for a round, I could wait?'

'Thanks Pa, but I won't, I've got some work to do. I'll see you later.'

'As you wish Rojay,' said his father. 'Rosa and Jack are off today, so you'll have to fend for yourself. I expect you'll find some food in the fridge.' Then, as an afterthought he added, 'Oh, and your mother said something about some diaries Alice left for you. Lots of nonsense probably, but still, if you are at a loose end, I expect they are in the drawer of her desk.'

A few minutes later the door closed behind his father and Roger breathed a sigh of relief. He had no plans to actually do any work, he'd only come back to get some books and enjoy the relative luxury of home for a while. Lounging about when his parents were around wasn't considered acceptable, but it was a pastime that came more and more easily to him since he had been at Kingston.

After a long snooze under a tree, Roger rubbed his eyes and went inside in search of food. He flicked the television on as he munched crisps and, in the absence of a beer, he drank cola. When he found nothing of interest on tv, he turned it off and sighed. Downing the last of the cola, he sauntered upstairs to get a book and as he passed his mother's study, he remembered what his father had said about Alice's diaries. He was still mystified by his unexpected inheritance and now there were apparently some diaries as well. Odd that his mother hadn't mentioned it.

He pushed open the study door and walked over to the desk, trying the two drawers, but both were locked. A brief search of the pots on the shelf revealed the small gold key. He tried the left hand drawer first, it was full of paper and envelopes, along with his mother's ink pen and a few stamps. The second drawer was more difficult and although the lock turned easily, he struggled to slide it open. It appeared to have very little in it, but something was caught on the desk frame inside, above the drawer. Getting down on his knees, he peered into the space and could see that a large, brown envelope was wedged there. He prodded and pushed it until finally, the drawer slid open and he prised the envelope out. When he eventually held it in his hands, he turned it over to read the four words in large loopy script on the front. It said simply; To Roger from Alice.

He pushed the drawers closed and locked them again, replacing the key. Then he made his way out into the garden. He tore the envelope open at the top, pulling out several large exercise books, filled with scrawling script. He slid the first one out from under the elastic band, opened it to the first page and began to read.

The story of Alice and his parents' young lives absorbed him for the remainder of the weekend, and he paused only occasionally for snacks and drinks. It was as riveting as any novel and he couldn't put it down. Who would have guessed that Alice had had such a racy past! Roger still had no idea what it all had to do with him, and he was no closer to discovering why Alice had left him everything when she died. Just then, he heard the front door open and his father called out, 'Roger, are you still here, old chap?'

'I'm upstairs Father, just about to pack my bag to go back to Kingston.' He thrust the journals quickly into his rucksack as his father entered the room.

'Good, I'll drive you, but first let's go out for a bite to eat, they do a marvellous roast beef at The Bishop.'

'Great, I'd like that, I'm starving,' said Roger, brightening at the prospect of a good meal.

SUMMER BREAK

A few days back at Kingston and into the final weeks of term, Roger was absorbed by Alice's journals. They had taken him through her life from the time her parents were killed, to Paris, then Normandy and London. He was longing to tell Julie about it and he smiled at the prospect of an evening with her, imagining the two of them laughing over a couple of drinks.

He hadn't seen her much since they got back from Paris. Usually she contacted him, but the last couple of times he'd missed her. He knew he should have made more effort, but his obsession with Alice's life story had overshadowed everything. Julie still went out drinking and dancing with her crowd, and sometimes he thought about joining them, but Julie seemed distracted and it put him off. He suggested coffee one day, but she said she was busy. Perhaps she'd given up on him, he would try and catch her later in the week.

The end of term was just around the corner and who knew what the summer might bring. Ashcroft had invited him down to Cornwall again in July, but he wondered now whether he had outgrown it. On the last day of exams, Roger walked across to Julie's block. He climbed the stairs to the second floor, walked along the corridor to her room and knocked. He waited a couple of minutes before knocking again and calling her name, self-consciously against the door.

'You looking for Jules?' a voice asked.

'Yes, I am,' he replied, turning to see a girl with short dark hair and wide set eyes,

'She's left for the summer.'

'Oh,' said Roger, 'do you know when she'll be back?'

'September I suppose.' Roger's heart crashed into his shoes as he took in this news.

'Don't suppose you have a number for her?' he said.

'No but you could ask around her friends or go to admissions if it's important.'

'Thank you,' he said, turning to walk away. Why hadn't he made more effort to see her?

'Hey Bones,' called a voice behind him, he stopped and looked round.

'Hey Sal,' he said half-heartedly. Roger carried on walking and Sal caught up and fell into step beside him.

'How did your exams go?' she said.

'Oh alright, I think I'll scrape through, you?'

'Bit of a disaster really, hopefully my project will pull me through.'

'Who did you research?' he said out of politeness, but wasn't really listening to her reply. His mind was on Julie, where on earth had she disappeared to?

'An artist called St Jacques, he painted an homage to the Victorian painter Millais. It's different to his other works, which are mostly conceptual in style. There is a mystery around this particular painting which made me want to know more.'

Roger realised she had stopped speaking. His mind was turning over the possibility that Sal would know how to contact Julie, but again, out of politeness, he asked,

'What did you say the painting is of?'

'I didn't' she said. 'It's of a woman floating in a stream surrounded by soup tins.'

' Oh, I think I saw that at the Hayward a couple of years back.' He paused, 'Sal do you know where Julie has gone?'

'She's left for the summer,' said Sal. 'Didn't you know? I thought you guys were seeing each other.'

'We were, I'm not sure what happened,' he said vaguely. Sal gave him a long look he couldn't fathom. 'Do you have a number for her by any chance?'

'I might, somewhere,' she said, 'but she won't be at home.'

'Where is she then?' asked Roger.

'No idea. She said something about spending the summer on a boat.' If Bones didn't know the details, who was she to tell him.

'Ok, thanks Sal, have a good summer,'

Roger walked back to pack up his room, there was no point in staying now. He would call Ashcroft and accept the offer of a month in Cornwall. He threw himself onto his bed, planning to tackle the packing later. First, he would settle down to read the last of the journals. He pulled it from his drawer and opened it, lying back on his bed and losing himself in it. On the last page it was as if Alice was speaking to him;

'After reading all about my life and quite a lot about your mother's life, I expect you are still wondering what all this has to do with you Roger.

Roger stopped short, surprised to find Alice addressing him directly; he had lost himself in her words, forgetting they had been written for him. He went back to reading,

'I had a marvellous life, with so many friends, but I lost the things that were most important to me. My parents were killed when I was only a child and I never had children of my own. The final blow was losing Xavier, the love of my life. He was a free spirit and that is what I loved about him. When we were together we were lost to the rest of the world, it was as if we became one spirit and one mind and nothing else mattered. The night he was killed, my heart broke into small pieces.

I didn't know it then, but the illness that will soon end my life was already brewing. Once I knew I was dying, I retreated into myself, living with ghosts in my mind as I roamed the quiet of the gardens and the woods. Then one day I was out walking and I thought I saw him. He looked as he did when I first knew him, sitting against the trunk of a tree in the woods. It was as if he had come back from the dead.

The illness and my longing for him made me believe it was a real possibility. I ran towards him wildly and desperately and when I reached the tree he was gone. That day, I thought

I must be losing my mind. Your mother came to my rescue, inviting me to join you all for dinner. I'm sure you remember the night I came to your house and reacted so badly when I first saw you. You must have thought me a mad old woman and maybe, in a way, I was.'

Roger looked up from the journal. He remembered the mad woman in the woods. So, it had been Alice and that was why she had been running towards him as if her life depended on it. She thought she was running to Xavier.

'That night changed everything for me. When the doctor found out that I was terminally ill, Juniper insisted I stay with her while you and Lydia returned to London. Those few days with your mother were the first time we had properly talked.

My relationship with Juniper was never easy, we were so very different on the outside, but on the inside it turned out we were not so very different after all. We talked about so many things, especially you Roger.

I urge you to speak to your mother. Only she can tell you the rest of this story, and she may choose not to, you will have to respect that. I hope that you will find a great love in your life one day, as I did.

Life is never easy, that is what I have learned, but if you are lucky, it comes with blinding flashes of joy and magnificence!

With love and kindness,
Alice xx'

PART 3

JUNIPER

Just before his trip to Cornwall, Roger was at home again for a few days. He wanted to bring up the subject of the journals with his mother, but was unsure how to do so, given that he had taken them from her desk and never mentioned it. Did she think they were still in the drawer?

It was awkward, and as he turned the situation over in his mind, he wished he could speak to Julie about it. She always knew what to do. Pity he didn't have a clue where she was or how to contact her. He sighed, and just then there was a light knock on his door.

'Come in,' called Roger. 'Ma!' He was startled when he saw her and wondered whether she had read his mind. 'Is everything alright?'

'Of course it is, yes, it's just that', she paused, 'there is something I need to discuss with you Roger.'

'Oh dear, she knows,' he thought. He knew if he was going to speak up he should do it as soon as possible, but initially words failed him. Then after a pause he spoke,

'Ma is it to do with Alice's journals by any chance?' Now it was Juniper's turn to look startled.

'Yes, as a matter of fact, it is,' she said.

'Well I'm sorry Ma, but Pa mentioned them to me a few weeks ago. He said that Alice had left them for me and that they were in your desk. I assumed that meant I could help myself to them, I should have told you.'

'Yes, you should have told me,' said Juniper, turning pale,

suddenly feeling the conversation running out of control. 'Have you read them?'

'Yes I have, but I'm none the wiser. Alice says at the end that only you can tell me the whole story. What is the story Ma, what does she mean?'

Oh, thought Juniper, this really is out of control, there was no going back now. Part of her felt relief that Alice's story was already out in the open, but she knew that the worst was yet to come, and that it could only come from her. She sighed, a long heartfelt sigh.

'It is a very long story Roger, today I planned to tell you about the journals and hand them over to you. I was not prepared for the fact that not only have you got them already, but you have read them as well.'

'I know, I'm sorry.' He looked at her, worried at how pale she had become.

'Well don't be, you need to hear it sooner or later, and we need to be alone. Come into the drawing room after supper, your father is away tonight, so we will not be interrupted.'

What on earth is going on, thought Roger, as his mother walked out of his bedroom, closing the door behind her. She seemed very unlike herself, almost frail, he thought, as if the strength had drained out of her.

After a light supper together they went into the drawing room. Roger picked up the Times and began to flick through it, unsure where all this was leading. Juniper settled herself in her usual chair and to his surprise, she kicked off her shoes and put her feet up.

'What I am about to tell you is not something I am proud of Roger but I want to be honest with you,' Juniper paused and Roger put down the newspaper,

'Sounds serious Ma, is everything ok?'

'It's a long story and I hope that in trusting you with this, you will begin to understand how it happened.'

'How what happened Ma? You're not making any sense.'

'You want to know why Alice left you everything in her will, don't you?'

'Well yes, of course I do, but I can't see what this has to do with you.'

'You will Roger.'

'Ok Ma go on, I'm all ears.'

Juniper paused and took a deep breath. 'It all started many years ago, when I was about your age. I met Alice around the time I met your father, I was still quite childish then. Outwardly I was pretty and elegant, doing and saying all the right things, your grandmother made sure of that, but I was a bit like a pretty doll. I had no depth, no compassion and little understanding of the world.' She looked at Roger and continued,

'Alice had just lost her parents in a car crash, she came to live with your father's family at the age of 16. I was just a few years older than her and I'm ashamed to say I was petty and jealous of her. Everybody seemed to like her without her even trying, and I resented it.'

Roger still couldn't see what this had to do with him or where it was leading, but said nothing. His mother continued, 'Once your father and I married, we moved to Normandy. After two years of being mostly alone while your father travelled, managing a new baby and enduring incessant rain, I was at my wits' end. I longed for some company and I missed my parents and my home in London. One day, out of the blue, I heard that Alice had inherited her mother's property on the estate, and was to become my neighbour. When she arrived, I did the usual polite things that neighbours do, took her some jam, tried to make her welcome and so on. I still resented her relaxed manner, the way she didn't seem to care about the things I had always cared about, but deep down, I think I wished I could be like her.'

'So, what was the problem,' said Roger.

Juniper continued as if Roger hadn't spoken, 'She was everything I was not and yet, despite wanting to be more like her, I couldn't let go of the expectations I had of myself and others.

I didn't realise quite how unhappy I was until one day, by chance, I came upon Alice and her boyfriend together, in the barn behind her house. I went to see her, I can't remember why, and I was intrigued when I saw a motorbike outside her house. There was no answer when I knocked and I should have just gone home. Instead, curiosity got the better of me and I walked around the back of the house and towards the barn, where I could hear laughter.' Roger began to listen more closely.

'When I got to the barn, the door was shut, but I found a gap between two boards and looked in. I could see that a man had been painting her. She was lying naked along an old couch, and as I watched, he put down his brushes and walked over to her. He leaned down to kiss her, and then, well, I'm sure you can imagine the rest.' Roger swallowed, as his mother continued, 'At first Alice giggled as he leaned over her, but soon she went quiet and I could hear her gentle sighs as he made love to her.

I know I should have left discreetly as soon as I realised what was happening, but I couldn't tear myself away, I just stared at them fascinated. You see, my experience of lovemaking had been so very different to what I saw in the barn that day, the joyful, playful union of two people in love. In that moment, I realised how it could have been for me and my heart began to break.'

Juniper paused and Roger looked awkward, unsure what to say. She continued, 'I am sorry if this embarrasses you Roger, but I have reached a point in my life where there have been so many secrets, that I simply cannot go on without honesty.' She reached for a tissue to dab her tears, trying to maintain her composure.

'What do you mean, how it could have been for you? I thought you and Dad loved each other.'

'We do darling, in our way, but things are not always as straight forward as that. Certain things happened to me when I was young that should not have happened. It has been a great sadness to me that some of those things have affected the life your father and I have had together, our private life I mean.' Roger blushed awkwardly.

'Mother there really is no need....'

'Darling, I'm so sorry but in order for you to try to understand what comes next, it is important for me to give you some context.' She continued, 'Anyway, as I ran from the barn that day, I cried and cried. It was a kind of grief for what I had missed, I believed it was too late for me you see. After that, I couldn't get the man out of my mind. I tried to imagine what it would be like to have him paint me, how it would feel to be in Alice's shoes. I'm ashamed to say that I began to feel so very jealous of her and her happiness.

Anyway, soon after that Alice held a house warming party. She invited her friends from Paris and London and of course, she also invited your father and I. He was away a lot then, just as he is now. I felt very alone with Lydia, and I certainly had no social life.'

'So, did you and father go to the party?'

'Your father was dismissive, but I felt that at least one of us should go to welcome Alice to the estate. As it turned out your father was still away, so I went alone. As I dressed to go out that night, my world suddenly felt full of possibility; I wanted to enjoy myself. When I arrived, Alice made me welcome and introduced me to some new people, scruffy, arty types. I felt free for the first time in years, as if that night, I could be anybody.' She paused to look at her son, 'Can you understand that Roger?'

'Actually Ma, I can,' he said. 'That's how I felt when I first started at Kingston. It was as if I could be anyone I wanted to be.'

Juniper looked up at him, surprised. 'Did you feel you wanted to be someone else Roger?' she asked, concerned. She realised it was the first time Roger had ever opened up to her.

'Not someone else exactly,' said Roger, 'but I felt able to come out of my shell among strangers. Nobody had any preconceived ideas or expectations of me, it was a fresh start I suppose. Sorry Ma, carry on, I didn't mean to interrupt.'

Juniper got up, 'I think I need a glass of wine, would you like something to drink Roger?'

'Yes please, I'll have a beer if there is one.'

'There you are darling,' she said a few minutes later, handing him a small chilled bottle and a crystal glass. He ignored the glass and put the bottle to his lips. Juniper sat down and took a sip of her wine, leaning back with a sigh as it calmed her.

'Roger, I am glad we are doing this.' Juniper realised sadly that she had never sat down to enjoy a drink with her son before. Roger put his bottle down on the table, and waited for her to continue the story.

'Do you really want me to carry on? We could do this another day if you prefer.'

'No, go on Ma.'

'Alright well, where was I?'

'You had just arrived at the party and met a couple of scruffy people,' he played back to her.

'Ah yes,' she said, 'well, I chatted to them for a while, then

I stepped away and made my way towards the kitchen, to see if Alice needed any help. I found her deep in conversation with a colourfully dressed man, he had shoulder length curls, and waved a long cigarette holder in the air as he spoke.' Juniper paused, 'Can you see Roger, these were not my usual crowd at all?' Roger could, and he grinned in amusement as he tried to imagine his mother at the party.

'Anyway,' she continued, 'As I approached, the man occasionally threw his head back and laughed before leaning conspiratorially towards Alice, to say something more. Alice laughed at whatever he had said, and then they saw me approaching. She beckoned me over, she was always so welcoming. I am ashamed now when I think of my petty jealousy towards her.

'Juniper, come on over!' she said. 'This is my friend Alexandre, Alexandre this is Juniper, my neighbour.'

'Enchanté,' he said, bowing theatrically as he kissed the back of my hand. I remember thinking that at last, somebody had some manners. Roger smiled as Juniper continued,

'Alice, can I do anything to help?' I asked.

'Not really, but thanks, have you been outside yet? It's such a beautiful evening.'

'No, but I will,' I said. 'Here, I've brought you a house warming gift.' I pulled a carefully wrapped package out of my shoulder bag and gave it to her.

'Oh do look daahling, what can it be?' said Alexandre, excited as a child. 'Don't you just love a present!' Alice pulled the paper off to reveal the beautiful, blue glass jar I had bought her with a pretty candle in it.

'Juniper I love it! Thank you,' said Alice as she leaned over to kiss my cheek. Just then another friend approached, and Alexandre introduced him as George.

'Who wants another top up of wine?' he said as he appeared from the direction of the fridge with a newly opened bottle. Without waiting for an answer he topped up our glasses before continuing to circulate, if only it had ended there. I was drinking more wine than I was used to and yet I felt a kind of thrill, and I didn't want to stop, I felt powerful and free.'

Juniper gazed into the fireplace as if in a dream. After a while, she looked back at Roger and said quietly, 'Darling, suddenly I feel tired, I hope you don't mind but I think I would prefer to resume our conversation tomorrow. Do you mind if I go to bed?'

Roger was initially disappointed. 'Come on Ma, it was just getting good,' he said, grinning.

'Roger try not to be so flippant, there is a lot more to come and I can promise you it will not be easy. You will not be laughing at the end of it,' she said. He hung his head for a moment, more confused than ever, as the drawing room door opened.

'Etty, you're back!' said Juniper jumping to her feet, wondering whether he had heard them? 'I wasn't expecting you until tomorrow.'

It wasn't until late the following morning, that Roger found a moment to speak quietly to Juniper, asking when they might continue their conversation.

'I'm sorry Roger, it will have to wait now until you are back from Cornwall, or perhaps I will write to you there, it may be easier for both of us.'

'Alright,' he said, disappointed, 'I'm just going to finish my packing and then I'll be off. Ashcroft and I are catching the sleeper train from Paddington.'

As Juniper waved her son off for a month, she sighed and went to sit in the garden. The lavender flowered abundantly and scented her path as she walked, the still cool morning air on her face. She breathed deeply, she had taken the first step and the rest would surely follow.

THE PARTY

The next day, taking a few thick sheets of paper from her desk, Juniper sat down to write. She would put down the events of those weeks as best she could remember them, not least to get it clear in her own mind. She could decide later whether or not she would post it to Roger in Cornwall. The next part, she knew, would have been particularly difficult to tell him face to face. She cast her mind back to the party and the scene in the kitchen, she was chatting with Alice and her friends when a man walked up to them.

Her pen hovered over the page, but she found herself unable to write. Emotion flooding through her, she got up from her desk and went to sit in her armchair facing the garden. She closed her eyes as she recalled the events of that night, wondering how she would ever be able to tell Roger the whole story. She hadn't thought about the details for many years. Now, as she leaned back in her chair, her mind drifted back to the hazy room, the thrum of the music and the heady feeling that she could be anyone she wanted to be. She remembered that she had drunk too much wine and as she turned to step outside for some air, she bumped into the man she had seen with Alice that day in the barn.

'God, I'm sorry,' I said. His eyes burned into me, and without thinking I added, 'I saw you in the barn with Alice.' I paused, continuing to look at him. He stared back at me and then, instead of waiting for him to speak, I said, 'I want you to paint me.'

His gaze was unwavering and he looked at me for a long time, before leaning in and saying quietly into my ear,

'You don't want me to paint you, you want me to fuck you.'

I gasped at his words and looked up at him, 'I just want... ' but the trouble was I didn't know what I wanted and my voice trailed off. Then he smiled, 'Come into the garden with me, let's get some air.'

From the kitchen, Alice had seen us chatting and gave me a brief wave, I suppose she was glad I was enjoying myself. A few glasses of cheap wine had made me feel powerful and brave, so I followed the blonde stranger out into the garden towards the barn. Once on the far side of it, he lit what I assumed to be a cigarette, it was only later I realised it was marijuana. He sat down on the grass, patting the spot next to him, 'Sit down,' he said. 'Here, take a puff of this.' He passed me the joint and I inhaled deeply.

'Now, lie back and look up.' I settled onto the soft grass and looked up at the sky,

'Oh my God, it's beautiful,' I breathed. I had never seen a sky like it, deep navy blue and filled with bright stars. It brought to mind Van Gogh's Starry Night and I knew in that moment, that this is what he saw over his head when he immortalised the sky. I drank in its beauty as my fingers played with the cool blades of grass at my sides.

'You know,' I said, 'I don't think I have ever really noticed the sky before, not like this.' He said nothing, but leaned over to kiss me, trailing his fingers from my throat, over my chest and belly and then back up to my face. I felt detached, aware of the feel of his unshaven face against my skin as his lips brushed mine. I sighed as his fingers moved over my thin dress, slowly circling my nipples. Then he brought his lips down and began to suck the mounds of my flesh. I could feel the fabric becoming wet as it clung coolly to my skin in the night air.

Juniper was jolted back to the present by a click of the door as Rosa came in to tidy the room. 'Oh I'm sorry Mrs D'Apidae, I didn't realise you were in here. Would you like a cup of coffee?' Juniper blinked in the bright light and instinctively smoothed her hair, half expecting to find a blade of grass in it.

'I would Rosa, thank you,' she mumbled, closing her eyes again. She could almost feel the soft grass through the fabric of the dress she had worn that night.

I closed my eyes and smiled, a little gasp escaping my lips

as he lifted my skirt, his rough hands gently pushing my panties aside and his fingers moving slowly over me.

'Open your eyes,' he whispered into my ear, ' and tell me that you want me to fuck you.' I looked into his eyes and then up at the stars as I said,

'Yes, I do, I want you to fuck me.' The words sounded strange to me, as if they were being spoken by somebody else. In a way, I was someone else that night, I realised. It was the first time I enjoyed any form of intimacy without memories of the past rising up in me. I felt pleasure as his fingers stroked my moist, secret flesh, tantalising me for moments longer, before he swiftly unbuttoned his jeans and slid on top of me. I gasped first with shock and then pleasure, as he thrust inside me. I lost myself in the stars over my head and began to move my hips in time with his rhythm. I heard myself sighing and moaning in a voice I hardly recognised as my own, as wave after wave of pleasure flooded my body. Finally, I cried out, gripping his shirt, as he too gave a grunt of relief and rolled away.

Have I really just let this happen, I vaguely thought, as if I was observing myself from afar. Next to me, the man buttoned his jeans and lit the joint again, taking another long drag before passing it to me.

'I'd better not,' I said, and I heard him laughing quietly to himself. We lay there for a moment longer and I had almost drifted into sleep when he said,

'Come on, we'd better get back to the party.'

'You go, I'll see you in there,' I mumbled. So he got up and walked off in the direction of the house. As I watched him leave, I thought to myself in a detached way, I have just given myself to a stranger in a field. I pulled a mirror out of my bag, struggling to see myself in the darkness. I brushed the bits of grass out of my hair then stood up to straighten my dress.

Juniper sighed as a small tear escaped from the corner of her eye and she looked up to see Rosa coming back in with her coffee. She hastily wiped it away and stood up from the armchair. 'Thank you Rosa, I'll drink it over here.' She sat down at her desk, picked up her pen and took a deep breath. Roger didn't need to know everything, but he did deserve the truth.

After slowly and reflectively sipping her coffee, Juniper spent the next hour setting out a version of events that would spare Roger the graphic details of that night; but finally, he would know the truth of what she had done.

Once she was satisfied with what she had written, she put down her pen and sighed, allowing her mind to drift. Juniper had always told herself that what happened with Xavier that night, was an inevitable consequence of seeing him with Alice in the barn. She wanted to feel what Alice had felt and naively imagined that by asking Xavier to paint her portrait, it would end with him making love to her, but he had seen through her. Sex with him had been so raw, combined as it was with the elements of the earth and the sky. She could still feel the damp grass in her hands and smell the wild mint in her nostrils as they crushed it beneath them. Even now, as she closed her eyes, she felt warmth rising in her belly at the memory. That night was a turning point for her, it showed her how to give herself up to pleasure. It enabled her to play her part to perfection with Étienne in Paris, and she surprised both herself and him at the change it brought about in her.

The bitter blow of hearing the news of Xavier's death, and the strain of having to hide her shock from Étienne, was something she would never forget. She covered her face with her hands for a moment and sighed. Reliving that time thus far had been enough for one day. She would continue tomorrow and then post the letter to Roger in Cornwall. After that, it would be up to him.

JULIE

Julie had been living on the narrow boat on the Seine for two weeks, when she received a call from Sal,

'Hey friend, how is Paris?'

'Sal! how great to hear from you! Everything is good, how are you, did you get your project finished?'

'Almost, I'm still trying to get to the bottom of something that could be important. I was thinking of coming over to have a look at the libraries in Paris. Do you want some company for a few days?'

'I would love some company! When can you come?'

A few days later, Sal arrived, staggering along the path with her bag. Julie jumped off the boat and flung her arms around her friend.

'I am so happy to see you!' she said, hugging her tightly. Between them they lifted Sal's bag on board and Julie took her down into the cabin to show her around.

'Wow,' said Sal, 'you are living the dream my friend!' Just then a scrawny looking cat stood up from behind some cushions and stretched, arching its back towards the low ceiling, before turning around and curling up among the cushions again. 'Who is this?' said Sal, reaching out to stroke his soft, ginger fur.

'This is Cedric,' said Julie, 'Commander of the ship!'

'Aye aye sir!' said Sal standing to attention and saluting, before dissolving into giggles. 'So,' she said, sitting down next to the cat, 'How are you really? Have you heard from Bones?'

'No, I haven't,' Julie said quietly, 'He has no idea where I am.'

'God he's a chump,' said Sal. 'He wanders about in his own world half the time. He wouldn't know a good woman if she stood naked in front of him,' said Sal loyally. 'He came looking for you actually.'

'Did he, when?'

'A few days after you left. I saw him in the corridor knocking on your door. He seemed to think everything was fine between you. He looked pretty gutted when I told him you'd already left.'

'Oh,' said Julie, 'Did he say anything else?'

'Not that I can remember,' she said. 'He talked to me for a bit, about art and stuff and then walked off. Actually,' she said, rummaging in her jeans pocket, 'Now I come to think of it, he gave me a phone number for his parents' house in Richmond.' She pulled a selection of screwed up pieces of paper out of her pocket and put them down on the table, struggling to smooth them out. 'Mostly old receipts,' she said apologetically, then, 'Ah, here it is.' She peered at the note, 'Have a guess what his surname is?'

'I know what it is, it's a bit unpronounceable. Dippy something isn't it?'

'Nearly, it's Dappy Day, spelt d'Apidae, he told me his father is French. Here you are,' said Sal, handing her the crumpled piece of paper.

'Do you think I should call him?' asked Julie.

'Well yes, if you want to see him again. Do you?' Julie's face lit up and she smiled,

'Actually Sal, I think I might be in love,' she said quietly.

'You dark horse!' she said. 'Since when?'

'Since Paris I suppose.'

'He brought you to Paris, when?' said Sal.

'A couple of months ago, he's very sweet when you get to know him, just a bit shy.'

'Why hadn't you seen much of him before the end of term then?' asked Sal.

'I'm not sure really. He had to go home quite suddenly because a relative had died, and soon after that he suggested coming to Paris. We had such a great time together. That was when I met Astrid, the owner of this boat and because of that, I am here now spending the summer on it.'

'Why don't things like that happen to me,' said Sal wistfully, as she watched a young couple strolling hand in hand along the bank of the river. She turned back to Julie, 'So what happened, with Bones I mean, if it was going so well?'

'I don't know, but soon after we got back to England, he seemed to go into his shell. The few times I saw him, he was distracted and in his own world. To be honest, I thought he'd lost interest in me. I was pretty upset about it, given the way I had begun to feel, but I made a decision to keep going out with friends and having fun, as I always have. He didn't even seem to notice,' Julie paused and sighed. 'Come on let's go and sit outside.' She took some wine out of the tiny fridge and they went to sit at the table on the stern of the boat. 'Cheers my friend, welcome to Paris! So, enough about me, what's with the Paris library search?'

'Well, it's a bit of a mystery actually. I'm researching an artist called Xavier de St Jacques, he's quite hot at the moment. Most of his work is conceptual in style, but there is one painting of his that is unlike anything else he has created before, and that's the one I'm interested in. It is a version of Ophelia, you know, the one where she is lying in the river, except St Jacques has her surrounded by floating soup cans, after Warhol.

Anyway, I've found more than one article suggesting that the St Jacques' version of the Millais painting, may be one of a series, even though only one has ever been seen.'

'Why do they think there are more?' said Julie.

'It's just a rumour, maybe someone who knew him saw the others and mentioned it in an interview, or something like that, but there's rarely smoke without fire.' Julie was only half listening, her mind had drifted back to Bones, she really did miss him. Sal had given her hope and she allowed herself to imagine what she might say to him if they spoke. She would call him tomorrow.

The next day, while Sal was at the library, Julie went to the old payphone on the quayside, and dialled Bones' number, it was engaged. When she tried a few minutes later it rang several times before being answered by a woman with a French accent. 'Hello,' said Julie, ' this is Julie Greenwood, I'm a friend of Roger's from Kingston.'

'I'm sorry but Rojay is not 'ere, he 'as gone away to Cornwall.'

'Oh,' said Julie, her heart sinking, 'Do you have a number for him? Do you know when he'll be back?'

'At the end of July,' said the woman, 'I am sorry but I may not give out the phone number without asking. I am Rosa, the 'ousekeeper,'

'In that case Rosa, would you be very kind and give Roger my number when he comes home. Perhaps he could call me back, it is a French number.' She slowly read the number off the front of the payphone and then Rosa read it back to her. 'Yes, that's it, thank you so much Rosa, goodbye.' Julie put the phone down, what did she expect, it was July and he was away on holiday.

Nevertheless, Julie was heartened by the fact that Roger had been asking after her. It made her hopeful when she had felt hopeless. Perhaps he did still care for her after all. Maybe he had been going through a difficult time. After all, his Aunt had died, they must have been fairly close, for her to leave him enough money to fund a trip to Paris. She felt guilty for not having considered this possibility before. 'Come on Cedric, let's get your food,' she said as the cat wove in and out between her ankles. Just as she put his food down, the phone rang and Julie stepped off the boat to pick it up. 'Hello,' she said.

A frantic female voice said something incomprehensible, and Julie said, 'I'm sorry but do you speak English?'

'Yes, yes I do,' she said, breathless. 'My name is Rachel, I am Astrid daughter, I call to tell you she is in hospital.'

'In hospital!' said Julie. 'Oh no, what happened?'

'She suffered a heart attack this morning,' then the woman broke down and began to weep.

'Oh Rachel, I'm so sorry.'

'She is worried about her cat. She says she had a premonition that he will be alone.'

'Cedric is fine,' said Julie. 'Please tell her not to worry. Her home and Cedric are in good hands. Send her my love and tell her to concentrate on getting well, everything is fine here.'

'You are so kind,' said Rachel, 'thank you. I will call again in a couple of days to let you know how she is.'

Sal arrived back at the quayside in the late afternoon, hot and flustered. The temperature had risen in the city and she stepped back on board with relief. The boat was moored in the shade of the trees along the river bank and a cool breeze blew off the water. 'Thank God!' exclaimed Sal, nearly tripping over Cedric as she dived into the cool of the cabin. 'It is so hot out there!'

'Hi Sal,' said Julie, looking up from her book, 'How did you get on?'

'Really good,' she said, 'I got chatting to one of the art experts at the library, and she thinks St Jacques had a muse. A close friend of hers spent quite a lot of time with him in the south of France, apparently he was very distracted in the last few years of his life. Uncharacteristically, he was spending a lot of time in the country with a girl he had fallen for in Paris. The friend says he was obsessed with her and that he spoke of little else, she believes the girl in the painting is the same person. She also said she thought it likely that there are more paintings, possibly unfinished.'

'Really?' said Julie, 'I wonder where they are.'

'You and the rest of the art world,' said Sal. She sighed as she poured herself a large glass of water and gulped it down. 'How was your day?'

'Not great,' said Julie. 'I got a call from Astrid's daughter, you know Astrid who owns this boat? Well, apparently she's had a heart attack, and she's in hospital.'

'Oh no,' said Sal. 'Is she going to be ok?'

'They think so, but her daughter was pretty upset, she's going to call me again in a couple of days.'

'Poor woman,' said Sal.

Later, over dinner, Julie told Sal that she had tried to call Bones in London.

'What did he say?' asked Sal.

'He wasn't there,' said Julie. 'He's away in Cornwall for the rest of July, according to their housekeeper.'

'Did you leave a message?'

'I left my number and asked if he could call when he gets back.'

'Did she say who he's with?'

'No, she just said friends,' said Julie, looking meaningfully at Sal.

'Well it could be anyone, no need to jump to conclusions.'

'Thanks Sal, I'm glad you're here.'

'Funny you should say that,' said Sal, 'but I was wondering if I could stick around for a while? London is crazy at the moment with the Charles and Diana wedding about to happen, and I'm loving it on the boat. It would help my research too.'

'Of course you can!' she said, delighted to have the company. 'Cedric loves you too Sal, I can tell.'

ROGER

Roger had been in Cornwall for nearly two weeks when he awoke, late as usual, the sun streaming through his flimsy curtains. The promised letter from his mother had arrived the day before and he was up late last night reading about Alice's house warming party and his mother's description of sex with a stranger in the garden. It was like reading a swinging sixties novel about somebody he had never met. He still had no idea why she was telling him this and was certain he would never be able to look her in the eye again. He picked up the letter and sauntered downstairs to make himself a coffee. A note propped up on the table told him that Ashcroft and their friends had gone surfing, so he had the place to himself.

He went to sit outside with his coffee, the Cornish sun already beating down with a vengeance, and pulled the letter out of its envelope. The second part was a much thicker wad of paper. He had been too tired last night to carry on reading, needing time to process his mother's revelations. He was still struggling to reconcile the strict, uncommunicative mother he had always known, with this version of her that was as unlike her as he could possibly imagine. He leaned back in his chair, taking in his mother's neat handwriting and wondered how there could still be so much more to say,

> *'Five weeks passed after the party, Étienne was away, and I began to feel unwell. I was tired much of the time, and noticed it particularly during the few days that Rosa was not at work. Lydia was exhausting, running me ragged and without Rosa, I was struggling to cope.*

The next morning a wave of nausea overcame me, and as I caught sight of myself in the bathroom mirror, a dreadful possibility dawned on me.

As soon as I was dressed, I phoned my mother in London to ask if we could come and stay for a few days. There was a lot I needed to tell her, and it couldn't wait. The journey was exhausting, and it was only once Lydia was in bed that I told her the real reason I had come home;

'Mummy I think I might be pregnant.'

Roger looked up and saw his friends coming up from the beach, waving as they approached, so he folded the letter and slid it into the envelope.

'Hey lazy bones you missed some great waves!' said Maria, plonking herself next to Roger on the bench. Ashcroft propped his surfboard against the wooden fence and lit a cigarette, while Sue and John went inside to get some coffee. 'Are you ok?' said Maria, 'You look a bit serious today.'

'I'm ok,' said Roger, 'Sorry I missed the surf.' He got up and walked into the house. 'See you in a bit,' and returned to his room, shutting the door behind him. He threw himself onto the bed and pulled the letter out again, finding the page where he had left off, and continued to read;

'Pregnant, is that all? Juniper, surely that is wonderful news!'

'You don't understand,' I said. 'Étienne and I haven't shared a bed for months,' Claudia blanched.

'Oh dear,' she said, falling silent for a moment,' in that case Juniper, who in heaven's name is the father.'

I didn't want to tell her and she tried to hide her shock, struggling to imagine the kind of party at which something like this could happen.

Roger stopped reading for a moment and paused to let this sink in. Christ, could it get any worse? He was grateful to be alone and so very glad he did not have to hear this from his mother face to face. He continued reading,

'I told my mother the whole story, holding nothing back. I told her how difficult my relationship with Étienne had been. You see Roger, something awful happened to me when I was a child and it affected us as a couple. I will spare you the details, but these days it would be called sexual abuse.'

Roger drew a sharp intake of breath, he could barely take in the magnitude of what his mother was saying.

Your grandmother was devastated, but she has always been strong. The next day she took me to see her gynaecologist in Harley Street, who quickly established that I was approximately five weeks pregnant. After the appointment, over lunch, Claudia lifted her glass and said calmly,

'To my next grandchild,' before taking a sip of wine and leaning back in her chair.

I still didn't know what to do, but she was very clear. She said I should go to Paris and spend some quality time with your father, she wanted there to be no doubt that the child was his.

My pregnancy was announced soon afterwards and of course Étienne assumed that it was a result of our time together in Paris. The beautiful baby, born nine months later, was you my dearest Roger.

Darling, I know this will come as an awful shock to you and I wish with all my heart there was a way I could have avoided the hurt that this will bring you. Your father has always believed you to be his child, and he has certainly loved you as his own, so very much. You are the apple of his eye.

Although I would like to tell you that I loved Xavier, I didn't. How could I when I hardly knew him? The next morning, it was as if the events of the night before had happened to somebody else, in a dream; but like many intriguing dreams, I couldn't get it out of my head. While one part of me wanted to push it to the back of my mind and pretend it hadn't happened, the other part of me was intoxicated by what I had done. You see, that night, I discovered my true self for the first time.

I confided in Alice before she died, I felt she deserved to know. I don't suppose I was the first person Xavier had slept with, their relationship was an open one. However, please know Roger that the knowledge of you made such a difference to her in the last weeks of her life. She could already see how like Xavier you are my darling, and that is because you are his son.

How I wish I had had the courage to tell you all this sooner, and in particular, the courage to tell you face to face, as was my intention.

As for Étienne, the man you have always known as your father, he will never know the truth unless you decide to tell him yourself. No doubt if you do, we will all suffer the consequences, but I am ready and it will be no less than I deserve. Of course Roger, this is your choice. I have lived with this secret since the day you were born and I no longer have the right to keep the truth from you. I have been alone for much of my adult life, despite being married to Étienne. I have also been lonely, but that is going to change.

Alice was one of the bravest and most unselfish people I have ever known. There was a spark within her, the light of goodness I suppose, it shone from her face. It may sound strange, but knowing her, finally seeing who she was after all these years, was like having an epiphany. I realised that for most of my life, I have thought of nothing but myself; and yet Alice, despite her ill health and misfortunes, was always thoughtful and kind, even on her deathbed.

Something within me has changed, Roger, and I want to build on that. I am sorrier than you will ever know for the hurt I have caused you. I have struggled over the weeks since Alice died, so very unsure of what to do for the best. I hope that one day you can find it in your heart to forgive me

Your loving mother,
Juniper d'Apidae

CORNWALL, THE LETTER

When he had finished reading the letter, Roger felt numb, as if he was sitting in the quiet aftermath of an earthquake. His familiar reference points were no longer there, the framework of his world was broken around him and he sat in the rubble of his life, unable to move.

He couldn't process his thoughts, his mind was frozen, his body inert. Only his heart felt alive, galloping and pounding in his chest and temples. He slumped back against the pillows and closed his eyes, wanting to shut it all out. He didn't know how long he lay on his bed, perhaps he slept, he couldn't be sure, but it was dark outside when he finally sat up.

He gulped down the water from the glass beside his bed and surveyed his room in the moonlight. His few belongings were scattered over the floor, and he slowly began to pick them up, pushing them into his small rucksack until there was nothing left. He quietly opened his bedroom door, and hearing no sound, made his way down the stairs to the kitchen, where he filled a flask with water. He scribbled a brief note, telling his friends he had been called home, then took some cheese from the fridge and some apples from the bowl, pushing them into his rucksack as he let himself out into the night.

He glanced at his watch as he walked, it was 3am. At the end of the lane he turned right, towards St Austell and the railway station, knowing that the walk would take him hours, but he didn't care. He needed to move and he needed to be alone.

It was lunchtime and the sun was high in the sky by the time he reached the ferry port in Plymouth. He bought himself a one-way ticket and boarded the ferry to Roscoff, deciding on impulse to get himself a cabin on board. He let himself into the small space, dumped his rucksack on the floor and kicked off his shoes as he peered out of the porthole. Then, exhausted, he threw himself onto the bunk and fell into a deep sleep, dreaming busy dreams as the engine thrummed beneath him, rocking his bed like a cradle.

After a series of buses and trains, during which at some point he slept beneath a hedge in a field, Roger's subconscious mind led him inevitably to the familiarity of Normandy and to home. He trudged along the lane towards the d'Apidae estate. Ironic considering he had never been a d'Apidae he thought now, but realised he would not have been gifted this house at all were it not for Xavier, his real father.

He began to walk more briskly, suddenly keen to see the house. He would move in there, he decided, allow his mind to settle and give himself time to come to terms with his new reality. If there had been any residual elements of his childhood within him, his mother's letter had chased them away, leaving a void he would need to learn how to fill. Bypassing his parents' home on the estate, which had a closed up air of desolation about it, Roger turned right along the narrow, wooded lane that would lead him to Les Lavandes. He didn't have a key, but hoped that he would either find one hidden, or that a window might have been left open. Otherwise, he would have to break in.

When he eventually arrived at the garden gate, he pushed it open and walked towards the front door. There were flower pots containing geraniums on either side of it, in the dappled shade of a tree. He pushed them to one side, hoping to find a key. When he found nothing, he looked above his head, feeling along the low beam of the porch. His fingers alighted on a large, old key, and turning it easily in the lock, he pushed the door open.

Once inside, he dropped his rucksack and looked around him. Despite the wooded approach, the back of the house was flooded with sunshine streaming in through floor length windows. He took off his shoes and walked through to the kitchen, opening the glass doors. A chorus of birdsong filled the room and for the first time, just for a moment, Roger's heart experienced something close to lightness.

He stepped into the sunny conservatory, where jasmine climbed the walls from large terracotta pots, their sweet fragrance filling the warm air. A bougainvillea overwhelmed its pot, its papery purple blooms pushing up pale pink, brick walls. Roger stepped out of the conservatory onto a long terrace which gave way to lawns and flower beds full of tall, summer flowers. In the centre of the lawn, a statue of a shepherd, his jacket blowing out behind him in the wind, appeared to move through an abundant swathe of miniature roses.

A childhood memory came to him then and he remembered playing here. He had forgotten that he would find such beauty behind the old stone walls of the house. This garden must have been Alice's great love before she died, he thought, and was surprised to realise that tears had begun to run down his face. It was nothing to do with Alice, or her garden, he realised later, but that the unexpected beauty of it had left his heart vulnerable and it flooded with the pain of his loss.

He had taken his parents for granted, never feeling especially close to them, more often believing himself a disappointment, but they had always been there. Now, nothing was left of what had always been. The framework of his life had crumbled and he felt exposed. His mother had lied to him, lied to them all for most of her life. Anger welled up in his chest, his father was not his father, his real father was dead and now he had nobody. A loud wail rose into his throat and burst from his mouth as he screamed his pain to the sky, railing at the unfairness of it all.

It was a couple of days later, during which he mostly slept, barely ate and neither shaved nor washed, that Roger was woken by the sound of the telephone ringing. He stumbled out of bed, squinting his eyes in the late morning sunshine, as he searched for it, finally picking it up. 'Roger, thank God, we have been beside ourselves with worry,' said his mother. 'Why aren't you in Cornwall? One of your friends called thinking you were here with us.'

'Mother, I've got nothing to say to you,' he said. There was a silence and then she said,

'I understand Roger, you've had a shock.'

'You lied to me and to Pa, just leave me alone.' After a sharp intake of breath Juniper said,

'There was a phone call for you last week, Rosa took a message.'

'Who was it?' he said flatly.

'A girl, someone called Julie.' Suddenly, Roger was paying attention,

'What did she say?' he asked.

'Just a minute, I will hand you over to Rosa,' said his mother.

'Ello Rojay, are you alright mon brave?' hearing Rosa's familiar voice made him want to weep and he took a deep breath.

'Yes Rosa, I'm ok. What did Julie say?'

'She wants you to call, she left her number in France.'

'In France,' he said, 'where?'

'Well it is a Paris number, that is all I know.'

'Hold on Rosa, I'm going to find a pen.' Eventually he returned holding a wax crayon and a scrap of paper. 'Go on Rosa, tell me.' He wrote the number down and then said, 'thank you Rosa, I have to go now.' He put the phone down and sighed, rubbing his eyes.

He was starving, there was nothing much to eat as far as he knew, but he headed hopefully to the kitchen. He would at least make some coffee, a nice strong pot of it. He opened cupboards and found a mug, coffee pot and some roasted coffee. Once the kettle had boiled, he added three heaped spoons to the pot and poured on the water, then searched the cupboards for signs of food. He found a tin of tomatoes, another of sweetcorn and little else. His heart sank as he pulled open the empty fridge and just as all hope had left him, he opened the freezer to find a treasure trove of neatly labelled meals. He had no idea how they had come to be there, and he didn't care. He pulled out two dishes labelled 'macaroni cheese', turned the oven on and slid them onto the top shelf.

Roger walked into the conservatory and pulled the doors open, taking his coffee outside into the morning sunshine. The birds sang and there was a gentle breeze, his world suddenly seemed brighter and he paused to take it all in. A tall plant with pink blooms swayed nearby, and he saw that it was covered in butterflies. He strolled across the lawn, not bothering to put on his shoes and felt the cool dew glide over his toes as he slowly approached a small herb garden. The mint and lemony fragrance rose up to meet him as he made his way round the perimeter, stopping now and again to sip his coffee. He passed roses and other brightly coloured summer blooms, spilling from the flower beds, and he found himself smiling. The sight of the flowers lifted his spirits and made him think of Julie. He let out a long slow breath, allowing his shoulders to drop and his chest to relax. He looked down at his feet, watching the blades of grass drag between his toes, losing himself in the rhythm of his footsteps as he walked back towards the house. He breathed a deep sigh of relief, everything would be alright.

Later, full and comfortable after his first hot meal in almost a week, he got himself organised. First he shaved and showered and then threw some clothes and his sheets into the washing machine. He found old jeans and a white t-shirt in a drawer and put them on. At least they were clean, which was more than could be said of anything else he owned. Once dressed he walked around the house opening windows, and unpacked the few remaining items in his rucksack. Finally, in the kitchen, he put the dishes he had used into hot soapy water.

His heart beat faster as he picked up the phone to dial Julie's number. He let it ring for a long time and when there was no reply he gave up, disappointed, she had probably gone away.

JULIE

Julie was filling watering cans along the quayside, returning to the boat with one in each hand, dripping water as she went, when her neighbour called from his boat.

'Bonjour Julie, ça va?'

'Oui Claude, et toi?'

'Ça va, ça va,' he shrugged. She put the watering cans down for a moment, he clearly wanted to talk. 'Comment va Astrid?' he asked. It had been nearly a month since news of her heart attack had reached them, and he was worried.

'Je ne sais pas,' she smiled at him sympathetically. Astrid had been his neighbour for years; he probably thought she would always be there, a solid presence in an uncertain world. 'I will pop in and see you later, when I have news Claude, ok?' He shrugged his shoulders again and shuffled towards his chair.

Julie heaved the containers on board, ready to water the hydrangeas. She and Sal had fallen into an easy routine over the past month and as she began the watering, she heard Sal calling up from below, 'Ju, the phone rang for ages and I was in the shower, couldn't get to it, sorry.' Julie immediately thought of Astrid, and wondered whether there was any more news. At that moment it rang again, and she jumped off the boat to pick it up,

'Rachel!' said Julie, 'What news?'

'Julie, it's me, Bones,' came his gentle, familiar voice.

'Bones!' her cheeks flushed pink with pleasure and her face broke into a smile. 'Where are you? How are you?' then she added more quietly, 'I've missed you.'

'Have you?' he said surprised.

'Yes,' she said quietly, 'I have.' He smiled with relief, and the silence stretched between them, until he realised he should say something.

'Julie, I would really like to see you.'

'Where are you?' she said.

'I'm in Normandy.'

'What are you doing in France?'

'It's a bit of a long story, something has happened, I need to talk to you.' This was unlike Bones.

'What's happened, Bones?'

'I can't say on the phone, would you be able to come to Normandy?'

'Bones, I'm in Paris, looking after Astrid's boat and her cat, I don't think I can leave.' As she said it, Sal came up out of the cabin nodding and waving.

'I'll look after everything,' she whispered. Then Julie said,

'Hang on a minute Bones, I may have found a solution.'

Two hours later, Julie was heading out to Normandy on the train. Roger got Alice's old car going and was waiting at the station when she emerged, wearing a floral cotton dress and flat sandals. She carried a small bag which she threw down as she flung her arms around him. 'Bones, I have missed you so much!' she said, squeezing him tightly. He basked in her embrace and for a moment, everything in his world felt right.

As they drove back to the house, Julie told Bones about life on the boat, new friends and her waitressing job. She longed to know what had happened with him, but accepted he would tell her in his own time. She was just so happy to see him again.

'So, where are we headed?' asked Julie.

'Not far now,' he said. 'I just want to stop off at the market to get some food, I haven't shopped since I arrived and the cupboards are bare.'

'When did you arrive?' asked Julie.

'I'm not sure exactly, it's all passed in a bit of a blur, a few days maybe.' Julie waited for him to elaborate, but he didn't. They pulled up on a pretty square, where the market was in full swing, and bought fresh fish, beautiful tomatoes and salad, a selection of cheese and some crusty bread. They bought butter, wine and strawberry jam from the épicerie and then headed out of town. About a mile further on, Roger slowed the car and they turned through tall wooden gates bearing a sign with three carved bees on it and the name d'Apidae.

'This is my family estate' he mumbled, as they turned in.

'Your family estate!' said Julie, 'Bones, you are full of surprises.' The long wooded driveway took them past a small lake, before winding through the trees, and eventually an imposing house came into view. It was built of soft yellow stone with shutters of pale turquoise blue.

'That's my parents' house,' he said, 'and where I have spent many summer holidays growing up.'

'I didn't know you had family in France.'

'My father is French,' said Roger automatically, then looked awkwardly at the floor. He realised that whichever of the two men he was referring to, the statement was true.

'It's beautiful!' said Julie. 'Is that where we are staying?'

'Not this time,' he said, turning to smile at her, as he continued past the house and turned down a lane to the right. Julie was intrigued as they drove slowly along the narrow, leafy lane. There was some woodland to the right, and she could see a stream running alongside it, overhung with wild flowers and grasses. Eventually Roger pulled up outside a house built of the same honeyed stone.

'Here we are,' he said. 'I discovered a few weeks ago that this house is all mine.'

'Yours,' she said, 'how?'

'It's part of a long and difficult story,' he said, and she could see the pain in his eyes. 'I'll tell you more later, but I'm glad you're here, thanks for coming Ju.'

'Come on then, let's go and have a look inside!' She jumped out of the car and stretched, reaching her arms towards the canopy of trees above, where sunlight glinted between the leaves. Roger pushed the front door open; sunlight sliced across the pale terracotta floor as Julie took in the pink sofas and bright rug. The sofas were draped with blue throws and overlooked the conservatory and garden. An old pine table stood on the far side of the room forming part of the open plan kitchen, 'Bones, this is beautiful!' said Julie.

Later, as they sat in the garden Julie sighed contentedly. The evening sun caressed her face and she closed her eyes for a moment, enjoying the feeling. Then her face became serious and she said, 'What's up Bones? You said something had happened.'

He looked stricken and hesitated before he replied,

'So much has happened in the last month, I don't know where to start. My whole life has changed,' he looked up at Julie.

'Do you mean this house?' she asked.

'Well, this house is a part of what's happened, but that's the good part, the rest is rubbish.' Roger covered his face with his hands and rubbed his palms over his eyes. He wanted to tell her, but couldn't find the words. Julie waited patiently, giving him her full attention.

Finally, he said, 'It's a long story, my Aunt Alice died a month ago and she left me this house in her will. I had no idea why, I hardly knew her. She wasn't an Aunt exactly, she was my father's cousin, but we thought of her as Aunt Alice. Anyway, as well as the house, she left me her diaries.'

'How intriguing,' said Julie.

'When I was last in London, I read the diaries from cover to cover, hoping to shed some light on it, but I still didn't understand. On the last page, Alice wrote that I should ask my mother to tell me the rest of the story.'

'Your mother? Was she close to Alice?'

'Not as far as I know, but when I asked Ma, she seemed reluctant to tell me. In the end, because I was about to go away to Cornwall, she said she would write to me instead. I received her letter last week.' He paused and took a sip of water, rubbing his palms across his eyes again.

'Bones, you don't have to tell me any more unless you want to, you know,' Julie said gently, putting her hand on his shoulder.

'Thanks Ju, but I need to say it.' He took a deep breath and then began to tell her about the letter, his shock and grief when he found that his life was built on lies.

'So the man I have always believed to be my father isn't my father and some random stranger is. Even my mother only met him once, and that was the night of the party. I see pictures of them in my mind that I'd rather not see, especially in the garden. How could she have betrayed my father like that!'

Julie stood up and put her arms around him, 'What a story, Bones, I'm so sorry. That must have been so hard on you. Have you told your friends about it?'

'No, I couldn't face them or anyone else. I just picked up my things and walked out. It was the middle of the night, I just walked and walked. Eventually I got on a train to the ferry port and made my way here, you're the first person I've seen.'

'So you haven't been back home?'

'No, I may never go back the way I feel.' Julie sat quietly looking into his face. 'Reading it all in a letter made it so much worse.'

'What made your Ma tell you after all these years,' said Julie. 'Does your father know?'

'Nobody knows except Ma and me, she's kept the secret all my life. Alice knew, but now she's dead.'

'How did Alice find out?'

'Just before Alice died, she and Ma became close and confided in each other. Alice never had children of her own. She was passionately in love with Xavier and when he was killed, she felt she had nothing to live for.'

'That is so sad. Did she know she was dying?'

'Yes, that was how she and Ma became close, Alice collapsed when she was visiting our house for dinner. Up to that point, she hadn't told anyone she was ill.

When Ma told Alice what had happened at the party all those years before, the fact that Xavier had cheated didn't matter to her, she only cared that he'd had a son. Ma said it made Alice really happy before she died. So now you see why she left me the house.' Roger was raking his big hands through his hair, struggling to manage his emotions.

'Everybody makes mistakes in their lives, Bones. Your mother was obviously unhappy and it made her do something reckless. It turned out badly for her and she handled the consequences the best way she could, at the time. You must know that in keeping the secret, she had your best interests at heart as well as her own. She was trying to protect herself and her family.'

'Her mistake changed my life, she had no right to take away everything I have always known and believed about myself. It was all lies!' he shouted, and put his face in his hands, raking his fingers through his dishevelled hair. Julie hugged him and said quietly,

'Bones, I know this is hard for you, but after all these years, it must have taken a lot of courage for your mother to tell you the truth and risk everything in the process.'

'I've always felt I didn't quite belong, and now I know why,' he said quietly.

Julie got up from her chair and came over to him, she took his face in her hands and said,

'Look at me, Bones.' She bent forward and looked into his eyes. 'Everything will be alright,' she said gently. 'You've had a shock, you need to give yourself time.' She leaned towards him and lightly kissed his mouth, feeling his shoulders relax as he breathed out. 'Come on, let's go to bed.' She took his hand and led him up the stairs.

NORMANDY

The next morning, after a leisurely breakfast, Roger felt better. The kitchen was warm and sunny, and a chink of happiness had entered his world; he sighed with contentment. Having Julie here gave him hope for the future and put things into perspective.

'Come on Ju, I'll show you round the garden.' Julie smiled and got up from her chair. They stepped outside and climbed the stone steps to the lawn. A small pink bud could be seen among thick, shiny leaves. 'This looks like a magnolia,' she said, pausing briefly.

They walked over the lawn admiring beds full of tall flowers, tangled together, covered in bees and butterflies. Further on there was an old greenhouse against one wall, housing a vine. Dozens of bunches of black grapes hung temptingly from the old glass ceiling, 'Wow,' said Julie, pulling one off to taste.

They sauntered on, rounding a small box hedge to the ornamental herb garden. 'Purple sage,' Julie said, bending to pick a leaf. As she rubbed it between her fingers she reached out to Bones, 'Smell this,' she said, 'it reminds me of the day we first met Astrid on the boat.'

At the other end of the garden, they followed a narrow path along a high wall behind the flowerbeds. 'Look there's an old gate in the wall,' said Roger. It was surrounded by plump peaches growing against the sunny bricks, some had dropped, overripe to the ground. Julie watched fascinated, as butterflies fed on the peach nectar, slowly beating their wings in the sun.

'Look at that,' she said. 'I didn't know butterflies fed on peaches. Did you?'

'No,' said Roger, distracted as he tried the gate. At first he thought it was locked but then, with difficulty, it opened. Beyond, was a small paddock of long grass with a barn on the far side.

'Does this field belong to the house too?' said Julie.

'I think so,' said Roger. 'Ma said that Alice had an art studio, that must be it.' They pushed their way through the long grass and when they reached the barn, it was locked. They tried to peer in the windows, but they were too high up. Roger walked round the back to where a piece of wood was out of line with the rest. Pushing it aside, he peered into the gloom.

'Anything?' called Julie, following him.

'I can't see much,' he said. Then Julie spotted a key hanging from a hook inside the wood store.

'Bones, I've found a key,' she called. He let the wood panel swing back and followed her round to the front. The padlock was rusty and it took several attempts before the key turned and it sprang open. She looked at Bones, 'We're in,' she said, undoing the catch. Roger slid the huge door open and the barn flooded with light. An old table was stacked with tubes of paint, bottles of turpentine and oils. A canvas on an easel stood beside it, covered by an old sheet. In front of it was a faded sofa with a few cushions on it. Numerous canvases, large and small were stacked against the walls. As Roger looked at the sofa, he had a vision of Alice with Xavier and he glanced at Julie, but she was peering under the sheet covering the canvas. 'Let's have a look,' she said, 'I wonder what she was painting.'

They carefully removed the sheet from the canvas, and gasped at the shimmering oil painting as it was exposed to the light. It depicted a young girl as she lay unconscious in a stream, her chest and arms bare, her palms open. A man leaned over her, his gleaming back exposed in the sunlight, his arm under her waist as he lifted her from the water. Her head and shoulders fell back, and tendrils of her hair floated on the current, as he gazed into her face.

Julie broke their stunned silence, 'Do you think Alice painted this?'

'That is Alice,' said Roger. 'A lot younger than I remember her, but I'm sure it's her. Maybe Xavier painted it.'

As he said his name, Roger realised that he was speaking of the man who was his father. It felt strange and yet oddly liberating. He could feel his new identity stretching inside him, trying to find its feet.

'It must have been here for years,' said Julie. 'I thought you said he died?'

'He did, but I'm not sure when.' Sadness came over Roger suddenly. If only he had met him, but now he never would.

A fresh wave of anger towards his mother rose in his chest and suddenly he needed some air. He strode quickly out of the barn and slumped against one of its wooden walls in the shade, taking some deep breaths.

'Bones, are you ok?' called Julie, slipping the cover back over the painting. There was silence, so she walked towards the door of the barn and slid it shut behind her, clicking the padlock shut. 'Bones?' she called, following the flattened grass round to the end of the barn. She found him sitting there, knees bent with his head resting forward on his arms. He wiped his face roughly across his arm as he sat up. 'Bones, I'm so sorry, that was really insensitive of me.'

'It's ok,' he said, 'it wasn't you. Everything in my life has changed. Sometimes I don't know what to do with the feelings that well up, they come at me out of nowhere.'

A dark cloud covered the sun and the air was cooler. 'Why don't we go back to the house,' said Julie. 'Come on,' she said, getting hold of his arm. Roger stood up, and draping his big arm across her slim shoulders, they slowly crossed the field together, retracing their steps to the gate and then pulling it shut behind them.

That evening, Julie lit some candles and Roger opened a bottle of wine for them to share. He had located a frozen spaghetti bolognese among the labelled packets and put the contents onto the stove to slowly warm through. He walked towards Julie carrying two glasses of red wine.

'I'm so glad you came Ju.' Her heart lifted and she smiled at him. 'I know this might seem a funny thing to say but,' he paused, unsure how to continue.

'But what?' said Julie. He handed her a glass and sat next to her at the table as she looked at him expectantly.

'I think,' he paused again, 'I think I love you.' Julie smiled with pleasure,

'I love you too,' she said softly. 'Now, come on Bones, talk to me, let me help you.'

Gradually, as they sipped their wine, Roger opened up to her. 'My feelings are so muddled and confused,' he said. 'On the one hand, I finally feel the pieces of me falling into place, and it all makes sense. On the other hand, more than anything, I feel sadness for the family I've always known and I feel I've lost.'

'You haven't lost them Bones, what do you mean?'

'I've always taken the comfort of belonging for granted, I suppose we all do that. I've never given my family much thought and now, I find myself longing for the stability of them, needing them, Ma and Pa, even my sister. I feel alone, as if I no longer have the right to their affection.' Julie got up and put her arms around him.

'First of all, you are not alone, you have me.' She kissed him, 'But mostly, although so much has changed for you personally, for everyone else it has remained the same. Your family love you as much now as they ever did. Why should that change?'

'Julie I can't live a lie, how can I be my true self without telling people who I really am?' he replied. 'Yet if I do that, it will ruin everything and hurt my family.'

'Bones, the person you are today is a result of the life you have lived. The people who have cared for you are your true family, nothing can change that,' she said, giving him another hug.

A couple of days later, they were lounging on the beach together at Deauville. The wide flat sand stretched out as far as they could see, to the deep blue of the ocean beyond. Horses galloped along the shoreline in the distance and Julie glanced at Bones and smiled, this was perfection. They had stopped at a boulangerie on the way and bought a picnic of generously filled baguettes, apples and water to enjoy on the beach. After lunch, they lay back on their towels and Roger fell asleep.

They had spoken so much over the last couple of days, or rather Bones had. Julie usually had to coax his thoughts from him, but he had so badly needed to talk. He'd said he had nowhere else to turn, and she was glad that it was her he wanted. She smiled to herself and looked at him sleeping beside her, no wonder he was exhausted, poor Bones; Julie wanted to hug him to her and take care of him. Just then, he opened his eyes and smiled up at her, reaching out for her hand and running his fingers along the inside of her wrist, before winding his fingers into hers and holding her hand.

He closed his eyes again and pulled her gently against his chest, where she could feel the steady thud of his heart against her cheek. When they awoke, the tide had come in and the sun was setting, spreading its golden light across the sand and the shimmering water.

JULIE

When Julie arrived back on the narrow boat in Paris, Sal had news. Astrid's daughter had arrived unexpectedly from Canada, to collect the cat and some of Astrid's things. Astrid was on the mend, Rachel explained, but was persuaded for her health's sake to stay on in Canada with her family. She was enjoying having her grandchildren nearby and finally admitted that life on the boat, had become too much for her. The only sticking point was her beloved cat.

'Astrid is not really well enough to travel at the moment,' Rachel told Sal. 'We have wanted her to come back to Canada for the longest time. It seems that fate has finally intervened.'

'Was that it?' asked Julie. 'What happened next?'

'She didn't stay long,' said Sal. 'She was flying back to Canada the same day, and even brought a cat box with her for Cedric. So, I let her take him. I hope that's ok,' said Sal, looking worried.

'You had no choice by the sound of it,' said Julie. 'What did she say about the boat?'

'She said it will eventually be sold, but we can stay on it for the rest of the summer if we want to, until arrangements can be made. She actually asked if we would stay on, she said she would appreciate it.'

'Wow,' said Julie. 'Typical that all this happened just as I was away for the first time, did she mind?'

'To be honest, she was distracted and tired, just wanted to get back to the airport with the cat. She left you this,' Sal handed her an envelope. Inside was a scrawled note signed by Astrid, mostly in French.

'Well this is helpful,' said Julie, mystified. I'll have to get my dictionary out and try to read it later!' she stuffed it into her pocket and sighed.

'Cup of tea?' said Sal.

'Love one,' said Julie, kicking off her boots and leaning back on the old sofa.

'So, how did it go with Bones?' said Sal. Julie smiled and said softly,

'It went well, very well.' Sal looked round at her friend,

'Oh God, I know that look. You're in love aren't you?' said Sal.

'I might be,' said Julie, winking at her. Then she looked up at her friend, 'Actually Sal, I think he's the one.'

'Cue violin music!' shrieked Sal. 'Are you serious? That's fantastic my friend!'

As Sal made tea for them both, Julie told her a potted version of Bones' story.

'Poor sod,' said Sal. 'That must have been hard for him. How is he now?'

'It's all still raw and new for him, but there are some positives. He's never been close to his parents, and always struggled to fit in. Now he's discovered he had an artist for a father, he said it all makes sense.'

'An artist,' said Sal, 'how so?'

'It's a long story,' said Julie, but that's why his Aunt Alice left him the house. She was passionately in love with this man apparently, and he died young. Even when she found out much later that he'd cheated on her, all she cared about was the fact that Xavier had a son.'

'Xavier?' said Sal.

'Yes, that was his name.'

'Xavier who?' said Sal.

'I don't know,' said Julie, 'I can't remember his last name. Anyway, the house is idyllic Sal, along a winding lane through woodland. It's open to the hills at the back, with a lovely walled garden.'

'It sounds amazing,' said Sal. 'Is Bones still there?'

'Yes, he has stuff to do,' she said. 'I think he's planning to make it his home, there is quite a lot to sort out. Alice had an old barn she used as a studio, and it's full of paintings stacked against the walls. We went in briefly when we were touring the garden.'

'Touring the garden!' said Sal. 'How big is this garden that you 'toured'?' She held her hands up gesturing commas around the word as she said it.

'Pretty big,' said Julie,' and quite overgrown in parts. We found a gate in the wall, and when we went through there was a field with an old barn in it. At first we couldn't get in, it was padlocked and there were no windows, but eventually we found a key.'

'What was in it?' asked Sal.

'It looked like his aunt's art studio, complete with a chaise longue, an old table and tubes of paint. We weren't in there long, Bones got upset and walked out, it was probably my fault.'

'Why your fault?'

'Oh, I said something about Xavier, I can't remember exactly. There was this painting you see, on an easel, covered with a cloth, Bones thought it was a painting of his Aunt Alice when she was young.'

'Was it a self-portrait?'

'No, that's the thing, Bones thought it may have been painted by Xavier. I put my foot in it, by talking about the fact that Xavier was dead. It was as if it suddenly hit him that he would never know his real father, and he got upset.'

'What was the painting of?' asked Sal.

'Oh, it was amazing, luminous, rich with blues and greens. It was of a woman, lying half naked in the river, with her long hair flowing on the current. A man was leaning over her, trying to lift her out,' Sal went quiet.

'Oh my God,' said Sal, her face suddenly pale.

'What?' said Julie.

'The painting!' she said, 'What was Xavier's last name, was it de St Jacques by any chance?'

'Yes, that was it,' said Julie, 'I remember now, I remember thinking that it reminded me of something I'd eaten in a restaurant.'

'Julie, do you realise what this might mean?'

'What what might mean?' said Julie, looking at her friend.

Sal leaped up from the table, 'Julie, it's Xavier de St Jacques, the artist I'm researching!' She grabbed Julie by the shoulders, 'Have you any idea what this could mean to the art world! They have been searching for the rest of his paintings for years.'

Julie looked at Sal, finally understanding, her eyes round in her face. 'Is it really possible that it's him, that the painting is one of his?' said Julie.

'Ju, is there any way we can go down there, so that I can see it for myself?'

'I'm sure we could, but do you think we should tell someone about it?'

'We need to be careful who we tell,' said Sal, suddenly serious. 'If it is one of St Jacques paintings, it will have enormous value. Did you say it was in a barn?'

'Yes,' said Julie, furrowing her brow, 'It must have been in there for years.' Sal put her hands over her face, trying to think what to do. Then she remembered the art expert at the library, she had given her a card and said to call if she needed more information. 'That's it!' she said, 'I'll call the woman at the library and arrange to see her, she'll know what to do.'

Things moved quickly after that. The expert at the library contacted the head of the authentication of paintings at the Musée du Louvre and explained the story. A few days later, the art experts, along with Julie and Sal, arrived at Les Lavandes. Julie had alerted Bones to the possibility that the painting could be of value, explaining that they would be coming from Paris accompanied by the people from the Louvre. The experts spent over two hours in the barn, while Julie, Sal and Bones drank coffee in the kitchen, awaiting their verdict. When they eventually emerged from the barn, it was to tell them that yes, the painting was indeed one of the lost works of Xavier de St Jacques. Furthermore, they had found the third in the series, stacked against the wall among many other works that appeared to be by the same artist. Sal was beside herself with excitement and she and Julie began to laugh as Bones looked on.

'Bones, this is incredible! Have you any idea of the significance of this?' said Sal. Roger nodded, his expression inscrutable. The expert turned to Roger,

'Monsieur de St Jacques am I correct in assuming zat zis

property belongs to you?' Roger didn't react until Julie nudged him and he looked up,

'Sorry, what did you say?'

'I was just confirming zat you are ze owner of zis property.'

'Yes, I am. It was recently left to me by my Aunt Alice, but my name is d'Apidae, Roger d'Apidae,' he said quietly.

'Monsieur d'Apidae, zere is a very valuable painting in your barn which despite being in an unfavourable environment, 'as remained in surprisingly good condition. Zere are potentially many more important paintings zere too. I suggest zat we arrange for some security as soon as possible until ze paintings can be removed, with your permission, to ze safety of ze gallery vaults in Paris.' Roger couldn't keep up,

'Security, here?' he said, 'but we are in the middle of nowhere and those paintings have been in the barn for years. What has changed?'

'Everything 'as changed Mr d'Apidae,' she replied. 'Zese are very important art works. Experts 'ave been searching for years to find ze paintings zat Xavier de St Jacques completed in ze months before 'e was so tragically killed. I sink we can also surmise zat ze mystery lady in ze paintings is your Aunt Alice. We would love to know more about 'er, but for now, may we 'ave your permission to look srough and catalogue ze ozer art works in ze barn? I would also like to get some temporary security in place.'

Roger went along with their recommendations, still struggling to comprehend the day's developments. After a few phone calls to Paris, the experts announced that they were going for lunch and would be back in the afternoon. A security van would be coming from Paris with special transport frames for the paintings and a security guard.

The experts booked themselves into a local hotel and over the next couple of days, they spent mornings and afternoons sorting and cataloguing the paintings. Their working days were punctuated by long, leisurely lunches, but they worked diligently. A few days later, Roger watched with relief as the security van made its way back down the lane with the paintings. The experts asked Roger to sign papers giving permission for the restoration and eventual exhibition of the paintings, before getting into their car and returning to Paris.

The girls had left the day before, and Roger finally closed the door on the last of his visitors with relief. He was grateful for the solitude and slumped into an armchair, closing his eyes, as the enormity of the events of the last few days hit him.

He reflected on the time he'd spent with Julie, and smiled. She was so wise; she'd helped him see things in perspective, pointing the way to reconciliation with his mother. Much as he liked the idea of having a motorbike riding artist for a father, instead of the formal, distant man he knew, that man was dead and he would never know him.

He sighed, thinking of the times he had spent with Étienne in the last few years, they had always had a bond of sorts. Roger tried to imagine the pain that the knowledge of his mother's betrayal would inflict on him, to discover that his only son was not his son after all. He flinched at the thought of it, and resolved to keep it from Étienne; that much he could control. Impulsively he picked up the phone and dialled his mother.

In Richmond the telephone rang and Juniper stepped into the hall to pick it up,

'Hello.'

'Hello Mother, it's me, Roger.'

Juniper sighed with relief, their last conversation, though not entirely unexpected, had been very hard to bear. She had known she was dropping a bombshell when she posted the letter to Cornwall, but would Roger confront Étienne? She accepted long ago that she was no longer the centre of Étienne's life, in truth, she hardly saw him. If he was to divorce her as a result of this revelation, her life would continue much as it was now, she imagined.

'Mother, are you there?' said Roger into the silence.

'Roger darling, yes, yes I am. I'm so happy to hear from you. How are you?'

'How do you think I am?' he said truculently, 'I still can't believe you would lie to me about something as important as who my father is; and what about Pa? He'd be devastated if he knew.'

'Roger, I've tried to explain it to you as best I can. Nothing will ever make what I did alright,' Juniper said quietly. 'But I felt you had a right to know.' She paused, allowing the silence to stretch out, before asking tentatively, 'Have you decided whether or not you will tell your father?'

'That's the main reason I called,' he said decisively, 'I've decided not to tell him, I want to spare him the pain.' There was accusation in his tone and Juniper flinched, before slowly exhaling with relief.

'I think you have made the right decision, it will serve no purpose after all.' She paused, then said quietly, 'Thank you Roger, this means a great deal to me.'

Feeling sorry for her, he said more kindly, 'By the way, I've got an invitation for you and Pa, there's going to be a big exhibition of Xavier's paintings in Paris. They want me to speak, I hope you'll be there.' Before Juniper could ask more he said, 'Anyway Ma, I've got to go.'

'Of course, well, goodbye Roger,' she said, resisting the urge to ask him to come home, to talk to her, to tell her how he was feeling. If only she could undo the hurt she had caused.

FAMILY

His conversation with Julie clarified things for Roger, helping him decide he would go ahead with the exhibition. He would invite his family and friends to the private view and say nothing. What he most wanted was to feel the comfort of them all around him, cocooning him with love. Trauma had a strange way of making you see things in a different light, perhaps seeing them all together once more would be enough, and he could move on.

In London, Juniper called Hermione to tell her the news. 'I don't suppose you would come with me would you? I could do with the moral support,' said Juniper.

'What about Étienne?' she asked, 'and Lydia. Won't either of them be going with you?'

'Hermione, I haven't seen Étienne in weeks, he's always away. To be perfectly honest, I'm quite happy without him. As for Lydia, she's made her own life and apparently I'm not part of it anymore. Ever since she had counselling at the Priory, she's cut me off, I try not to dwell on it.'

'Are you sure you actually want to go?' said Hermione.

'Yes,' said Juniper, 'I'm curious to see the paintings Xavier made of Alice, and in particular the talent of the man I brazenly lay down on the grass with at a party! Please say you'll come.'

'In that case, what the hell, yes! I'll come with you,' she said, 'I can't pass up the chance to meet the players in the ongoing drama of your life. Have you always known he was famous?'

'No,' said Juniper, 'I didn't even know his name when I met him at the party.'

'You hussy,' said Hermione winking, and Juniper grinned.

'It was only when I was helping Alice get her affairs in order before she died, that I found out his surname and put two and two together; so I haven't known for long. Most of what I know about him has come from reading the papers over the last few weeks.'

'Did you know about the paintings in the barn?'

'I knew they were there, but had no idea of their significance. To me, Xavier was just another struggling artist. Don't forget, I didn't know Alice particularly well until recently.' There was a pause then Juniper added quietly,

'Do you really think I'm ready to do this, go to the exhibition I mean?'

'Up to you my friend, but if you want to, I've got your back.'

In Paris, the researchers knew far more about Xavier de St Jacques than Roger ever could have known. They said he was a radical and a rebel; he would frequently ride out of Paris, disappearing for weeks at a time. Only his very close circle knew about his obsession with Alice and even they didn't know where she lived. The discovery of Xavier's last paintings filled in the final pieces of a puzzle that had intrigued the art world for years. Newspaper articles fuelled the mounting excitement around Xavier and Alice's story, and the unveiling of the newly discovered works in Paris.

Once the wheels were set in motion, arrangements progressed swiftly. The Palais de Tokyo beside the Seine was chosen for the exhibition. It described itself as a 'rebellious wasteland with the air of a palace, an anti-museum in a state of permanent transformation'; a bit like Xavier then, thought Roger.

Xavier's work would be shown in the east wing, a large light filled gallery overlooking the river and the Eiffel Tower. In the basement, and running concurrently, another exhibition would feature a graffiti covered space, focusing on inner demons and urban violence. It was definitely edgy and he smirked to himself as he imagined his parents and their society cronies attending the event.

The researchers wanted as much information as possible about Alice, the mysterious muse of Xavier's paintings, as they compiled the exhibition. There would be a brief summary of her life with emphasis on the poetic tragedy of her early demise and that of Xavier's some years before, in the light of the passion they shared. Roger provided them with limited information from Alice's diaries, as well as the names and addresses of many of her friends for the guest list. Along with these, the gallery invited patrons, collectors and contemporaries of Xavier de St Jacques. The exhibition promised to be one of the highlights of the year.

Roger personally sent the invitations to Clémence in Paris and to his parents in London. He was not to know that his father stayed there less than ever these days, and wouldn't see it.

Julie was his rock over the weeks leading up to the exhibition. She was a regular visitor to Les Lavandes, helping him navigate the practicalities of setting up his home, and fielding questions from the researchers. She returned to Paris regularly to check on the narrow boat, a responsibility made much easier without the cat. Their final pieces of course work, submitted early in the summer, were expected back with their results any day. Those last days of term felt like a lifetime ago, and now Roger wondered how he had ever managed his life without Julie by his side.

The head of the gallery and exhibition organiser, invited Roger to come and see the progress while there was still time to make changes, but he declined. After all, what did he know. They were the experts and he said he would leave it up to them. As the owner of the paintings, he would open the exhibition, and in this, he felt rather out of his depth. Julie promised to help him work on the wording and they practised together on the narrow boat, in the days leading up to the event.

THE EXHIBITION

Roger wore a beautifully cut, light blue suit with a white T shirt and Julie wore a short, beige dress decorated with blocks of tan and yellow. Her short hair framed her face as she looked up at him, 'This is it!' she said, smiling confidently, as they stepped into the gallery. The swell of conversation and clinking glasses rose to meet them as the gallery director stepped forward to greet them.

'You are most welcome, Monsieur d'Apidae et Mademoiselle, I hope you will enjoy the evening.' A waiter appeared with a tray bearing two glasses of champagne, and the director led them towards his team for the exhibition, before melting into the crowd. They briefly ran through the plan for the evening and then, spotting his mother, Roger made their excuses and they moved towards her.

Julie stopped in her tracks, grabbed Roger's arm, saying in a stage whisper, 'Bones, look over there, have you seen your portrait?' Roger turned and saw that the backdrop to the podium where he would make his speech, was a huge black and white photograph of, he stared at it, it couldn't be.

'Oh Christ,' he said as the colour drained from his face.

'What is it?' said Julie grinning, 'Don't you like it?'

'That's not me,' he said quietly, and was about to continue when he heard his mother's voice as she approached.

'Roger darling, at last, how lovely to see you!' said Juniper, walking towards them in an elegant silk dress and neat jacket. A plump woman in a voluminous, colourful dress sailed along on the other side of her. 'Darling, allow me to introduce my friend

Hermione. Hermione this is my son Roger.'

Hermione stepped forward smiling and shook his hand firmly.

'Delighted to meet you, Roger,' and turning to Julie she said, 'And who is this?' Roger, still pale, but jolted by the handshake remembered his manners, just as Julie stepped forward with her hand outstretched.

'Mother, Hermione, this is my friend Julie.' Everyone smiled as Hermione kissed first Julie and then Roger on both cheeks. Juniper took Julie's hands in hers.

'I am so pleased to meet you Julie,' she said smiling. The conversation flowed, Julie told them about her adventures on the narrow boat and how much she had enjoyed her recent visit to Normandy. Roger's mind drifted to the consequences of his having to stand in front of the photograph to make his speech.

'Mother, is Father here with you?' said Roger.

'No darling,' said Juniper. 'He's been away on business, I don't see much of him these days.' Roger breathed a sigh of relief. He regretted that he had not taken up the offer to visit the gallery in advance of the exhibition. He could have prevented the now inevitable questions that would be asked and the conclusions that would be drawn.

'Mother, may I have a word?'

'Of course,' she turned to Hermione and Julie, 'Will you excuse us for a moment.' Roger led her to the side of the room where there were some screens with benches along the wall behind them, 'What is it Roger, is everything alright?'

'Just come and sit down for a moment Mother, I need to ask you something.'

Mystified, Juniper sat down beside her son and he was about to speak, when wide eyed she put her finger to her lips. Further along the wall and still hidden from the crowd in the gallery by screens, Juniper could hear the unmistakable voice of her husband. She indicated that Roger should stay put, then she got up and made her way quietly along the back of the screens, intending to surprise Étienne.

When she heard a woman's laugh, Juniper stopped in her tracks. Curious now, she made her way carefully towards the sound, peering around the long curve of the wall, then she gasped, pressing her hand over her mouth. Folds of red chiffon cascaded over Étienne's right hand as he pressed his fingers into the small of a woman's back, pulling her towards him. Her ruby earrings glinted in the gallery lights as he ran his hand up her back to stroke the nape of her neck. She laughed again, low and throaty, as Étienne leaned to whisper something into her ear, lingering there for a long moment. Juniper stood rooted to the spot as Étienne lazily lifted his head, and their eyes met in shocked recognition. Before he could react, Juniper turned on her heel and walked swiftly back to where she had left Roger seated on the bench, her heels echoing on the marble floor.

'There you are Ma, what was it?' Juniper looked pale and her hands were shaking.

'Nothing darling, don't worry.' She took a deep breath and sat down. 'Now, what did you want to speak to me about?'

A few minutes later, Roger thought how well his mother had taken the news of the portrait and the awkwardness of his having to stand in front of it to open the exhibition. He feared that her secret would be revealed to everyone, and to his surprise, with a glint in her eye and the shadow of a smile on her face, Juniper seemed to come to a decision. She linked Roger's arm as they made their way back through the throng, and when they reached the others, Juniper took Hermione to one side. They conferred for a moment, and then Juniper moved over to speak quietly to her son. Julie wondered what was going on, Roger was due to make his speech at any moment and he would need to make his way to the podium. He turned towards Julie, an anxious look on his face, just as the gallery director emerged from the crowd beaming. 'Suivez-moi Monsieur d'Apidae, we are ready for you now.'

As Roger walked across the gallery, people moved aside to let him pass and he heard intakes of breath and murmured comments. He strode towards the podium with increasing confidence, no more lies, tonight he would speak his truth. There were low gasps and murmurs as he stepped up before the assembled company, looking out at them from below the huge black and white image of Xavier, in the prime of his youth. Tall, tanned and broad shouldered, his tousled, blond hair fell across his moody face, as he looked straight into the camera. Tonight, infused with his spirit of reckless confidence, Roger began to speak.

'Ladies and gentlemen,' he began, 'Welcome to this exhibition of previously unseen paintings by Xavier de St Jacques. It is my great honour to be able to share these works of art with you, for the very first time this evening. Nobody was more surprised than I to discover them at the house I recently inherited from my Aunt, Alice Gardener. Alice lived in France for most of her life and almost as soon as she met Xavier in Paris in her twenties, she became his muse. You will see her image in many of the paintings on show this evening.

Xavier was a spirited adventurer and we can only try to imagine his life. He was a private man who refused to live in the way society expected him to. As you know, he died young, in a tragic motorbike accident. When I heard a few months ago that Alice had left me her property in Normandy, along with her diaries, I thought there had been a mistake. It was several months before the reason became clear to me.

Before I say more, I first want to thank my parents, Juniper and Étienne d'Apidae for giving me every opportunity in life and in particular for allowing me to follow my passion for art. I am not sure that they ever really understood it, and I'm sure they would have liked me to take a different path, but in the end I followed my heart.'

Roger paused and Juniper waited, her breathing shallow, as her eyes scanned the room for Étienne. Then, she saw him, the woman in red beside him, half hidden by a pillar. Étienne's eyes were fixed on Roger as he continued,

'It will not have escaped your notice that I bear more than a passing resemblance to Xavier de St Jacques. So many of us have secrets that are meant to remain hidden, but then something unexpected happens and the truth is out. What I am about to tell you would have remained a private matter, were it not for the picture behind me and my mother's assurance that tonight, it was important to finally tell the truth.'

As if he sensed Juniper watching him from across the room, Étienne turned and met her unflinching gaze, then Roger delivered her coup de grâce.

'I discovered through Alice's diaries and subsequent

conversations with my mother, that Xavier de St Jacques was my father.' There was a collective intake of breath and then stunned silence in the room, before people began to clap and cheer. Juniper watched the colour drain from Étienne's face, he opened his mouth and doubled forward for a moment as if he had been punched. It was only then that she saw Clémence, standing ashen faced beside them, and she reached out to Étienne.

Juniper continued to look straight at him and their eyes met once more, before he turned and escorted his mother quickly out of the gallery, the surprised woman in red hurrying after them. As the applause began to quieten, Roger finished, 'Thank you all so much for coming this evening, and for your support. I hope you enjoy the exhibition.' The clapping began again as Roger stepped down from the podium, shaking the hands of well-wishers as he passed.

The next morning, the papers were full of photographs and the sensational story that emerged at the event. A picture of Roger standing in front of the photograph of Xavier dominated the front pages. "Xavier's Love Child Inherits His Fortune" ran the headlines, declaring him the living image of the artist. "Wealthy Society Couple, their Secret Affairs and the St Jacques Love Child" was another, bearing a photograph of Étienne leaving the gallery with a statuesque woman in red on his arm.

When Roger looked back on the glittering evening, he struggled to believe how quickly the fallout from that event had led to his parents' decision to divorce. Given his mother's lies and his father's obvious affair, he shouldn't be surprised; but he still wondered if he was, in some way, to blame. His mother had actively encouraged him to tell the truth that night, and it turned out that his father had been there to hear it, and his grandmother too. She must have arrived late, perhaps with his father. Had Juniper known they were there? Who was the mystery woman with Étienne as he left?

'Penny for your thoughts,' said Julie, smiling at him.

'What, oh sorry, in my own world, just thinking about stuff, you know.'

Roger was searching for a pen and paper among a pile of magazines and essay notes and he came across a hand written letter on creamy yellow paper, he picked it up.

Ma Chère Julie,

J'ai retrouvé en toi la jeune femme que j'étais: sensible, aventureuse et attentionnée.

Ce bateau a été toute ma vie depuis des années et aujourd'hui, c'est le moment de passer à autre chose. Je te l'offre en remerciement et je te souhaite une vie heureuse, prête à rencontrer la personne qui partagera cette vie que je te souhaite pleine d'amour et d'aventures.

Merci et bises, Astrid x

Crikey, thought Roger, does she even realise? 'Ju,' he said.

'Mmm?' she answered, her head in a book, 'What is it?' Roger held out the letter,

'Have you seen this?' she looked up briefly, recognising the pale yellow notepaper.

'Yes, of course I've seen it. That's the letter Astrid sent to thank me for looking after her cat, her sister left it for me.'

'Have you actually read it?' said Roger.

'Of course I've read it,' she said. 'Didn't understand a bloody word mind you, apart from merci, which I know means thank you.'

'Julie, she's actually written you a lovely letter and at the end, have a guess what she says?'

'What?' said Julie, putting her book down in her lap.

'Astrid is giving you her boat, this boat!'

'You can't be serious!' Julie jumped up and grabbed the letter from him, scanning it for clues. Then she looked up at him, her face flushed and her eyes wide as she took in this news. 'Are you sure Bones?'

'Of course I'm sure, this is what she says;

My dear Julie,

I saw in you the person I was when I was young. Sensitive, adventurous and kind.

My boat has been my life for many years and now the time has come for me to pass it on. I gift it to you with thanks and I hope it will lead you to many happy times and adventures, with the person you love.

Thanks and kisses, Astrid x

'Oh my gosh, I can't believe she has done this for me. I knew we had a connection that I couldn't explain, Astrid must have felt it too. When I think about it, do you remember she told my fortune that day?'

'Yes, I do, although you never told me what she said.'

'That's because it seemed so far-fetched. She told me that one day I would come into an unexpected inheritance. She said I would sail away into the sunset with the love of my life.'

'I wonder who that will be,' said Roger, looking worried. As he hovered uncertainly, Julie flung her arms around him,

'It's you, you ninny!' He felt her small, capable body pressed against his and he knew in that moment, he had found his heart's home. Julie pulled her head away from his chest and looked up at him, 'Come on Bones, let's sail away and have an adventure.'

A note from the author

Did you enjoy Parisian Legacy?

I hope you enjoyed it as much as I enjoyed writing it. I lived alongside the characters and their worlds as I wrote, and I can tell you, their story is far from over!

I am working on the sequel *Windsong*, and can promise you more captivating settings and a wonderful family story, woven with the rich and complex tapestry of life.

* * * * *

WINDSONG

A story of hope, love and family
by Rosalie James

From the healing white sands of Captiva Island, to the rugged cliffs of coastal England and a beautiful French Chateau in the Loire Valley

Windsong will be available in 2023

* * * * *

If you have a moment to review Parisian Legacy on Amazon and/or Goodreads, I would really appreciate it. Thank you so much!

See you on Captiva Island!

ACKNOWLEDGEMENTS

Thanks to Lynli, Harry and Jules for lending me their home in Montmartre to write.

Thanks to Philip and Ink Academy for pushing me to be my best!

Thanks to Caro for helping me brainstorm this book title.

Thanks to Deanne and Sylvie for helping with my French.

Finally, thanks to my husband and lifelong friend Tim, and my children James and Camilla for their unstinting support and encouragement on my writing journey.

They make me proud, every day.

About the Author

Rosalie has been telling stories since childhood, excited by new places, new ideas and change. Her mother was brought up in India, and later began modelling for Dior. When she married, the family moved to the Bahamas, where Rosalie spent her childhood.

Rosalie raised her own family in Sussex, England and in Normandy, France. She is a regular house sitter in Paris, London and overseas, which inspires her writing.

Her stories take readers on a journey that transcends everyday life, yet with themes we can all relate to; tragedy, hope, love, misplaced trust and new beginnings.

Parisian Legacy is Rosalie's first book. The sequel, *Windsong*, will be available in 2023.

For further details and the latest information please follow her on Facebook and Instagram:

instagram.com/rosaliejamesauthor

facebook.com/Rosalie-James-Author-110882358036939

or go to:

rosaliejamesauthor.com